To Kathy

The Accidental

BAD GIRL

MAXINE
KAPLAN

Dear Reader,

If you're like me, you love *Veronica Mars*, *Raymond Chandler*, *The Disreputable History of Frankie Landau-Banks*, *Gone Girl*, *Brick*, snappy dialogue, girls who refuse to be put into little boxes, and books that tell twisty stories that also pack an emotional punch. If you're not like me . . . I bet you'll still like *The Accidental Bad Girl*.

You'll get to meet Kendall Evans, whose tarnished reputation gets her in trouble in ways she couldn't imagine—but also allows her to be free for maybe the first time in her life. You'll meet Mason, the young, privileged drug peddler who entangles himself into Kendall's life. You'll also meet Gilly, stage crew dork and man of hidden depths, and Simone, independent loner who doesn't want to be anyone's victim.

I'm so excited to be publishing Maxine Kaplan's debut novel, which is surprising and sexy and thought-provoking. If you're like me—and I hope you are—you'll find a lot to love in this story.

Best,

Maggie Lehrman

Maggie Lehrman
Senior Editor

Cataloging-in-Publication Data has been applied for and may be obtained from the Library of Congress.
ISBN 978-1-4197-2858-7

Text copyright © 2018 Maxine Kaplan
Jacket illustrations copyright © 2018 Catherine Casalino
Book design by Siobhán Gallagher

Printed and bound in U.S.A.
10 9 8 7 6 5 4 3 2 1

ABRAMS The Art of Books
195 Broadway, New York, NY 10007
abramsbooks.com

PROLOGUE

IT WAS A GAME, AFTER ALL. It made sense that eventually we'd make it to the school gym.

Grant Powers pulled me down the hallway by the wrist, laughing as he hitched up the black gown pooling around his khakis. The tassel tickled my nose as his cap nearly fell off my head in the mad dash through the double doors to the bank of athletic offices, high on the fifth floor of Howell.

It was empty. Of course it was. Grant stopped short and I crashed into his broad back, briefly breathing in the grassy, detergent smell of him. He reached backward and pulled me into a one-armed embrace, squashing me against his chest.

He bit my ear and I squealed.

"What now?" I asked, my voice still muffled in his gown. "Does the prom king have any last requests before he abdicates the throne, in, oh, about an hour?"

Grant spun me outward and his cap finally did fall.

"Let me think about that," he said, with a wicked grin. Then he nodded to something over my shoulder.

I turned my head and saw the equipment cage, the chain-link enclosure in the most shadowy corner of the room.

Before I could answer he had maneuvered me into the rusted-out metal box.

The next thing I knew, I was flat on my back, my butt squeaking against the nubby, padded nylon of a gym mat. Grant was on top of me, unbuckling his belt. The sunlight pouring through the big, glass windows flashed across something on his wrist, momentarily making me squint.

The sun moved and I saw that they were cuff links. Specifically, they were 14-karat gold cuff links engraved with his initials. Etched onto the back of each were a heart and the letter *A*.

I knew that because I was there when Audrey bought them for him, as a present for his eighteenth birthday.

I pushed that out of my head and concentrated on Grant, arching my back, trying to lose myself in the heat from his palms on my skin.

We weren't technically having sex yet, but my underwear had been flung to the side and a condom retrieved. He went to unzip my skirt.

"Wait," I said, lifting my head off the floor.

"What?" he asked, his voice excited, even hysterical.

I shook my head, concentrating, but it was gone. "I thought I heard something," I told him.

"Like what?"

I looked at him, suddenly suspicious. His voice was too casual to match the glitter in his eyes. I pushed him off me and sat up, holding my half-unstrapped bra to my chest, straining to hear. The gym was empty.

Then the heavy, metal doors leading up from the locker rooms boomed open—and the gym was decidedly *not* empty.

The entire senior class, capped and gowned, breathless, cheeks rosy with excitement, thundered in. I stumbled to my feet, twisting my underwear around my ankles, needing this not to be happening.

But it was happening. The distracted bustle in the air could protect me for only so long, and eventually, like dominoes, their eyes fell to the equipment cage and to me, stumbling back into my clothes. And, also, to Grant, who was laughing sheepishly and buckling his pants at a leisurely pace. A boyish whoop blew through the room. Someone yelled, "Fuck, yeah, Powers!"

I couldn't speak. I couldn't think. All I could do was try not to melt, and then Grant put his mouth next to my ear. "Hey, Kendall? Don't worry," he breathed.

"How . . . ?" I couldn't finish the query, looking wildly from person to person, identical in black and blue, and not recognizing any of them, just the look of witness-to-a-train-wreck delight on their faces.

I finally turned to Grant. "You knew?" I squeaked. "The seniors . . ." I tried to shake some focus into my head but failed. "You knew they would be here?"

He had been grinning at his friends, but then he looked at me, affection in his eyes. "You're really cute when you're nervous," he said. He bent down and kissed me on the cheek.

He sauntered away, pausing only to pick up his graduation cap, leaving me alone and unprotected in the cage.

Actually, scratch that: in high school.

CHAPTER ONE

No one was looking at me.

Or, more accurately, everyone was very carefully *not* looking at me.

My locker was in the basement level, the undercroft, and I had figured that if I cut in early and through the back, I'd get the chance to steel myself in the peace of an empty hallway.

Sadly, I had been mistaken. The senior class at Howell Preparatory School held enough overachievers that about fifteen kids had beaten me there. None of them were my friends, but I had known almost all of them since the fifth grade.

I stood there for a minute, just idling at one end of the corridor, waiting for someone, anyone, to acknowledge my existence.

Nope. I exhaled heavily, suddenly aware that I had been holding my breath.

I had just hooked my combination lock into place when the stairwell door swung open and out spilled a full-court press—including my volleyball teammates, Amy and Alexis. The summer before junior year, a few of us had gone on a couple of day trips to

Long Island, so we could practice while also relaxing on a beach. That hadn't happened this past summer. I smiled at them and waved. Amy nodded a little but then turned away to her locker. Alexis offered an almost silent "Hey" before looking away, too, embarrassed.

The full class shuffled into the corridor, and they all continued to not speak to me. I watched the door, but she—the only one I really wanted or needed to see—didn't show. I fished the glitter-edged mirror out of my backpack and stuck the magnetized back on my locker. With a touch of desperation, I applied lip gloss and mascara. I moved my hair, to temporarily hide my face. "Just one more year," I mouthed at my reflection.

I redid the hopeful math I'd been doing in my head all summer—in approximately six months, or thirty-two weeks, minus winter vacation, so make that thirty and a half weeks, I'd be accepted into college and, for all intents and purposes, not here anymore.

Of course, if my plans laid out over the long, lonely summer, came to pass, I'd escape even sooner. But I couldn't afford to get my hopes up, so I concentrated on the probable over the possible. *Thirty weeks, Kendall,* I thought hard, trying to will it into reality. *You can survive anything for thirty weeks.*

I surveyed my reflection and buttoned the top button on my cardigan. I shifted, and the lace neckline on the pastel blue camisole puckered. I had carefully selected this outfit: pale colors and soft fabrics, nothing moody or confrontational. The outfit had been neatly folded on my desk chair for a week, like empty paper doll clothes.

I unbuttoned. Maybe no one would even care about last year.

My senior year commenced. Nobody yelled at me or laughed at me. Nobody hit me or anything like that. But every time I stepped toward someone, they stepped back. I walked up to a group of student government kids hanging out by the vending machines and they simply evaporated around me, recongregating by the water fountain.

Third-period English class was divided into separate tables, each seating four. Lucia, Amy, and Raisa were sitting together and I joined them. One by one, they shouldered their backpacks and discreetly relocated.

For the whole of the morning, literally no one under the age of thirty spoke to me, and the ones who were over thirty barely did. Once it was clear that they were ignoring me, I was too proud to force a conversation with anyone in my clique and too timid to try to initiate contact with the other kids in the class, especially since I'd pretty much ignored them for the past three years.

I just wasn't there.

As I signed out at the front desk during lunch to get a bagel, my spirits sinking under the pressure of being mute and incidental, I tried to look on the bright side: The school was probably too small for anyone to get away with outright bullying. As cold as I felt when I imagined being excluded from everything that had been my life, if this benign ostracism was all that was coming my way, in terms of teens having it rough in American high schools, I was getting off tremendously light.

I attempted to cheer myself up with more math as I bought my lunch. Two hours and forty-five minutes until I could go home. Thirty minutes left of lunch, so only three more forty-five-minute blocks of having to be where people could see me. One hundred and thirty-five minutes total.

Eat. Then count to sixty, repeat one hundred and thirty-four times, and you're done.

I hurried back down to the senior lockers—I needed to pick up my bio textbook before next period.

Crouched in front of my locker, I sensed the world go quiet behind me. I looked up and locked eyes with her. Audrey Khalil, coming right at me. I had imagined seeing her all summer, knowing that she held my fate in her hands. If Audrey—the beautiful, the benevolent, the wronged—decided to forgive me, things could go backward and be OK. If Audrey was still *my* Audrey.

I stood.

Audrey looked at me directly, her chocolate eyes harder than I'd ever seen them. Her body was relaxed and loose; she wasn't nervous to see me.

As always, Audrey looked perfect. Her beige knit skirt fit perfectly over her legs—long, but not skinny or knobby. Her red sweetheart top was just bright enough to highlight the rich coppery undertone her warm brown skin had acquired in the summer. And her hair was tucked up in a simple twist, not a single strand out of place.

She looked me over coolly, but without investment or engagement. There was no quirk of the mouth, no dip of the head, no wave, no flipping me off, nothing. Just that cool, hard, appraising gaze.

But still, she walked slowly in my direction, looking like she was coming to see me, until, at the last second, she gave me a wide berth and slid her eyes away.

Something in me broke.

Audrey turned to the girls with her as they got to the stairwell door. And then she said, achingly lightly, "That's our dear little slut." There was a disdainful chuckle in her voice. "First day of school and she still can't keep her tits to herself. Gotta love her."

I was in rigor mortis.

Gulping for breath, I struggled to retreat, barely feeling the floor under my feet. The atmosphere in the hall felt tangible, thick and chilly, and blood pounded in my ears.

I ran.

I made it to the bathroom, locked the first stall behind me, and sank to the floor. I tried to cry but couldn't find the oxygen to do anything but gasp.

The worst part was the nauseous feeling that I deserved it. No one was lying about me. I *had* had sex with my best friend's boyfriend. Every chance I could for a whole week. And then I had been caught. The whole senior class saw me do it. Their descriptions of my half-naked, sweaty, shamed self on Facebook posts were all the proof my class needed. The likes and OMG comments proved it. I *was* a slut. A few of the seniors had even taken pictures on their phones. Once I saw those, I stopped going online.

Before, I had been happy enough at Howell. I heard no evil, saw no evil, and spoke no evil. I hadn't rocked the high school boat.

Except for that one week. Grant had white teeth and pillowy lips and this way of suddenly catching me up in his arms and wrapping them around my entire body. I never saw him hug anyone else like that. Not even Audrey. Just *once* I saw something I wanted and took it without thinking.

I drew my knees up and put my head down on them, sucking as much air into my lungs as I could. I had broken the rules and now I was alone.

The bathroom door opened and I squeezed into myself tighter, hoping that whoever it was wouldn't notice the pathetic heap behind the stall door.

There was a weird clicking noise and then silence. Whoever it was, they were still right at the entrance. *What are they doing?* And then I realized: Whoever it was had locked the door.

Heavy heels echoed off the tiling as the person walked slowly toward where I was sitting. Then stopped. I inched away from the door, trying to see underneath it.

Silence.

Just when I thought I was being paranoid and some girl was only checking her makeup in the mirror, a combat boot slammed the stall door into my back, twisting the hinges and knocking me forward. I caught my head on the ceramic toilet tank as I toppled forward into a face-plant on the linoleum floor.

CHAPTER TWO

DIZZY, FEELING LIKE MY HEAD WAS ON FIRE, I SLOWLY LIFTED MYSELF FROM THE FLOOR. I touched my fingers to my hairline. They came back bloody.

"What the hell is wrong with you?" I scrambled to my feet, wincing as I bent my banged-up knees.

I turned, expecting to see one of Audrey's toadies, but I was wrong. I had never seen this girl before in my life.

The girl was very tall and very thin. Everything about her was long, from her hair—pin straight and heavy—to her waist, to her legs, to her mouth, oddly made up: lined in a severe heart shape with a rich dark red, but with no lipstick filling the gaps. Even her eyes, narrow and bright blue, seemed longer than a normal person's eyes.

The Long Girl smirked at me. "Sorry, Kendall," she said in an offhand way, as if she had just tipped into me on the subway. "Didn't mean to hurt you."

"Oh, really?" I pushed past her to get to the sink and wet some paper towels for my head. I glared at her reflection. "Are you new?" I asked. It was always possible someone had dared a new girl to maim me.

"Yeah, no," she said, coming up next to me and rearranging her hair. "I don't go here."

My head still pounding, I saw cobwebs start to make their way across my vision. I blinked, trying to shake them away.

Balancing a hand on the mirror, I took a shaky breath. "So, how do I know you?"

"I'm hoping that you don't, actually." She pulled a cell phone out of her pocket and held it up to her eye. "Say cheese!"

The flash of light sent me swaying.

"Cute," she deadpanned, checking out the shot. "You're really smizing. Hey, Kendall, are you doing OK? You're looking a little blurry."

My vision faded for a second and I clutched at the sink. "How do you know me?" I mushmouthed: My tongue wasn't working so well.

"We have mutual friends. I really think you should sit down." The Long Girl pushed my shoulders down until I was sitting on the floor. Then she made herself comfortable, cross-legged in front of me.

"Basically, I wanted to come by and see you, to tell you in person, for both me and Mason, that this has gone far enough," she said. "No harm done or anything. We are, as of yet, cool. But we are very soon going to run out of cool."

I shook my head. "You have the wrong person. I don't know anyone named Mason."

"Kendall, please. If you're going to lie, at least set your Facebook profile to private. Hide the photographic evidence. That's kind of basic."

My Facebook profile is *set to private*, I tried to say, but everything was going gray, like a fade to black in an old movie. The Long Girl's face flickered in front of me like static as she tucked her phone in her back pocket. "In a nutshell, Mason is done with this, I am done with this, our friends are done with this, and you are done with this. Or the next time you hit your head, you won't be twenty feet from a nurses' station."

The Long Girl hauled her arm back and I heard a pop, as if from a distance. And then everything faded away.

A shrill alarm went off, jolting me awake. *Oh god, school starts today.* For five precious seconds, this day hadn't happened yet. Then Nurse Keckler walked into the dim, antiseptic-smelling room to pick up her cell and I plunged back into my body. This was reality.

"Hi," I said weakly. "Can I have some water?"

The nurse started and clutched her hand to her chest. "You startled me! I was just calling your parents."

Awesome. "Why? Am I in trouble?"

"Trouble? Honey, no. You slipped in the bathroom and hit your head pretty hard. A van is coming to take you to the hospital, just to be safe. How are you feeling now?"

I swallowed and it felt like a brick was trying to escape from my skull, Zeus-birthing-Athena style. "Totally fine. If I promise to see my family doctor as early as possible, can we call off the ambulance?"

"It's already on its way. I'm going to try your mother again." She left the recovery room. Without getting me any water.

I lay back down, the fluorescent ceiling light pulverizing the space between my eyes. I closed them. "Great. I'll just lie here and screw myself."

"Would you like some privacy?"

I didn't open my eyes right away. It was easier to pretend that this wasn't happening if I couldn't actually see him lounging in the bed on the other side of the room.

Michael Gilbert, commonly known as Gilly, was sprawled on the opposite bed, twirling a thermometer between his thumb and forefinger. His wiry limbs stuck out at their customary awkward angles. He was looking at me with a bemused half-grin spreading across his face. A half-grin was the only kind Gilly had, as far as I could tell. Normally, he was scowling.

I was hanging on to my composure by a toenail and I did *not* want to break down in front of Gilly. I gritted my teeth.

"That would be great, thanks. See you later."

Gilly stuck the thermometer in his mouth. "But I'm sick," he mumbled.

"Yeah, no doubt."

He laughed with his mouth closed, so it came out a snort.

Nurse Keckler came back into the room. "Kendall, I got a hold of your dad. He's going to call your mother and they're going to meet you at the hospital, OK?"

Oh god, this is actually happening. I nodded miserably.

"Do you want me to get one of your friends excused from class, to go with you in the hospital van? It should be here any second."

I opened my mouth automatically to ask for Audrey, but then remembered and shut it.

"No," I said. "Nobody." She went back into her office.

Gilly took the thermometer out of his mouth. "Well. Awkward."

The pain in my head increased. "Please, stop talking."

His mouth twisted meanly as he began whistling the theme from *Jeopardy*.

"*Stop.*"

Gilly paused. "Just trying to be helpful." He was silent for a moment and then began whistling "All by Myself."

"Goddamn it, Gilly," I snapped, sitting up.

He sat up too and looked at me, eyebrows lowering. He started humming again, this time a minor cord melody I couldn't place at first. Then he added the lyrics.

"I've been a bad, bad girl . . ."

Fiona Apple. "Criminal."

That toenail slipped. Without keeping track of what my limbs were doing, my arm swung back and I slapped him hard across the face.

Gilly fell against the wall and I fell back on the bed, dizzy from the sudden movement. Maybe I did have a concussion. What was I thinking, hitting someone like that?

I looked over at Gilly. He appeared surprised but not angry. Slowly rubbing his jaw, he cocked his head to the side and looked at me with focused, inquisitive eyes, like he was peering through a microscope at something he couldn't quite identify.

"What?" I said. "*What?*"

"There's really none of your friends who would go with you to the hospital?"

I hesitated and then, for no reason other than it seemed easier, decided to be honest. "I don't think so, no."

Gilly's foot began to jiggle up and down. I had noticed that before: He always seemed to be in motion.

Something occurred to me. "Do you know why . . . ?"

He pulled a *duh* face.

"Right," I sighed. Stage crew guys were practically their own ecosystem, autonomous and unconcerned. If Gilly had heard the details, my disgrace was complete.

"I'll go to the hospital with you, if you want."

I looked at him, surprised. He had stopped jiggling his foot and was looking at me weirdly seriously. I met his eyes and wondered if I'd ever actually made direct contact with them before. They were unusual: layered flecks of gray and silver and very, very clear.

Gilly blinked and looked away. I quickly did the same.

"You just want to get out of class," I said. "I'll go by myself."

He shrugged and lay back down, still not looking at me. "Worth a shot, right?"

Nurse Keckler came in. "OK, Kendall, let's go."

I gathered up my bag and my body and headed for the door.

"Hey, Kendall?"

"What?" I turned around.

Gilly caught my eye for a microsecond. Half-grinning again, he sprawled across the bed. "You look really pretty."

CHAPTER THREE

"THAT ASSHOLE." It was later that night and I was examining my reflection in the full-length mirror hanging on my bedroom door. I was not happy.

There was a gash on my forehead, still lurid, barely scabbed over. My cheekbone was rosy and swollen. And, on top of that, the Long Girl had given me a black eye, which was swiftly turning green. I flopped onto my bed in disgust.

The Long Girl. Every time I ran through the scene in the girls' room, she got longer and longer, looming over me, all lips and lashes and legs.

I felt bad for whoever the Long Girl was really looking for, because I was pretty goddamn sure it wasn't me. To my knowledge, I had never pissed anyone off until recently, and though someone at Howell might have been tempted to attack me in an effort to impress her, it didn't seem likely that Audrey would conscript a total *stranger* to beat me up. I had considered it in the van on the way to the hospital but concluded that it wasn't her style. Violence was too vulgar for Audrey, too obvious; even calling me "slut" was a little raw for her.

And it wasn't Grant. Grant had no reason to care. He wasn't the one in trouble. On the contrary, Grant had been forgiven. Nobody even remembered that Audrey and Grant had in fact been broken up when our "affair" had happened. Before I had put the moratorium on social media, I saw the unofficial Facebook album announcing their reconciliation. It was called "The Night Audrey and Grant's Relationship Became Officially Inappropriate" and contained a collection of portraits of her and Grant at the graduation party. The nine pictures told a story, but I only needed to see the first one: Grant kissing her high up on the cheekbone, arm slung around her waist; her leaning toward him, dark auburn hair hanging over his chest, smiling at the camera with an eyebrow raised.

That was also the night I saw the picture of me in my underwear. I had logged out and hadn't been back.

I frowned. The Long Girl had called me Kendall. She *recognized* me. Something wasn't right.

I reached for my laptop and went to the Facebook log-in page and hit enter, since my log-in username and password were set to automatic—and reached an error screen.

Please reenter your password. The password you entered is incorrect. Please try again (make sure your caps lock is off).

"What the hell?" I went back to the log-in screen and entered my e-mail address and password manually.

Please reenter your password. The password you entered is incorrect. Please try again (make sure your caps lock is off).

I entered my username again and typed the password into Word first,then copied and pasted it into the entry box, making sure I got it right.

Please reenter your password. The password you entered is incorrect. Please try again (make sure your caps lock is off).

I sat back, stunned. I was locked out of my profile. Someone had hacked it.

Swallowing the bile that had suddenly risen in my throat, I typed my name into Google and clicked on my public Facebook profile. All that was available to me, not being signed into Facebook, was my profile picture. And I stared at it for a long time.

There was no doubt that the girl in the profile picture was me. The room I was in was dark, but a light was shining on me, creating a golden halo around my face. I was looking off to the side of the camera, smiling at something. My eyes looked like embers, shining black against skin made glossy in the glow. My mouth was red and tilted upward in a slightly feral grin. My neck arched to the left, my hair flipped all to the other side in one thick stream.

The girl in the photograph was me, but I had never seen myself look so . . . lit up. So alive. I had no idea where or when this picture had been taken. Or who took it. But, for just a moment, I loved my hacker.

There was a knock at the door and I snapped my laptop shut.

"Come in," I said and my dad opened it. He leaned against the doorframe and looked at me thoughtfully.

"Hi, honey."

"Hi, Dad."

He didn't say anything.

I sighed. "What's up, Dad?" My father had this habit of starting a conversation and then stopping midstream, mid-thought, until you brought him back to the present. Living with him, I got used to repeating myself as needed. Or just handling whatever needed answering myself.

He started and entered the room, sitting at my desk chair.

"How are you feeling? Your head hurt?"

"A little, but I'm fine."

"Did you take the aspirin? Do you want any tea?" Tea was my dad's remedy for everything. My mom's was to ask if I was getting my period.

"I'll make some in a bit."

"I'll bring you some," he said, crossing his arms. He scratched his bald head. "Rough first day back, huh?"

"You think?"

He chuckled. "Well, your mom and I were talking . . ."

"Yes?"

"About the incident at graduation."

He paused again.

"For god's sake, Greg." My mom appeared in the doorway. Without skipping a beat, she pushed past him until she was standing in front of me, arms crossed in front of her, hip cocked, in full-on lawyer mode. "Ken Doll, did that snotty she-who-shall-not-be-named take a shot at you today?"

"The accident had nothing to do with Audrey. I swear, you guys. That was a completely unrelated mishap."

My mom leaned forward and examined my face closely. Greg and Judith Evans were not disciplinarians in any sense of the word, but if she was in the room with them, my mother could always tell when someone was lying. This bothered me at the beginning of adolescence, until I realized that, short of intravenous drug use and fucking with their stereo, I could do basically whatever I wanted without getting in trouble.

"OK," my mom said, sounding cautiously satisfied. "Please be more careful, Kendall. You scared us today. I mean"—she added, sounding mystified—"I was actually scared."

"I promise, Mom. I'm fine."

"Good." Then she smiled broadly. "We have something that might cheer you up." She nodded to my dad, who grinned and handed me a thick, padded manila envelope.

The return address said, "Young Astronomers Talent Search."

I looked down at the package in my lap, my brain fizzing. "It's heavy," I said, trying to keep my voice calm.

"Open it," ordered my mom.

I ripped open the seal and dumped three brochures and a folded letter, on fancy, textured stationery, into my lap.

My shoulders cramped with anticipation as I picked up the letter.

Dear Kendall Evans,

We are pleased to inform you that you have been selected by the Young Astronomers Talent Search to participate in next year's Accelerated Astrophysics Senior Semester, to be held on the campus of Rice University in Houston, TX, in conjunction with NASA, staring January 10. Information about housing is enclosed . . .

I dropped the letter. "I got in," I whispered.

"What? What does it say?"

"I got it." I started shrieking. "I got in!"

My mom's eyes got wide. "You're going? You're going to Texas?"

My father smiled passively. "Of course you got in. Why are you two surprised?" He wrapped his arms around me. "Congratulations, Kenny!"

My mother joined him, hugging me around the neck. "We're proud, Kendall. You earned this."

I sat there, pinned down in their arms, feeling like my brain was in suspended animation. I had known about the YATS program since they came to our Academic Enrichment Fair last year. The moment I saw the NASA logo at their booth, something lodged deep in my heart said: *Oh. Oh I want that.* But I would never have thought to give up my senior year of high school for it. Until this summer, that is.

My father let go first. "Honey, you look like you need a minute. I'll go make tea." He shuffled out of my room, placid as ever.

My mother looked like she was going to protest and opened her mouth, but, for the first time I could remember, she didn't seem to have anything to say. She smiled a little too widely at me and hurried after my father.

A sudden roar of sheer relief flooded over me and I reopened my laptop to e-mail Facebook, as I knew I should. I wasn't exactly sure of the procedure, but I assumed some measures would be taken to restore my name to me. But as I looked at the girl in the photograph—me—something in my brain sputtered and stalled. I didn't want to take her down yet. It was entirely irrational.

I shut the laptop. *Tomorrow,* I decided. *I'll take her down tomorrow.*

CHAPTER FOUR

THE GOOD NEWS WAS THAT NO ONE WAS IGNORING ME ANYMORE. It's kind of hard to look away from a girl whose face looks like it got run over by a bicycle.

"Damn, girl," whistled Dennis as I opened my locker that morning. "You fucked yourself up. You OK?"

I had to hold myself back from leaping on top of him, throwing my arms around his shoulders, and wrapping my legs around his waist out of sheer gratitude for any attention at all. Instead I smiled and said, "I'm fine. It's just a few bruises."

Dennis took off his Knicks hat and dropped it on my head, a gesture of great honor. "That's our fighter. Toughen you up for volleyball season."

Lucia slammed her locker shut and cracked a grim smile in my direction. "Off to some year, huh, K?" She walked past me before I could respond.

Dennis shrugged at me, plucked his hat off my head and trotted after her.

The good news was that my friends were no longer pretending

I was invisible. The bad news was that they still considered it a bad idea to stand next to me for too long.

Gilly didn't seem to have that problem.

All of a sudden, he was everywhere. Every class I went to, Gilly sprawled himself out in the desk next to mine. When I tucked myself into a corner near my locker for my free period, Gilly and his friends colonized the opposite wall. And I thought I saw Gilly staring at me. Never at my face, but at my shoe or my elbow or my ear.

His scrutiny bothered me. I didn't know what was behind it. I liked knowing what I was dealing with, and I didn't get Gilly. I was used to getting people.

I don't like not knowing things. This thought ran through my head all day like a mantra, and my mind naturally drifted toward my hacked Facebook profile, now inaccessible to me.

I had used my Howell e-mail address to send a notification to Facebook, but by that afternoon I hadn't gotten a response. I still couldn't see my own profile. It was like an itch I couldn't reach.

While grabbing my books for last period, I snuck a look at Gilly—he quickly looked away. He frowned at the wall as he slammed his locker shut and bolted up the stairs. I watched him go and thought back to our moment in the nurse's office. He had been a dick and I had slapped him. But then . . .

I couldn't see what the hacker had done to my profile without someone signing into Facebook and showing me. Last year I could have asked any number of people. This year the only person who had offered to do me a favor was Gilly.

So I steeled myself and followed him to the auditorium.

The fall play was still a few weeks away from auditions: The amphibian population would be in hibernation and I would have to seek them out in their own environs.

I had never been backstage before, but I found Gilly burrowed as far away from the door as possible, sitting in a nest of cables. He, Lemon, Drew, and Dave were snickering at some video on a laptop.

"Um . . . hi."

The crew looked up at me, in unison. Lemon politely asked, "Can I help you with something?" Dave, an abrasive dork with a crew cut and a hideous ball chain necklace, snorted and snatched the laptop out of Gilly's hands.

Gilly himself was quiet, looking at me with raised eyebrows.

I felt like a telemarketer. "I was hoping to speak with Gilly?"

He cocked his head to the side, as if he was suspicious of my intentions. "Here I am."

"OK." My palms felt sweaty and I wiped them on my jeans. "I could use a favor."

Dave was drinking out of a silver thermos. He choked on his laughter, and a little bit of liquid dribbled out of the side of his mouth.

I ignored him and sat down. "Someone hacked into my Facebook and changed the password."

"And you just assume *I'm* a hacker and can fix it."

Smartass. "No, no, I didn't assume that," I said, keeping my tone light. "I just thought I could look at Facebook with your log-in, see if anything in my profile got messed up. So I can do damage control."

"You want his log-in?" squeaked Drew. From his horrified expression, you'd think I'd asked for his firstborn child.

"No," I said patiently. "I thought I could just sit here and look at it on Gilly's laptop."

I tried to catch Gilly's eye, but he was too fast for me. He grabbed the laptop out of Dave's grasp. "Sorry, the computer's not available," he said. "We're watching *Peep Show.*"

He pressed the space bar and that was that. All four boys snapped their heads back toward the screen, away from me.

I gathered myself off of the floor and made my way to the exit. I thought I heard Gilly say my name, but I didn't look back. My instincts in the nurse's office had been right: When he makes eye contact, look away. Beware of techies bearing gifts.

I pushed open the heavy door and collided with Simone Moody, knocking her shoulder bag to the floor.

"Fuck! Watch it!" she said in her distinctively soft, flat voice, as she bent down to pick up her bag. She stood and pushed dark bangs out of her eyes. "Oh, it's you."

"It's me," I said cautiously. "Hi, Simone."

Simone rearranged her shoulder bag, pulling her neckline down with a practiced hand. Simone Moody's body was legendary and, if accounts were true, widely and thoroughly appreciated.

"I was looking for you today," she said huskily. "I had a question."

I didn't really know much about Simone other than that she didn't give a fuck—and that she liked to party. But she made me nervous. She made most people nervous, because a quarter of the way through sophomore year, she completely lost her mind.

It started with her slamming her fists into her locker. No one paid it that much attention—at first. It was midterms, people were frazzled. The real action started when she abandoned her fists and started using a chair. When she had demolished the locker and moved on to the window, the teachers called the cops.

She was out of school for a month.

"What's going on?" I asked, super casual.

"That girl you were talking to yesterday."

I froze. "What girl?"

Simone folded her arms. "The one I saw follow you into the bathroom. The tall girl. How do you know her?"

"I don't."

She looked at me hard.

"No, really, I don't know her."

Simone licked her lips and stuck her tongue through her teeth. She seemed to be thinking.

"What?" I asked. "Do *you* know her?"

She shrugged. "Not really." She sounded as calm as always. "But I do see her around my building most days. Every afternoon this week actually. I think she goes to Columbia."

"She hit me," I blurted out.

Simone raised her eyebrows.

"I don't know why, but she hit me."

Simone was quiet for a while. I watched as she seemed to process the information. Her face was beautiful but a little confusing: unreadable and ethnically ambiguous. I was staring, trying to parse whether she was part-Asian—maybe Vietnamese?—when she said matter-of-factly, "She's kind of scary. I think you should stay away from her if you can. Just my opinion."

We stood there, surveying each other for another moment, not talking.

"I'm going to get going," she said eventually, turning around. "But I guess I'll be seeing you around."

"Yeah," I said, distracted. "See you tomorrow."

Simone opened the door and then turned around abruptly, smiling a rare, wry smile. "Hey, Kendall? It's going to be fine."

"Huh?"

She shrugged a little. "I've been where you are. Don't worry, you'll get used to it."

She started to leave when, to my surprise, I stopped her. "Simone?" She turned around. "Could you log in to Facebook and show me my profile?"

Simone's brow crinkled, but she pulled her phone out of her bag, flicked her fingers over it, and held it out to me.

I stepped toward her and took it. "Thanks."

Surprisingly, my hacker hadn't touched most of my profile. There were no new likes of any creepy alt-right pages or links to pyramid schemes. The only items Kendall Evans had contributed to the News Feed in three months were pictures. There was the profile picture of course, but there was also a whole new album called, "My New BFFS."

I clicked on the first picture. It was a squat stone building somewhere by the water, with colorful posters partially obscuring the one, wide window. As far as I could tell, there was nothing special about it. It looked like one of the faux-dive bars in Red Hook.

The second picture was of a shiny, green Prius, illegally parked next to a fire hydrant. A medal hung in the window; I couldn't make out what it said.

The third was hard to figure out. There was a slick, red leather sofa and a decrepit, scratched-up wooden coffee table. The dingy white walls looked like they were made of cinder block.

The fourth, and last, was that same coffee table, only this one had a single white capsule on it. Someone was also tagged in this picture, somewhere in the vicinity of the coffee table: Mason Frye.

Mason. I clicked on his name. It was a private profile. No profile picture. But at least I had a last name. Mason Frye.

I turned toward Simone and handed her the phone. "Thanks."

Simone hesitated a moment before taking it back. "It's not a problem."

We stood there silently until Simone seemed to lose patience with the awkwardness. "Anything else?" she asked, crossing her arms.

I studied her carefully. It was as direct an offer of help as I could imagine receiving, and I didn't know what to make of it. Whether it was because I had never needed help before or because it was coming from Simone, I wasn't sure.

"You said you think the Long Girl—I mean the tall girl—" I took a deep breath and re-collected myself. "You said that you think she's scary."

"I said that, yeah."

"Any particular reason?"

Simone tossed her hair out of her face. "She plays with pocket knives while glaring at everyone and hanging out with the sketchiest people on the Upper West Side," she said mildly. "That's why."

"Huh. That'll do," I agreed.

"So you're going to stay away from her then?"

Gingerly, I brushed the skin around my eye socket. It still stung. "I don't know. I'd like to know why she hit me. I've never been hit before."

Simone sighed and walked away.

I watched her leave. I still didn't know what to make of Simone, but I knew I liked having a clue. When she was out of sight, I went to the office and looked up her address in the school directory.

After school let out, I rode the subway to the Upper West Side. Simone's building was a freestanding structure of gray stone, with classically coiled moldings, a slate blue awning, and a doorman.

I studied it from across the wide, clean street, not entirely sure how to proceed. It occurred to me that in movies, stakeouts usually involved cars. I had to settle for huddling on a fire escape partially hidden behind a wall across the street, keeping my hoodie up, and praying that no one looked out the window and started yelling at the vagrant on the wall.

You need information, I told myself sternly, trying to get comfortable. *Information is armor.* I was already being crucified for something I had actually done. I couldn't handle being beaten up for some mystery offense on top of that.

But after an hour and fifty-six minutes had passed uneventfully, I started to stop feeling stern and just felt stupid. Stupid and sad. What was I doing here? I was not a spy; I was not a detective. I was no kind of threat to the kind of guy who would plan an assault on a seventeen-year-old girl or to his scary henchwoman. I was no kind of threat to anybody.

I stood up glumly and accepted the truth: This was a distraction. I would e-mail Facebook again that night, I'd wipe the fake profile, and I'd start building a new one. I'd build a new profile saying that I was going to be leaving soon anyway, to study astrophysics in Texas. *I can confirm what people probably always thought: I'm just a harmless nerd. I'm not even a popular girl fallen from grace, just a fraud and a nerd.*

I owed the Long Girl and Mason a thank you for helping me to forget for even twenty-four hours the voice Audrey had used when she called me a slut.

Just then, as if my anger at myself had conjured her out of thin air, the Long Girl stepped out of a cab.

Dressed in all black, with sunglasses and silver jewelry, she seemed older than she had at Howell, when I had mistaken her for a high school student. But that might have just been the way she was walking—her slinky, straight-ahead stride toward the doorman, who let her in without a second look.

Ten minutes later, she came out and headed to the side of the building, unlocking a gated entrance to what was probably the boiler room. And then she was gone.

I crossed the street and circled the block, hoping to find an unlocked back entrance to the building. There was a narrow alleyway between Simone's apartment and the one on the other side of the street, but the gate there was as high and locked as the one in front. Dead end.

I grabbed the bars and swung back on my ankles, shaking the railings, frustrated at being so close, and my elbow slipped through the bars.

Easily.

My heart starting to beat fast, I pushed my whole arm through the gap and then, my shoulder. I moved slowly, finally getting stuck on my lower ribcage.

I extricated myself and took a closer look at the gate. The bars were all uniform and they would all stymie my ribcage. Except, I noticed, moving closer, where the building met its neighbor. There, the middle of the bar had become slightly warped. The warped area was only about a foot high, but it might be just wide enough to get my torso through. If I got that far, I could easily wriggle the rest of my body across. Just like taking a dive for the volleyball.

I turned around and moved my back over the gap in the bars, trying to gauge my chances. My torso would fit.

I waited for a car or two to pass by, and then, when the street was quiet, I launched myself through the gate.

It was not graceful.

I got the top half of my body through right away, but the momentum from my leap sent it plummeting to the ground while my ass got jammed in the narrower part of the bars. The unwieldy gravity of the situation telegraphed the inevitable to the part of my brain not thudding with adrenaline, but there was nothing I could do. I toppled to the cement on my back, and for the second time that week, knocked my head.

But I had made it.

I struggled to a sitting position. It was awkward to do while still wearing my backpack, but I was grateful to it for cushioning my head somewhat, and, anyway, I couldn't have just left it on the street. Overall, it was a vast improvement on the last time I had been knocked off my feet. I wasn't bleeding, for one thing.

I also felt sort of . . . giddy. Excited. As I got to my feet, I couldn't help but congratulate myself on my perseverance and resourcefulness.

Then someone grabbed my hoodie and yanked backward.

CHAPTER FIVE

I WAS HALF DRAGGED, HALF THROWN THROUGH A DOORWAY. The door slammed shut with a bang and the light was gone.

"Oh god, it's girl detective," said a familiar, smoky voice behind me. The Long Girl. "Great. What do you think? Do we, like, blindfold her?"

There was a deep sigh and then a pair of quick hands tied something silky and narrow tightly around my eyes. The extra fabric flapped against my nose and mouth, and light appeared at the top and bottom of my vision as someone flicked on the overheads.

"Well, what do we do with her now?" said a new, exasperated, male voice.

"We wait for Mason."

The hands pulled me to my feet by my elbows and, after a second, dusted me off lightly, grazing my back and butt. I stiffened, but he moved backward a second later.

"He's supposed to drop by in about fifteen minutes," said the Long Girl. "Might as well bring her back."

The guy grabbed my hand and started to pull me forward. I

couldn't seem to make my mouth work, but I planted my feet and strained in the opposite direction. He stopped and for a second I thought I'd won. But then he asked, not speaking to me, "Wait, you're not coming?"

The Long Girl said, "No, I have to make a phone call outside. I'll head in when Mason gets here."

"What? I'm *babysitting*?"

"Don't whine. I'll be back there in a minute."

I heard the door open and shut again. There was another deep sigh and I was pulled down the hallway again.

"This is honestly a really big misunderstanding," I bleated, grimacing when my voice rang out as a shrill, anxious echo of its former self. I rolled my eyes under the blindfold and tried again. "I—"

He cut me off, "Chill out for a minute. OK? I need to find my keys." Again, there was a sigh. "This is such a waste of my time," he muttered. "So not what I signed up for."

My guard led me into a bright room and sat me down on a chair. My makeshift blindfold's extra flap tickled my nose and I tried to twist it to the back.

"You can just take it off. It was a stupid idea. Girl's nuts. Here, let me, I tied it pretty tight and it's in the back." Arms reached around my head, little hairs tickling my ears. He smelled like smoke.

Little by little the silk loosened around my face until it dropped to my collarbone in a loop. I opened my eyes. It was a red plaid tie, presumably taken directly from my jailor's neck, judging by the popped collar on his preppy white button-down.

He struck a match and I looked up. He was ripped, with heavy, bulging shoulders, but his face looked young. He lit a cigarette and looked me up and down.

To my surprise, I realized that I wasn't actually scared anymore. I might find the Long Girl terrifying, but this fed-up guy with the creased forehead and the curious gaze *wasn't* terrifying. Just big.

"What's your name?" I asked, sitting up a little straighter.

He took the cigarette out of his mouth with long, well-groomed fingers and jerked his head back toward the door. "I don't think the sergeant would like us fraternizing." He smiled wryly, and a little grimly.

He didn't like the Long Girl. That was clear. I might be able to press him for some information. Usually, I was good at getting people to tell me things.

I considered and unzipped my sweatshirt. I knew that the glimpse of the fierce, illuminated girl in that photograph was a fluke, an illusion. But I kept her wolfish expression in my mind as I looked him in the eye and bared my teeth in a smile.

"Well, of course, I can see that," I said, pitching my voice low and amused. "She wants you to follow her sterling example. After all, she's so careful I was able to track her down less than two days after she was seen by at least a dozen people talking to me at my school. Is she as stealthy as that when she's climbing up Mason's ass?"

He choked on his cigarette smoke, laughing. I got nervous as he continued, not sure if he was laughing at my fake bravado or my joke. But then he shook out a cigarette from his pack and offered it to me.

"I'm Jerry," he said. "And you're funny."

I didn't smoke, but I accepted it and stuck it behind my ear, as if for later. "I'm Kendall," I said. "And I appreciate you taking off the blindfold."

He shrugged. "You knew where you were. What was the point?"

I answered in as nonchalant a tone as I could manage. "Got me. I was just visiting a friend who lives in the building. Any reason you guys threw me in here?"

Jerry slid his eyes away and shrugged.

"Hey," I said, impulsively leaning forward and grabbing his sleeve, using my real voice. "You seem nice. You can help me."

"I don't see that," he said, removing my hand gently. Jerry put my hands back on my lap and then, very quickly, so quickly that I almost missed it, he glanced downward.

Out of habit, I glanced down myself, frowning at the pale skin visible at the top of my shirt. I was in a constant battle with my larger-than-average boobs. Show any cleavage at all and I looked slutty. Cover it up and I looked dumpy.

The first time I was catcalled, I was thirteen years old. My dad had sent me to the corner bodega for a liter of Diet Coke. I was slouching down the street in beat-up Reeboks and a Sponge-Bob T-shirt, hands in my pockets, thinking about whether I was too scared to get my ears pierced, when a laughing voice called out, "Hey, girl, turn around!" Not knowing why I shouldn't, I obliged.

It was a skinny boy, barely older than me, but tall, standing in front of a trio of smirking comrades. He cupped his hands in front of his chest and pursed his lips in a kiss.

"That's our dear little slut. First day of school and she still can't keep her tits to herself."

I zipped up my sweatshirt.

The Long Girl slammed the door open and strode back into the room.

Jerry sighed. "Well?"

"He's just finishing a phone call."

A heavy door slammed in the hallway. I could hear keys jangling and a raw, tenor voice humming. And then Mason stepped into the room.

He was tall, thin, and pale, and had a dark blue tattoo of looping, interlocking lines snaking up his arm. There was something squirrelly and mischievous about his face with its hooked nose, high, uneven cheekbones, and sharp chin. He didn't look like he could be older than twenty or twenty-one, and he was wearing jeans and a plain gray T-shirt.

Mason quirked a blond eyebrow in my direction and leaned against the doorframe with his arms crossed. He smiled at me. His teeth were slightly crooked and very white.

He uncrossed his arms, lifting one hand up, palm out. "Hi," he said.

Without thinking about it, I found myself copying the odd gesture. "Hi."

He closed his mouth, pursing his lips.

"Jerry, Jo, could you guys give us a minute alone?"

At the sound of her name, the Long Girl snapped into a straight posture. She shot me a dirty look, but said, "Sure," in a pleasant tone of voice and headed out. Jerry looked from Mason to me. I locked eyes with him for a second. He shrugged as he looked away, like he was physically shaking me off, and followed Jo out of the room. A few seconds later, the door slammed once again.

Mason walked into the room and stood in front of me. He bent to the side and, grabbing the chair in one tapered hand, deftly flipped it over so it faced me. He sat down.

"So," he said, pushing his heavy, straw-colored hair back and then forward, so it fell around his face in pieces. "You're Kendall. *The* Kendall."

I couldn't help laughing, but I was nervous, so it came out as a snort. "You would think so, wouldn't you? There seem to be a few of us floating around."

He gestured around his cheek and my hand flew to mine—I had forgotten I was still bruised. "Was that all Jo?" he asked.

"Yes." I looked him in the eye. "Thanks for getting me out of school early."

He grimaced. "Sorry. I didn't mean for that to happen. She's got anger management issues."

"She should take up knitting."

Mason grunted out a brief chuckle.

It was quiet in that room. I started to count the seconds, trying to look anywhere but at Mason as he unabashedly studied me. I could see him out of the corner of my eye, his gaze flickering over my face, my arms, even my backpack. *What does this guy want from me?* I thought. *Please just tell me, so I can get out of here.*

He startled me out of my count at forty-two. "You know you're moving your lips?" he said. "Are you om-ing or something?"

I opened my mouth to deny it, but then stopped and shrugged. I bent down to retie my shoe, trying to avoid his eyes.

"I didn't take the pictures you saw on my Facebook," I said carefully. "I didn't post them. I don't even know what those pictures are of." I straightened up and looked him in his pale blue eyes. He seemed like he was listening, so I went on. "Someone else is messing with you, using me to cover their ass. It's not me. I've been hacked."

He nodded, looking thoughtful. "I did a little independent research on you. I found out some interesting things; coincidences."

"Oh?" I asked.

"Oh," he agreed. "And I know a bunch of kids who went to Howell, so I asked around, too. Got the scoop."

"That was probably pretty boring."

"No, actually," he said, rocking his chair back and then forward. "People had real opinions about you. Thoughts."

"What did they—?" I bit my lip and blushed at the eagerness in my voice.

Mason laughed again. It was a funny laugh, tight, but drawling, going all the way up and down the register.

Suddenly, he snapped his chair all the way to the floor with a crack and leaned forward on his knees, invading my personal space with his long neck.

Mason said, "I hate being so dramatic, but you *did* come looking for me and you're here, so . . . I do actually need to ask you something," his voice casual, as though merely curious. "I don't care about the pictures. Jo was the one who got all upset about them. To be honest, there wasn't anything in those pictures you couldn't find out by just asking around. But when a batch of doses goes missing right after I receive incriminating photographs purportedly taken by you, I have to wonder . . . well, I have to ask."

I waited for him to go on, but he didn't. It was my turn to raise my eyebrow. "You're serious?"

"Well . . . yeah. I guess I'm serious."

"You think I *stole*, what, 'doses' from you?" I asked, putting finger quotations around doses. "I don't even know what *doses* are. What, like, Ritalin?"

He grinned. "Ritalin? Pedestrian. You trying to insult me?"

"No. If you asked around about me, you probably know that I don't go out of my way to insult people."

"Tell that to Audrey Khalil."

"You dick." The words flew out of my mouth unpremeditated, but they felt good and I found I couldn't stop them. "Audrey Khalil is a hypocrite, Grant is pathetic, Jo's a loser, and you are, in fact, a huge drama queen. I don't know anything about your dumbass little drug operation and—" I rose out of my chair and stomped my foot. "I don't care."

Mason's head cocked to the side and he considered me. His face was impassive as Jo bounded back into the room, fuming.

"Jesus, could she be any fucking louder?"

Blue eyes still fixed on me, Mason suddenly smiled, his face lighting up like a particularly sinister sunrise. "Ask her yourself, Jo," he said. "She's right in front of you."

Jo's mouth flapped open and shut like a hungry guppy. Her eyes narrowed at me and I flashed her a toothy, sweet grin. I had sort of run out of my supply of verbal vitriol, but I felt like I was on a roll with Mason and I didn't want to lose my swagger before I had a chance to get out of that basement and possibly burst into tears.

Mason abruptly got up and headed for an old-fashioned roll top desk in the corner. He opened it and picked out a bottle of brown liquor. He poured himself a shot and then looked at me, his eyes still shining.

"You can go if you want," he said, gesturing to the door. "Thanks for answering my question. Sorry if I freaked you out."

Moving slowly, I bent over to retrieve my backpack. I nodded at Jerry, who had slunk in, and headed for the door. My foot was at the threshold when Mason said, "You want a shot before you go? You're having a hell of a week, I'm betting."

He poured a shot into a cream-colored mug and held it out to me.

Alcohol didn't glow with glamour for me the way it did to some other kids in my class. I had always attributed that to permissive parenting and the fact that I was given access to beer and wine from thirteen on, meaning I didn't have what I tended to think of as puppy-let-off-the-leash syndrome.

But I did have a secret relationship with alcohol. A sort of friends-with-benefits thing. I didn't get drunk often, but I *did* have a small glass flask of bourbon swiped from my kitchen hidden in my sock drawer. If I had a bad day or felt somehow bereft or bored, I would just look at it. Every so often, I took a swig. And it made me feel better.

I wanted that shot.

I walked toward Mason and extracted the mug from his fingers, briefly entangling his and mine awkwardly. I drank it in one go and started to leave.

Before I could reach the door, my nerve endings began to bubble and fizz. Giggling, I reached out for the couch. "Whoa," I said, every single sound in the room with the volume turned up to eleven, every detail in high-def. "Strong shot."

I whirled around toward the door and then the room flickered. As quickly as the colors had brightened, the world turned black from the outside in, tunneling my vision until it disappeared completely. My legs vanished from the knees down and I felt wiry arms catch me just before I cracked my head for a third time in as many days.

CHAPTER SIX

"Miss Evans! Kendall Evans!"

The voice was loud and peevish. I rolled over, cushioning my head on my arms. "Alarm clock didn't go off, Dad," I mumbled. "I'm not late yet."

"Kendall, *wake up*. Before the other children get here."

I opened my eyes. Principal Myers and Ms. Lowery, his assistant, were leaning over me, blotting out what appeared to be very bright sunshine. Shading my eyes, I looked to the side to see the glass double doors of Howell Prep looming overhead.

I bolted upright and immediately slumped back, my head aching with the exertion.

"Kendall, do your parents know where you are?"

I was sitting on the stone steps of my high school. My backpack was lying on its side where my head had been moments ago. I rooted around my pocket for my cell phone, fumbling under the red hoodie spread over my waist.

The battery was dead. I squinted up at the teachers. "I'm guessing not."

Half an hour later I was sitting in the principal's office, head down on the desk, trying to draw sustenance from the smell steaming out of a mug of cheap teachers' lounge coffee but feeling ill at the thought of moving my head to take a sip. Although, with my nose facing downward, I could smell myself, creating my own grim, bodily catch-22. I reeked of whiskey and sweat and sported a damp, brown stain on my top, making the cotton stick to my chest.

The door opened and my parents rushed into the office, kneeling down on either side of me.

My mother was pale and wild-eyed. "Kendall! Ken Doll, are you OK?" I nodded mutely. She narrowed her eyes at the obvious lie. "Kendall, are you crazy?" she continued in the same fast, breathless voice. "What are you doing? Are you being hazed or something?"

I moaned involuntarily. "Mom, please take *Pretty Little Liars* off your Netflix queue."

My mother shook me by the shoulders and when she spoke again, her voice was harder. "This is not about me, Ken Doll. You are damn lucky this is a private school and no one called the police. And no one's going to." Here she shot a stern look back at Principal Myers, who put his hands up.

My dad patted my head. "Judith, of course this is about us as well. We need to have more talks with Kendall. She's at a transitional epoch."

Helplessly, I swiveled in my chair to Principal Myers, silently begging him to just start yelling and get them out of there.

"Mr. Evans, Mrs. Evans, please take a seat." He pulled out two chairs from the row by the wall. My parents sat on either side of me, locking me in. Dad put his arm around my shoulder and Mom sniffed my hair, muttering, "Oh, Jesus," under her breath.

Principal Myers cleared his throat. "To be honest, Kendall, you've been the topic of some discussion among your teachers and I'd be lying if I said they weren't somewhat concerned about—"

My mother cut in. "Her grades are perfectly acceptable. She got honor roll all last year, as you know, and there is no reason she won't achieve the same level of excellence this year. That is, before she leaves Howell to attend one of the most prestigious math and science programs for high school students in the country. I believe my assistant faxed over her YATS acceptance letter. The list has also been published on the program's website, so feel free to put her accomplishment in the alumni magazine."

He grimaced and continued, ignoring Mom's barbs. "I know that last year we made the decision to put the incident at graduation behind us, but . . . I may have been misguided there. Especially as it seems to be the harbinger of a somewhat worrying new pattern of behavior—'acting out,' if you will."

"What sort of behavior?" my dad asked calmly. Even I had to give him a "you kidding me?" face.

"I'm not interested in re-hashing the incident at graduation," said my mom tersely. "Let's focus on the situation we find ourselves in this morning, please. What are you saying in real terms, Principal Myers? Is Kendall going to be suspended?"

"I'd like to interject one thing here," I said. All three of the grown-ups looked at me.

I struggled to find the words. "Last night wasn't my fault. I didn't get drunk. I mean, I had one drink," I admitted, looking into the unbelieving eyes of my parents, "but that's not why—"

Principal Myers cut me off, waving my mouth shut with his hand. "I understand that things get out of control sometimes, Kendall. Everyone knows that you're a well-intentioned and bright young woman. But we can't ignore present behavior just because you've always been a good kid."

"No, I swear, this wasn't me, it was—"

This time, my mother cut me off, squeezing my arm and entering the conversation in the deep, authoritative tone that meant she was going to get her way. "Kendall, I think you should go wash your face and get ready for school while your father and I finish our conversation with Principal Myers. Since you're *not getting suspended.*"

My mother's agenda clear, I left the room and headed for the little bathroom in the main office, wanting to avoid gen pop for as long as possible.

I looked in the mirror. My bruise had healed a little over the last couple of days, but I looked wrecked on a whole different level now. Feeling slightly ashamed, I shucked off my sweatshirt and wiped my underarms and chest down with damp paper towels.

I was still wearing Jerry's tie around my neck. I threw it in the trash. As I swung my sweatshirt around my shoulders, a piece of paper, neatly folded into a cootie catcher, tumbled into the sink. My name was written on it in black sharpie.

Here's what the note said:

Hi Kendall.

Don't be mad.

I slammed my fist into the mirror and then swore as I examined the raw skin of my knuckles, followed by the completely undamaged mirror. I took a long, deep breath and continued to read.

Don't be mad. I mean, be mad for a little while, sure, why not, but don't stay mad.

I believe you when you say you have no idea where the missing doses are. I am even willing to give you the benefit of the doubt on the pictures. You probably have nothing to do with this, or you didn't mean to anyway.

But here's my problem: Someone at Howell does have the doses. And someone at Howell has decided to pin their shit on you. And as I don't have the time or desire to trawl high school social media tracking the activities of everybody at that school who's got issues with you and cross-reference any connection with me, I have a proposition for you.

I want you to find out who took my doses. I don't like getting robbed. If you do this for me, you'll have a new friend and I can be a very good friend.

If you refuse, I can get you kicked out of YATS.

I sucked in my breath and blinked a few times, sure I couldn't have read that right. How could he even know about YATS? I hadn't told anyone. But I looked again and there it was: *I can get you kicked out of YATS.*

I kept reading.

I bet you think I'm bluffing, the letter went on. *Like, how would I even be able to do that? But, the thing is, it would actually be easy. This is your bad luck, but I spent all summer in Houston, specifically on the campus of Rice University. I had some business with a post-grad who's going to be a TA at YATS. This TA owes me a favor. And there are any number of ways I can cash in. Would you rather you get caught cheating or failing a test? Would you rather it happen once you've already gone out there, or should I have the TA in question get an anonymous tip from a teacher at Howell about how he suspects you cheated on the entrance exam, trigger a re-test, and have you fail* that *one, so your parents save on airfare?*

Think about it, Kendall. What won't *people believe about you at this point? Do you really want to test it?*

—Mason

There was a knock on the bathroom door. I knew I needed to answer, but with each new, horrifying word, icicles had formed in my head, blocking rational thought.

But, there was no solution except the one Mason had given me. I could keep my dignity and do what he said, and go to YATS. Or I could refuse and be even more disgraced than I already was. Principal Meyers has just made clear that my school was already primed to believe the worst of me. They were *expecting* more scandal, not less.

Fear is a zero-sum equation, I told myself sternly. *Fear has a value of zero.*

"Kendall!"

"Yeah," I said, stuffing the note in my jeans pocket and turning on the faucet. "I'll be out in a second." I counted a full four seconds, one for each month until YATS. When I was done, all I felt was determined.

I turned back to the mirror and tucked my hair back behind my ears. My face looked calm. My eyes were bright. "Here we go," I whispered at my reflection.

I reentered the office and stood behind my parents.

Principal Myers looked exhausted and annoyed. "Well, Kendall, you are not to be suspended. And please do accept my congratulations on YATS. But all three of us want it understood that you're on a very real probation. Any more disciplinary problems at all and you will be suspended, at the least. Is that clear?"

"Yes. Thank you for not suspending me."

He sighed. "I think I interrupted you earlier. If you have something you would like to tell us, please do so."

Voices from the hallway began to pour in through the open door. Naya Muñoz, our sharp-eyed student council president with uncannily sleek, pitch-black hair, walked in to drop something off with Ms. Lowery. She stopped in her tracks when she saw me.

Naya looked at me with an expansive, all-seeing gaze. "Good morning, Kendall," she said, in her loud, bell-like voice. "Should I tell Mr. Krieger that you'll be late to homeroom?" I pictured that voice reverberating against the ceiling and careening endlessly throughout the school like a ping pong ball.

"Nope," I said, cheerfully. "I'll be right there." I turned back to Principal Myers and my parents.

"It wasn't important. Thank you for your understanding. I'm going to do my best to make this better. I promise."

I meant it. Whatever it took, I would get myself out of this. I fingered the note in my pocket and made myself a promise:

Whatever it takes.

CHAPTER SEVEN

BY FIFTH PERIOD, ALL I HAD TO DO WAS LEAN BACK IN AP AMERICAN HISTORY AND ALL EYES WERE ON ME. Every move I made was leapt on by my viewing public, which was just dying to see me do something crazy. It had been a long time since Howell had seen a good downward spiral. And now there was blood in the water. If anything, my sophomore effort was even more exciting than sleeping with Grant Powers in the gym—just where had I been last night?

"She was definitely out with Grant. He's still in the city."

I was in the locker room bathroom when I heard the first rumor. Of course, Naya had busted me right away.

"No way. Audrey's got him on lockdown." That was Ellie Kurtz—I'd recognize her whitewater rapid of a voice anywhere. "But you're right, I'm betting it was some NYU freshman orientation thing. Where else is she going to find a party that doesn't card on a Wednesday night?"

"Did you see her before homeroom?" Naya again. "Totally wrecked," she went on. "I can't believe they didn't send her home right then and there."

"Wait. I just thought of something. You don't think she *did* anything? Like, on the steps?"

"Well, we know she's not conscientious about cleaning up the condom wrapper, so my guess is we'll find out."

"Oh god, that's traumatizing. You should send a PSA out in your student council minutes, suggesting we all exit out the back, at least until it rains."

"Ugh, if only."

As soon as they swung out into the locker room proper, I banged my head against the wall. Now I had slept with some college guy on the steps of Howell. At least I was still using protection.

It was a relief when I finally got to lunch—a blessed free period. I headed to the computer room and pulled up my Facebook profile. Facebook had sent me a new log-in that morning, so I had access to the whole account, but I stopped at the profile picture. Again, I studied it closely, but this time for clues.

I copied and pasted it into Photoshop. Blew it up. Tried to ignore my giant, glowing face and focus on the background. I highlighted the negative space between my tilted head and shoulder and zoomed in.

There was something there. I squinted at the screen and tried to make it out through what seemed like a cloud of brown-black dust. It was as if someone had laid a film over the image.

A thought occurred to me: I looked lit up. What if I was? I drew a line around my head and chest and lowered the brightness in that area, and then heightened it in the area around me. Darkened, brightened. Darkened, brightened. Eventually the picture was in equilibrium and I saw the whole image.

I wasn't looking into the light. I was looking into Audrey. More specifically, I was looking up at Audrey, previously too dark to see, who had just thrown her arms around my waist. She was smiling widely at the camera, wearing a gold-sequin-lined-and-laced, black silk tank top, with thick straps and a heart-shaped neckline that showed off her collarbones. That night was the first time she'd worn it.

I knew where the picture was taken.

The picture was taken on one of the first really warm days of the year last spring, a Friday. After school that day, I sat on Audrey's tidily made-up bed, messing up the formerly folded orange sunburst throw, and watching her try on the black-and-gold top.

"Well?" she had asked, twisting in front of the mirror.

"Looks good," I said, watching how she sparkled at her edges as she dipped and twisted, evaluating the angles. I plucked at my black cotton V-neck, feeling plain. "So where are you and I and your new top going tonight?"

"We're going to a party in Red Hook." She looked over her shoulder at me and smiled. "A warehouse party. Grant knows the people who are throwing it."

"Audrey, is this a rave? Are we having a very special episode?"

She just laughed.

So of course I ended up going to the stupid rave.

Three hours later, we met Grant and some of his buddies at the Carroll Street subway station.

"Hey, I've got a surprise for you," said Grant, his arms still around Audrey's waist. He whispered something to her and she made a face like she'd smelled something bad. She squirmed out of his grasp, grabbing my arm and drawing me to her side.

Grant made a pouty face. "OK, buzzkill. You're lucky you're so cute. Come on, ladies."

"What was that about?" I asked her as we walked.

"Nothing. He's just being an idiot."

We arrived at the party, which was in a cleanish, unadorned, gray building, pulsing with electronic chords and beats. I remembered wishing that I could go to the comparatively quiet-looking bar next door. I hadn't been feeling myself at parties lately. It was as if I were watching people interact through glass at an aquarium or a zoo. I could wave at the walrus in the tank, but I couldn't swim with him.

That bar, I realized, pulling up the photo album on Facebook, was the one my hacker had tacked onto my profile.

I hadn't been feeling myself at parties, but I'd had fun at that party. The music made me happy. Audrey, for once, let Grant do his own thing and stuck with me. We danced together and that was unusual for us. With Audrey off with Grant at parties, normally I didn't dance. It meant dancing alone. Dancing with boys at parties wasn't really dancing—it was more like sexual judo.

That night I felt every tiny exertion of each muscle, really *felt* it from the top of my skull to my toes, and every motion filled me with the pure pleasure of being in my body. And yes, I had had a shot of tequila, and the air was shimmering and bright. But it wasn't just that; the connective tissue in my body was clicking into place. I had assumed it was because I had Audrey with me.

But, come to think of it, I didn't feel lonely when Audrey went to the bathroom. I kept on dancing. Alone.

Grant pushed his way through the crowd. "Hey, you having fun?"

"Yeah," I said, looking up at him and grinning. "Thanks for inviting me."

Grant smiled his wide, easy smile. "Of course," he said, knocking me on the shoulder. "You're my bud."

I reeled and punched him lightly back. "Damn it, Grant, I'm a girl."

He leaned in close, suddenly, and whispered with his face right against my ear. "Can you keep a secret?" A stream of warm air hit my neck, just between my earlobe and my chin. I shivered.

"Sure."

"I got some ecstasy. I already did it, but Audrey won't. Want to get happy with me?" Just as abruptly as he had leaned in, he grabbed me around the waist and hugged me roughly, clumsy and sweet and—as I suddenly, insanely, noticed his thick, deep brown eyelashes—dangerous. Like a pit bull.

Just then, Audrey showed up and spun me away from Grant into her own arms. "Don't hog my friend!" she shouted.

Back in the computer lab I gulped, looked at the picture, and decided that the "doses" had to be ecstasy. It was the only lead I had. And there was only one person who I could think of to ask for help.

I caught up with Simone after school as she was loading up her backpack at her locker.

"Hey, Simone," I said, sliding into a sitting position next to her on the floor.

She flipped her bangs out of her eyes and smiled slightly at the sight of me. "Hey," she said, zipping up the backpack and turning to face me, legs crossing gracefully under her. "How's it going?"

It was amazing how much subtext Simone could convey with a hair flip and the flat delivery of a generic question. I had to smile back. "OK."

"Rough night last night?" she asked, archly.

"Didn't quite go as planned." I swallowed and barreled ahead.

"I want to ask you something, but I don't want you to judge me."
I added quickly, "or think that I judge you."

Simone crossed her arms and waited, her face impassive.

"So . . . do you know where I can buy some ecstasy?"

Simone quirked her nose and left eyebrow, twisting up her face.

"What?" I asked, shrinking at her expression, thinking: *Oh no, she never did any drugs, all that partying was just a rumor, shit.*

She shook the expression out of her face, flickering back to normal, and said, "Nothing, I just figured you would know. You hung out with all those seniors and I know they did ecstasy."

"Oh," I said. "No, I never did. But they're the only ones I know who did it. And, um, I didn't want to ask them."

She looked down at her fingernails and bit at one. "I once went in on a buy with Pete Morrison. I didn't really like it that much. But then I did it with Pete and he's a dick." Her voice went up a few decibels higher than usual at the word "dick," and I winced.

"From who?" I asked, trying to keep my voice cool. She looked up at me blankly. "Who did you buy it from?"

She stared for a moment before responding, in that unnerving way she had. "Can I ask why you're asking me?"

"Why I'm asking you or why I'm asking?"

She shrugged. "Either."

I cast around my mind, searching for one of any number of plausible reasons. But her face was so open and neutral, that I heard myself say the truth, "You're the only one I could think of who would tell me and also not tell everyone else I asked. You're the only one who wouldn't enjoy being asked."

She didn't visibly react, but she did take out her phone and scroll down. She handed it to me and I copied the number under "Trev" into my phone. I handed it back to her and she broke into a genuine smile as she stood.

"What?" I asked. "What did I say?"

She laughed. "The truth! At long goddamn last, someone in this school speaks the truth." She stalked out the door, stiletto heels clicking across the linoleum.

Quickly, before I lost my nerve, I took out my phone and sent a text to Trev:

Hey, this is Ken, a friend of Simone's. Is there a good time to pick up a dose?

CHAPTER EIGHT

I WASN'T SURE WHAT TO EXPECT WHEN I GOT HOME. I had never been "in trouble" before. When there aren't any rules, it's kind of hard to break them.

But what I definitely wasn't expecting was the smell of burnt sugar and the Who's "Baba O'Riley" blasting on the stereo.

"Hello?" I called out, shutting the front door. "Who's home?"

There was no answer, so I followed the bittersweet smell into the kitchen.

My mom was sitting alone, a glass of red wine in front of her, along with a tray of perfect, steaming Rice Krispies treats. There were two pans of failures piled on the stove behind her.

This was unprecedented.

"Hi, Mom," I said awkwardly, sitting across from her. "What's going on? Decided to come home early?"

She nodded and took a swift, solid gulp of wine.

"What's with the baking?"

"I do know how to bake, you know," she said, huffily. "We used to bake all the time when you were little. Don't you remember?"

"Not really." I picked up a square and took a bite. Caramelized marshmallow oozed over my tongue.

She stared at me. "You don't remember making a gingerbread house with me?"

I didn't know what to say. "Vaguely?" I offered.

My mom's shoulders sagged a little. She picked up her wine glass again. "This is weird, isn't it?" she asked flatly. "I meant this to be nice, but it's weird."

My dad wandered into the kitchen in bare feet and a T-shirt. "Oh, hi! School's out already?"

I sat back. "Yes," I said cautiously. "It's 4:30. What are *you* doing home?"

"Just kicking back. How's AP Bio this year?"

I was nonplussed. "OK, do you guys have something you want to say to me? What are you doing home?"

At this, my mom sighed and stood up. "Not really, I guess. I just thought . . . I don't know. Never mind. I thought I should be home? It was stupid, maybe. I'm going to order dinner. Chinese OK?" She left the room without waiting for an answer.

My dad called out, "Judith?" and went after her. I sat in the kitchen for a minute, finishing my Rice Krispies treat. Then I excused myself and sent myself to my room.

Fridays at Howell, every senior had last period free, although we were supposed to use it for study hall or college counseling. But this was the first week of school, so everyone was just hanging out by the lockers.

I slid down the lockers to a sitting position and nodded to Lucia, who had Dennis's head in her lap. "Hey, guys," I said, boldly.

"Kendall." Lucia smiled tightly and kissed Dennis on the forehead. Dennis looked contented to the point of being asleep. I felt a familiar stab of jealousy at how safe they looked with each other.

"Hi, Kendall." I froze at the familiar voice, not quite believing it. There was a rustle of fabric and then the familiar scent of lavender soap washed over me as Audrey sat down.

I looked at her. She was smiling calmly, as if nothing at all had happened. "Where've you been all week?" she demanded. "I haven't seen you at all."

"I've been here," I said cautiously.

Audrey sighed dramatically and put her head on my shoulder. I exhaled sharply. Audrey went on blithely, "I was so not ready for this week. My sleep is so off, Kendall. I'm going to get *duffel* bags under my eyes."

My chest tightened, but I made myself speak. "You always say that, but you never do."

"So what are we doing this weekend?"

A warm glow began to inflate my ribcage, flooding my system with a deranged hope. "Besides sleep, you mean?"

"Yes, mother, besides sleep."

My brain started to catch up to my body, tried to send it a warning, but I couldn't stop the flood in my chest. "Movie?"

Audrey adjusted herself on my shoulder, flipping her hair back. "We could do that tonight. Tomorrow, Ellie's having a party though. It's at her older brother's apartment."

"Oh, cool. Does he still live in that loft by the water?"

"Yup! Out of town and the liquor cabinet is all ours."

"Thanks for telling me. What time?"

"What do you mean?"

"What time does the party start?"

Audrey laughed. "Oh, you're not invited, Kendall."

I stiffened.

Audrey nuzzled in closer. "Ellie's got to return the apartment exactly as she found it, or no more parties there," she said. "She can't risk anyone bringing a bunch of strangers and trashing the place. I mean, her brother's coming back really early on Sunday. You understand, right?"

I shook her off. Audrey pouted and I noticed that the hallway was oddly silent. I looked around at everyone pretending to not look at us. Audrey did the same and went on, raising her voice as she did so.

"Kendall, talk to me," she said earnestly, grabbing my wrist. "I'm your friend."

"Get away from me," I hissed at her, trying to extricate my arm.

Audrey suddenly let go and buried her face in her hands. When she looked up there were tears in her eyes. I would have been impressed if I hadn't been there the first time Audrey cried on demand, to get out of trouble when she snuck into the hotel pool on the eighth grade field trip to DC. But I had been the only one there, so when she did it now, a hush fell over the hallway as Audrey hunched over and her shoulders shook.

"When you did what you did with Grant, I was angry, but I hoped our friendship would eventually get past it," she said. "Don't get me wrong, it was a real betrayal, but I told myself to remember how frustrating it must have been for you, to watch your friend with the guy you secretly wanted. I felt bad for you. But it's because I assumed you liked him, not that it was about sex!"

She drew a raggedy gasp and continued, with narrowed, clear eyes staring straight at me. "Now I'm just worried about you, Kendall. Despite everything, I still care about you and I don't want you to put yourself in dangerous situations. Grant is one thing, but strangers? Where are you meeting these guys? How old are they? Are you being safe?"

At each question, her voice went an octave higher, painting pictures in my head—and in everyone else's heads. "Look, just be careful, sweetie," she said. "I'm still here for you. It's senior year, after all. Promise you'll come to me if you ever get into trouble?" I stared at her, horrified, petrified, as she sighed and pulled a Duane Reade bag out of her backpack.

"Here," she said, unwrapping it. "Please, be careful. For me, if not for you."

Audrey dropped the contents of the bag on the linoleum floor with a clatter and walked away, giving everyone a clear view of the pile of Plan B boxes at my feet.

I picked up one of the boxes and examined the price tag: $20. I looked closer and counted nine boxes. Audrey had spent $180 on this demonstration.

The silence thickened with whispers and muffled giggles until finally the bell rang. As people charged around me out the door, I arranged the boxes into a neat stack and waited. I sat where I was, trying to turn myself into a boulder in the river, immovable and uncaring.

My eyes on the stack, my ears burning, straining to hear my name and praying not to at the same time, I waited until the doors swung shut with a final clang and the bustle faded away.

I stood slowly, picked up one of the boxes, tossed it in the air, and served it as hard as I could, sending it flying down the empty hall. I rammed the light box so hard I jammed my arm socket. But after doing it once I couldn't stop, so one by one, I sent the boxes spinning and skittering down the hall, spiking, drop-kicking, and pitching until I was sore.

When I was out of boxes, I rammed my elbow into the locker next to mine and spat, "Future housewife flunky fake-ass bitch in a padded bra!" I kicked the lower locker, making a visible dent. "Shit!"

Someone snorted behind me. I spun around as Gilly unfolded himself from his corner, stood up, and crossed his arms, his mouth twisted in amusement.

"Great," I said, still shaking with rage. I spread my arms out wide. "I'm all yours, douchebag. Go ahead. What lame, but still completely hostile, tidbit do you have to add to my total humiliation?"

Gilly seemed to consider his answer before speaking. "'Flunky' should really enter the everyday lexicon," he said finally. "It's a good word. Nice one."

"Thanks." I slammed my back against the locker and slid down, trying to relax my keyed-up muscles.

"I can't really speak to the padded bra—they look OK to me—but I wish you had said all that to her face. Or at least spiked the Plan B into the back of her head."

This time I snorted. I looked up at him, accidentally making eye contact. Immediately, he jammed his hands in his pockets and looked sharply away.

"Thanks for the support," I said, reaching out my arm for a hand up. Gilly stared for a minute, confused, and then got it, grabbing my hand with a jerk. I clasped it, lacing my fingers with his. As he lifted me up, his fingers tightened and I was surprised at their wiry strength.

Face-to-face, still holding my hand, he shrugged and said, "I don't like her much."

"Yeah, not like me, right?"

"You're already having a bad week. I feel like the pain is due to be spread around. Audrey's on deck, karmically speaking."

I looked down at our hands, still clasped together, and back up to Gilly's scornful but direct face. He dropped my hand as if it had burned him.

"So why'd you stick around?" I asked, my heart rate finally slowing. "Just to critique my improv skills?"

He smiled wryly. "Oh, I was going to collect the Plan B. I was running really low."

I laughed a little. "Oh, yeah, me too."

"Like you have any use for it."

I looked at him and saw that he was looking at me with what seemed strangely like understanding.

"That *sounds* mean," I said slowly. "But are you trying to be . . . nice?"

"By saying I don't believe you're getting laid on the reg? If you want to interpret that as me being nice, go ahead."

My cell phone vibrated in my pocket. I fished it out.

Hi Ken. 11 p.m. at the Fish Hook. I'll be behind the bar.

"Who's that?" asked Gilly.

"Uh, that would be a really good friend of mine named 'None of your business.'"

Just then, my phone started ringing in my hands. I picked it up. "Hello?"

"Hi, hon, it's Dad."

"Hi. What's going on?"

"Well, Ken Doll, your mother and I have decided that you should probably be grounded. So I wanted to catch you before you made plans."

I shook my head. "I'm what?"

"Grounded."

"What does that mean? I mean, what do *you* mean by grounded?"

"I think it means you're not going out this weekend. Is that OK?"

"Actually, Dad, I just—"

"Oh damn it, honey, my patient just got here. We'll talk about it at dinner, OK?" He hung up.

"Goddamn it!" I yelled.

Gilly started whistling. I turned to him and he looked down at me with wide eyes. "I'm sorry," he said with exaggeration. "I know how important your relationship with none-of-your-business is. I don't want to intrude."

"Oh, shut up." I looked at the boy leaning against the lockers, waiting for me to tell him what was bothering me. "Why are you always here when I'm losing it?"

He shrugged, a real smile hiding behind his smirk. "Just lucky, I guess."

I scowled back at him. But rather than leaving or deepening that smirk, he turned his face into a parody of my angry face, bringing his eyebrows all the way in and scrunching up his nose.

Involuntarily, I laughed and his true smile crept out further, like the sun peeking around a storm cloud.

"You really want to know why that call made me mad?" I said, looking into his abnormally silver eyes.

"Sure. Why not?"

"I'm supposed to meet someone at a bar in Red Hook at eleven o'clock tonight. A drug dealer, actually," I added, stumbling over the words slightly, but he didn't react. "So time and place are kind of non-negotiable. But my dad just called to inform me that I'm 'grounded.'" I put up finger quotes around the grounded part.

"So what's the problem?"

I stared at him. "Isn't it kind of obvious? 'Need to go somewhere' plus 'can't go somewhere' equals 'problem.'"

"Sneak out."

"My parents don't exactly go to bed at eight. I don't know how that's going to work. What? Why are you laughing?"

He shrugged, his mouth twisted up again. "I just think it's funny that Miss Popular Party Girl doesn't know how to sneak out."

I snorted. "Dude, my mother bought wine coolers for my fourteenth birthday party. I have never had to sneak out. I just . . . go."

"You've snuck back in though, right? Quietly, so you won't wake them up?"

"I guess. But that's not the same thing."

He made his patented Gilly duh-face. "The skill set is the same," he said. "The only difference is you need an alibi. You need to give them a reason to believe you're still in the house, but also a reason not to check on you. Develop a narrative."

As I listened to him, I was doing the algebra in my head. What plus what equals: I'm in my room early on a Friday night, but don't check on me? What equation would they believe?

An idea started accreting in my head. A disturbing idea. But an idea that might work.

I turned to Gilly, this time with an appraising eye. If you ignored the social tics and the constant aura of gloom, as ever present as the chain with a million keys clipped to his belt, he was well-constructed. Wide shoulders, muscled arms. Must be all the climbing around in the rafters and carrying heavy wires.

And, actually, now that I was noticing things about Gilly, his mouth was . . . acceptable.

"What?" he asked. His voice jolted me out of my stare and I

quickly looked away from the deep dip of his upper lip. Among other things, his voice had reminded me that Gilly didn't like me.

"Nothing," I said, relocating my attention anywhere other than his mouth and his shoulders. "I had an idea for a second, but it's not going to work."

He opened his mouth and then shut it. He turned to leave. I rolled my eyes at his predictable awkwardness.

He turned back and, jaw visibly clenching, said, "I'm not busy tonight. I could help you sneak out."

I made my voice as skeptical as I could. "You could?"

"I could. I mean—look, I'm not hitting on you."

"Don't worry, I'm not getting any ideas."

"I could just hang out with you and you would be credibly socially satisfied that if you said you were going to bed at ten, your parents would believe you. Or if they're really as relaxed as you say they are, I could just . . . stick around. And they wouldn't, you know, *want* to check on you."

He added, "And I wouldn't tell anyone."

I took a step closer to him, now trying to catch his eye. "Why would you help me?"

He avoided my eyes. "I'm making a documentary: How to destroy your reputation in six months or less."

"No, really, why?" I touched his arm.

Eventually, after we'd stared at each other for a moment, he sighed and shook my hand off. "I don't know. Maybe I feel bad for you. Maybe I'm bored. Maybe it's morbid curiosity. Now do you want my help or don't you, Barbie?"

CHAPTER NINE

So that's how, half an hour later, I was standing on the front step of my brownstone, fishing for my keys in my backpack with Michael Gilbert of all people by my side.

"So, this is it," I said, opening the door and waving him in. "Mom? Dad?" No answer. "Oh, thank god, they're not home yet." I swung my backpack to the floor.

Gilly had been hanging back on the stoop, but following the parental all clear, he strode quickly past me, looking all around the dusty woodwork of my foyer. "Your room upstairs?" he asked, heading for the stairwell.

"Yeah—hey there, wait a second, cowboy. Who said you were going up to my room?"

"I can just leave if I'm not welcome."

I rolled my eyes. "Fine, go ahead. First door on the right. I'm going to get a soda. Do you want anything?"

"Yeah." He bounded up the stairs before I could ask specifics.

A couple of minutes later, balancing two Diet Cokes, I hip-bumped my way into my room to find Gilly sitting on my bed, going through my nightstand drawer.

"What exactly do you think you're going to find in there?" I asked, coolly putting his glass next to his hand. The only stuff in that drawer was hairbands, Q-tips, my sleep mask, and Dead Sea mud. That's not where I kept the incriminating stuff.

He took a sip of his Coke, fiddling with a frayed scrunchie. "Not much," he said. "Especially since I've already been through your desk." He fished my secret bourbon out of his pocket. "Can I have some?"

I snatched at the flask, but he held it high above his head. Even sitting down, he was too tall for me.

"I'm not judging," he said, with a friendly-ish quirk of his mouth. "Relax a little. I'm on your team, remember? Today."

I sucked it up. "You're right, I'm sorry. Go ahead." After watching him pour, I sat down next to him and held my glass out. "Me too."

Leaning over me slightly, Gilly obliged. We sat for a moment in silence, not looking at each other.

He turned to face me. "So what's so important about this dealer?"

I cocked my head at him. "What, you don't know? I'm a drug-addicted slut, spiraling towards rock bottom." Gilly didn't respond except to shake his head a little.

Downstairs, a key turned in a lock.

"Kendall?" my mom yelled up the stairs, slamming the front door.

"Well, at least she sounds normal today," I muttered. Gilly had bolted upright and was downing his drink like there was a fire drill.

"You really don't have to do that. At least. . ."—I hesitated, remembering that all of a sudden grounding had entered my life—"I don't think you do."

Gilly slammed his glass down and wiped his mouth. "I'm just getting in character," he said.

"What?"

Mom pounded up the stairs to my room, carrying my bag. "Ken Doll, I know this is really bad-mommy of me, but I'm kind of looking forward to your first grounding." She stopped short when she entered my room and saw Gilly sitting on my bed.

She looked from him, to me, and back again. "Hello?" she said/ asked, seemingly keeping an eye on each of us. "I'm Judith. You are . . . ?"

I opened my mouth to preempt whatever wackiness Gilly was about to commit, but before I could, he jumped to his feet and bounced over to my mother, arm outstretched.

"It's so nice to meet you, Judith." Gilly enthusiastically shook her hand. "Are you sure it's OK that I call you Judith? I didn't want to call you Mrs. Evans, in case that's not your name. I apologize for coming over on the spur of the moment like this, but Kendall is so much better at calculus than I am and we have a test on Monday. Oh god, sorry, here's your hand back."

As he gave this speech, my mouth opened wider and wider. This was not Gilly. This was an eager, friendly boy with a confident handshake and a smooth, upbeat cadence to his speech. I looked at my mother and saw her eyebrows raised in pleasant surprise.

"It's no problem . . . Michael? It's Mikey Gilbert, isn't it? Kevin Gilbert's son?" I had no idea what she was talking about.

My mom went on, "I used to work with your father at Brader & Hayden. I've seen your picture on his desk and of course I remember that you go to school with Kendall. I'm so glad you two are finally chilling."

I winced. "Yeah, well, we haven't had any classes together before," I said quickly—I know an opportunity when I see one. "One of those weird things. I know I'm grounded, but can Mikey stay for dinner?"

My mom looked perplexed. "Well if you don't go *out*, that means you're still grounded. Those are the rules, right?"

"Sure?"

"Is pizza OK with you, Mikey? No dairy allergies or anything?"

"Bomb dot com, Judith. Pizza's great."

My mom grinned and Gilly turned around to look at me. I

nearly fell off the bed when I saw his teeth-to-face ratio. Gilly with a big, gleaming grin was a disturbing sight.

"OK. Awesome! I'll go make the call. It was nice to finally meet you, Mikey."

"You, too, Judith. Thank you for inviting me to dinner, that's really generous of you."

My mom left the room, crossing in front of Gilly to hand me my bag and mouth, "I love him," punctuating the statement with a surreptitiously pointed finger.

As soon as she was gone, Gilly transformed again. He shivered slightly, not in disgust, but as if he were cold. He shook his head to the side, like he was trying to get water out of his ears and collapsed onto the bed, kicking his feet at the floor.

He looked over at me. "What are you staring at?" he asked irritably.

"Uh . . . what the *hell* was that?" I leaned forward, trying to find that sweet, open, silly boy in his current face. "That was some serious acting! That was . . . kind of *awesome*. Where did you learn to do that?"

Gilly just shrugged, but I thought I detected a smile. "It's no big deal. I just wanted to make sure your mom let me stay for dinner."

"But your whole body, the entire way you carry yourself changed. Can you do other characters, too?"

"Oh, whatever."

I studied him. "Why do you just do tech? Why don't you try out for the plays? I bet you'd be really good."

His face hardened. "That's not going to happen. And it's not 'just' tech, OK?"

I put up my hands. "Sure, *Mikey*."

He groaned. "Ugh, that was awful. But it was a lucky break. I was hoping she'd remember me."

"I don't think I ever knew they worked together. My parents are a little forgetful about telling me stuff like that."

He gave me a look. "Yeah, well, you can forget you ever heard someone calling me Mikey."

"You actually like people calling you Gilly?"

Gilly swigged directly from the bourbon bottle, coughed, and sputtered. "Not really," he said in a choked voice. "But it's better than a lot of other things they could call me. For example, Mikey."

"You really know how to look on the bright side, don't you?" I held my hand out for the bottle. He handed it over and I stowed it under the bed. I did not need a drunk dork on my plate tonight.

"So you never answered my question," he said, turning to face me..

"What question?"

"What's so important about meeting this one drug dealer, at this one bar, tonight? You're pretty desperate to score, for somebody I would lay money on not being that into drugs. And I don't have to know you well to know that," he added as I opened my mouth to interrupt. "You just put the nearly full bottle of bourbon away after not even finishing one weak mixed drink. So what's going on?"

He caught me off guard. I knew it would be careless to trust him, but his face was earnest and concerned. And he was here.

Try him. The words imprinted themselves across my brain.

"Have you ever done ecstasy?" I kept my eyes down but sensed him shift on the bedspread.

"No," he said, shortly. "Ecstasy makes you love everyone. I have no interest in participating in that."

I looked up and locked eyes with him. "You have to promise not to tell anyone. Even if you don't believe me, you can't try to get me committed, or anything. Or I start calling you Mikey really loudly all over school."

He grimaced and nodded.

I drew a deep breath and started the story. "The first day of school when I got hurt . . . I didn't really fall. There was this stranger, this tall girl, who attacked me in the bathroom."

I kept checking in with Gilly as I talked, trying to read his reactions, but his face stayed mostly impassive and he didn't interrupt. His mouth tightened a little when I got to meeting Mason in the basement, but other than that, he didn't move.

"Simone seemed like the best bet for knowing who supplies

Howell kids or, at least, the best bet who's still talking to me," I finished. "And it looks like I was right. This bar I'm meeting Trev at, the Fish Hook, is the one in the picture on my profile. It's right next door to where the warehouse party was. It's the only lead I've got anyway."

Gilly stood up and paced around my room. He stopped in front of the mirror. When he spoke, he directed it to my reflection.

"Am I missing something? Why aren't you going to the police? You have Mason solid on accessory to assault, kidnapping, and drug dealing. You know where his office is. You can identify two of his people, names and everything. And you know where one of his probable dealers operates. Case closed."

"Going to the police just gets Mason arrested. It doesn't solve *my* problem."

"Yes, it does!" he insisted. "Mason's gone, game over."

Startled at the fire in his voice, I took a moment to collect my thoughts. "First of all," I said slowly, "stop yelling at me. Second of all, Mason getting arrested does not solve my problems. It is not my problem that Mason sells drugs. My problem is that my future is on the line. Mason has given me two options: I help him and I get to keep my future, or I don't and he takes it away. I don't think him getting arrested would dissuade him from screwing me over. And I don't know how much more getting screwed over I can handle." Gilly was still staring at me. "What?" I asked.

"You are unbelievable. Does the fact that turning him into the police might be the right thing to do factor into your math at all?"

I felt my face flush. "Of course it does. I'm not an idiot and I'm not a bad person. But this is *my* life and frankly, making any world but my own a better place right now is not my top priority. And if I have a chance to get out of this bullshit situation, I'm going to take it. I have my own problems."

His lip curled. "Your problems. Like what?"

I pulled my backpack over and picked out a box of Plan B. I took his earlier suggestion and spiked it at his head. He dodged just in time.

"You don't know me," I said.

We stared at each other furiously, tension tangible in the space between us. I clenched my fists and noticed him doing the same.

My mother called up the stairs, "Ken Doll, your father's home. Why don't you and Mikey come down and join us?"

I stood up and faced Gilly. "No one's forcing you to be here. Back out now if you want."

"I said I was in," he said brusquely, heading for the door. "But you're going to owe me, Barbie."

By the time I got to the bottom of the stairs, Gilly had put his mask back on. And on it stayed throughout dinner. I really did have to hand it to him: He was a natural actor.

I mean, by the time dinner was over, he was helping my mom

load the dishwasher and chummily asking far-too-pointed questions about my childhood propensity for dressing in my dad's clothes and pretending to be an old man, and whether any pictures existed.

"You know, we really should get started on the calc homework," I cut in, stepping between him and my mom. "We're going to go upstairs, OK, guys?"

"Well, it was great to meet you," called Gilly over his shoulder as I dragged him back up the stairs to my room and slammed the door shut.

"I wanted to see you as a grandpa," said Gilly, his smirk still twisting his face.

"Forget it," I said, sliding to the floor. "I think I've made myself vulnerable enough for one day. You want to talk about our plan for getting out of here?"

He dropped to the floor too, losing his smile. "Let's do it."

I checked the clock. "OK, it's eight now. I should leave for Red Hook at about ten fifteen. So maybe around ten, we should make an appearance in front of my parents, go down for tea or something, so they know we're going to be hanging out for longer. They'll probably start watching a movie in their room around then anyway, and we can sneak out fifteen minutes later."

"Will they buy it?"

"You know what? I think they will." I looked up at him. "I have to thank you. You seemed so sweet. They're going to be so glad I'm making nice friends, they won't question anything."

"Nice friends?"

It was a pointed question. "OK, sure," I said, raising my hands. "They never liked Audrey that much and now they really don't. What of it?"

He scooted backward, hopping onto my bed. "So. How do we kill the next two hours?"

That particular problem hadn't occurred to me. Then I had an idea. An evil, excellent idea.

I crawled to the other side of the bed and retrieved the bourbon bottle. I grabbed our used glasses and poured out two shots, asking, "Do you know how to play blackjack?"

"Sure . . ."

"Ever play for confessions?"

CHAPTER TEN

GILLY LOST FOR THE FOURTH TIME. "You're cheating," he declared. "I don't know how, but you're cheating."

I smiled to myself and took a dainty sip of my drink. "Me? Cheating? That's absurd!"

He put his head in his hands and groaned, "OK. Truth. What this time?"

Truth or Dare Blackjack was a game I had invented in ninth grade. Right after I taught myself how to count cards.

"Let's see," I said, reshuffling the deck. "What do I already have on you? Shall I inventory it?"

"That's not necessary," he said, his face still down.

Expertly fanning out the cards and flipping them back together, I pretended not to hear him. "We have your first crush at Howell— Ellie Kurtz is kind of unconscionable, Gilly. I'd be embarrassed, too. We have your first wet dream, involving some *Battlestar Galactica* character, which is so sad, I don't think I would have the heart to use it against you. And we have your first kiss, which I conveniently have no way of verifying—some girl at film camp, indeed."

"You know something, Barbie? You're the horniest girl I've ever met. Do you ever think about anything but sex?"

"What are we doing here if not dealing with the fallout of that exact tendency?" I replied, ignoring the sting. "Just for that, I'm going to ask how far you've gone."

He looked behind me and pointed. "No deal. It's ten. Time's up."

I checked the clock and dropped the cards. "So it is. Went faster than I thought it would."

"Yeah, well, I'm glad you had fun."

I decided to take pity on him. "Don't worry. You're not the first I've beaten. The things I know would frighten you."

I stood up and held out my hand to help him up. He gripped it with both of his and gravity pulled me forward until a moment later he was standing and I found myself locked against his chest.

"Your heart's beating fast," he said quietly. "Are you up for this?"

I swallowed and extricated myself. "Yes." I didn't have a choice. I prepared for the incredibly uncomfortable task of faking sexual tension in front of my parents. It made me feel slightly dizzy. I was willing to do a lot to get what I wanted, but this felt, well, like a lie. It *was* a lie.

And I didn't lie to my parents.

As we hit the bottom stair, I ran smack into my dad carrying a bowl of popcorn.

"Hey, guys," he said brightly. "Guess what? Mom called the Gilberts and Mikey can stay for the inaugural viewing of the—wait for it—remastered, Blu-ray, unbelievably good-looking *Star Trek: The Next Generation* discs! At least for a few episodes."

Gilly hadn't had a chance to put his Mikey mask on and he stared at me, shocked. I felt myself go pale. Everyone knew I was good at math, but nobody knew that I was a dork to the point that those Blu-Rays had been preordered for my birthday present. That was just for me. I had kept my public persona and private life separate. I wasn't used to being myself in public. I didn't know what that looked like, and I wasn't sure I liked the look on Gilly's face.

I grabbed his hand and hoped my mother wouldn't walk in. "Actually, Dad, Mikey and I were going to watch a movie on my laptop," I said. "Is that OK?"

My dad looked at us quizzically. "Why wouldn't you want to watch it on the good screen?"

Mom walked into the hallway and immediately zoomed in on our clasped hands. Her eyes narrowed and I felt Gilly flinch under my fingers.

"What's going on, Greg?" she asked, casually rubbing my dad on the shoulder. But there was a knife-edge to her voice. She had spotted fresh meat.

Dad, oblivious, answered, "Well, for some reason, Mikey and Kendall would rather watch a movie in her room than on the big TV!"

"Interesting," said mom, side-eyeing us.

I took a deep breath. She really liked Gilly, or Mikey, rather. I'd pay for this in mockery later, but it needed to be done. "Yeah," I answered, shifting closer to Gilly. "We won't be too late. You can still watch something, we'll be quiet."

Mom held up a finger and went into the kitchen. When she came back she was carrying another glass of wine. She took a long drink, swallowed and announced, "No, you won't. You'll either keep that bedroom door open or Mikey goes home."

I dropped his hand, appalled. "*What?*"

She sniffed primly. "It doesn't seem appropriate. It's late."

"You have to be kidding," I declared. "Tell me this is a joke. Dad?"

He gulped. "Um—"

"We're serious," my mom cut him off. "Not tonight, Kendall."

I was so angry I started laughing. "Gee, I wonder why all of a sudden you care who I have in my bedroom and when."

"I *always* care what you do."

"Please," I scoffed. "Only when it starts to embarrass you or intrude on your day."

"I'm going to go," blurted out Gilly. When nobody said anything, he nodded and bolted down the last step and out the door.

As soon it shut, my mom hissed at me in a quiet, deadly voice, "I will not be spoken to that way."

"Yeah, well, neither will I," I shouted. "You wanted to spend my whole childhood treating me like an adult, you had better damn well treat me like one now." I turned and stomped up the stairs.

"Come back here," Mom screamed after me. "We're going to talk about this!"

"No! Leave me alone!" I turned back and, my eyes stinging now, said, "I thought at least you would be on my side." I slammed my door and flung myself onto my bed.

I wasn't crying. I almost never did. But, I was gasping, just reaching out for every breath. My knees were tucked up around my middle. I rolled over until I was lying with my stomach against my thighs and stretched out my arms.

I felt the familiar buzz of panic build up behind my ears. I started to count.

One. Two. Three. I took a deep breath. *Four. Five.*

The clock said ten thirty. I had to pull myself together, so I did.

Plan A was out the window. Plan B, I decided, was probably for the best anyway. I'd just sneak out by myself.

Eventually, my parents' door closed and the buzz of the television started. That was one thing I had counted on. That sound had been my lullaby since I could remember.

After I had changed my clothes, I picked up my shoes with one hand and stepped slowly toward my bedroom door. I kept my socked feet on the floor, moving from heel to toe as smoothly as possible. I gripped the doorknob so hard it hurt my hand and, centimeter by centimeter, pulled it open and shimmied through. I pushed the doorknob to close it and winced at the inevitable click.

The stairs: They were carpeted, but they made noise even when nobody was stepping on them.

I crouched by the top landing, contemplating my best route down, but then the hallway flooded with light as my parents' door opened. I instinctively hit the floor, flattening myself and tumbling my torso down two steps, with a muffled *thump-thump-thump*.

"Ahem-auugh-ahem." My dad cleared his throat and, with the TV on pause, walked to the bathroom as I panted, prone across the stairs.

My mom started to say, "Greg, did you hear—?" and was cut off by the flush. This was my window—with no time to stand, I grappled my way down to the bottom of the stairs and landed *smack* on the hardwood just as my dad yelled, "What?"

"Did you hear something?"

"We don't have mice, babe, I've told you."

Their voices faded and I let out a breath. I rolled up to my feet. I had landed right in front of the door. I reached out and unlocked it carefully. Finally, I stepped into the cool night air, locking up behind me.

I hurried down the stoop and sat on the lowest step, slipping on and buckling my high-heeled Mary-Janes.

"You made it." The voice made me jump. I whipped around and saw Gilly emerging from behind a parked car.

"Yeah," I said, relaxing. "Only to be given a heart attack." I leaned down to adjust a buckle. "What are you still doing here?"

He leaned against a streetlamp, turning his light hair into an incongruous halo. His forehead creased as he said, "You didn't think I was going to just go home, right?"

I stood up and headed over to him. "Actually, I did." His expression stayed irritated and confused. "I really appreciate all your help tonight. And it was . . . kind of . . . fun, I guess. But I can take care of this part myself."

"Not a chance," he said flatly and headed down the block toward the F train.

I checked my phone. We were running late. I didn't have time to argue. "I'm OK, you know," I blurted out. He looked at me. "That fight thing. Everything's fine. You don't have to stay because of that."

His only answer was to shout, "Taxi," and run into the street with his arm raised. A yellow cab pulled up out of nowhere. He opened the door and made an ironic bow.

"After you, Barbie."

"Enough," I muttered, frustrated. But I headed to the cab.

The cab driver was blasting what sounded like a Bollywood musical score, too loud to talk over. I was relieved. I needed to get my head together. I leaned back against the worn leather seat, shut my eyes, and tried to do just that. But neither calm nor order would come. When I closed my eyes, I saw Audrey as she looked over her shoulder and called me a slut. That image was quickly replaced by Jo's fist coming toward me. Finally, I saw Mason leaning close, seeming to loom over me, even though our faces were level. That last image wouldn't leave. It kept coming at me and at me and at me, like a filmstrip caught in a loop.

Gilly put his hand on my arm and my eyes opened. "We're here," he said and paid the cab before I could reach my purse.

As the taxi sped off, I surveyed the bar from across the street. The Fish Hook was squat, dim, and unremarkable, until someone opened the door to go outside for a smoke. Yellow lighting and intrigue briefly flooded the street as the swinging doorway revealed a glowing room filled with dark-clad people standing in close, loud clumps.

"OK," I breathed and crossed the street. I had reached the other side when I realized I was alone. I spun around. "What? What are you doing over there?"

Gilly fidgeted, looking more like his normal self than he had all night. His normal self with a tinge of . . . *what is that? Fear?*

What does he *have to be scared of?* I shook my head, suddenly filled with contempt. After all, I was the one taking risks here. "Great," I muttered. "Very helpful. Fine, you wimp. I'll do it alone." I raised my voice. "Have a good night," I called, with my widest smile. He started as if he'd been slapped.

I turned around. This was it. I straightened my back as tall as it would go, strode to the door, swung it open, and walked into the musty-smelling light of the Fish Hook.

Luckily, the bouncer was distracted by two fratty guys in the corner and didn't even look in my direction. I headed to the bar and stood awkwardly against the scratched oak, until the bartender made her way down the line to me.

"What can I get you?" she asked, moving fast in about three different directions, putting a credit card here and pulling a glass out from under there.

"Um. Trev?"

She stopped what she was doing and turned to actually look at me for the first time, pointing at me with a shiny green fingernail.

"Are *you* Ken?" she asked. "Simone's friend?"

"Yeah," I said, embarrassed. "Kendall. I don't know why I said Ken in the text."

She laughed. "Trev told me to look for some high school dude named Ken. I didn't expect *you*." She opened the hatch and said, "Come on through. Trev's in the back."

She took my hand and led me to another door, ushering me though. "Just holler for him. He'll hear you." The door slammed in my face.

I was in a dank, unfinished passage, piled high with cardboard boxes and plastic kegs, forming a sort of tunnel. It was shadowy and dusty. "Hello?" I called. No answer. "Trev?"

I took a few steps down the hall, my heels clicking across the rough cement floor.

"Trev?" I called again. There was a hacking cough. I followed the sound around a corner and reached the source.

It was an alcove overflowing with papers and boxes. There was no desk, just a saggy leather couch and a matching, albeit patched, armchair arranged around a coffee table. A softly rounded body was doubled over at the waist, racked with coughing. All I could see of him other than his skinny jeans and Timberland boots was hairy arms, a mop of brown and black waves, and what looked like very impressive sideburns.

I crouched down in front of him and put my hands on his shoulders, trying to steady them. "Are you OK?" He put up a hand as if to say, "Give me a minute."

"Do you want some water?" I said, digging into my purse and pulling out a bottle. "It's kind of old—"

He grabbed at the water and threw his head back, swallowing it with a theatrical gargling sound. "Whew . . ." he whistled, still bent over backward above me. In a final, convulsive hack, he stretched his shoulders back, then forward, thrusting his face into view.

Trev had enviably smooth skin, bright and terra-cotta brown.

He had a pointy, substantial nose and a triangular chin. He smiled down at me and his black eyes sparkled. "Whew," he said again. "Thanks, lady-friend. I needed that. Did Kitty send you back to look for me?"

So this was Trev.

I pulled myself up to my feet, smacking the dust off of my black leggings.

He pointed at me, but in a friendly way. "Who are you?" he said, looking me up and down. After completing his circuit, his eyes lingering curiously on my bruise before smoothly moving on, he smiled. "Whoever you are, I am very, very pleased to meet you."

I felt myself relax. I tossed my hair over the left side of my face and smiled.

"I'm Ken," I said, raising my eyebrow at his surprised expression. "Simone's friend."

He stuck his hand out. I took it.

"I should have expected a friend of Simone's to be both a pal and a total smoke show," he said, shaking my hand vigorously.

"And instead you were expecting some bro with creepily styled hair and inappropriately fancy cufflinks?"

He laughed. "Hey! You hear Ken, you get a certain mental image, you know?"

I smiled. "I know. Malibu beach houses."

He dropped my hand and pointed at me with a wagging finger. "Exactly, exactly. OK, take a seat," he said, patting the couch and sitting back down. "Tell me what I can do for you."

A familiar sweet, piney, manure smell hung over everything. I couldn't place it until I spotted the bong hidden discreetly under the table.

So that's why he was coughing. I took a seat on the couch, and Trev sat down next to me.

"You weren't very specific in your messages," he said. "All I got was 'dose.'"

I rolled my eyes self-deprecatingly. "I'm sorry. A friend of mine always calls it that, got in the habit. No, I was looking to roll on what you sold to Simone and Pete Morrison."

"You go to Howell?"

"Aw, come on, don't make me admit I'm a high schooler at a bar on a Friday night."

He grinned. "Hey, I'm not the cops. You look older than high school, is all."

I planted my heel on the table. "It's all an illusion. When you're as short as I am, you learn fast that dark leggings, high heels, and a too-short skirt will get you as far you're going to go." I grinned at him, hoping he wouldn't laugh in my face.

He didn't seem like he was going to laugh though. He looked up my leg quickly and then back up to my face. "Well, mission accomplished. I look older than I am, too," he said quickly. "I'm twenty-three."

"I wouldn't have guessed," I said, moving my leg back to a more comfortable position, inwardly exalting. I hadn't had much of a plan other than to go to the Fish Hook and find out what I could. And Trev seemed more than willing to chat. That seemed like a liability for someone with his side hustle,, but who was I to complain?

"Yeah," he said. "And I grew up around here, so I know a lot of Howell kids."

"I got that impression. You sell to a lot of kids in my class, right?"

"Oh, sure. Your girl Simone for one thing. A bunch of guys who graduated last year—you know Grant Powers, right?"

"I know him."

"Well, him, Burke, Ryan, Dougie, those guys. In your class—you're a senior, right?" I nodded. "In your class, obviously Pete Morrison, some chick named Ellie that Grant's girl brought into the bar, Ricky, Lucas, Danica, and also this guy Lemon."

"Jacob Lemon?" I asked, surprised.

"Yeah, yeah, sweet kid. All sunshine and rainbows, practically didn't need the E. Had this really grumpy, mean-eyed little friend, though. Guy was kind of a pain in the ass."

I pictured the aggressive, angry Drew and grimaced. "I know

the guy you're talking about. I sympathize. I guess Howell's such a small school, you're probably our only connect, huh?"

He leaned back with his arms behind his head and gave a smirky little shrug. "Maybe I have some influence," he said, moving one of his arms to rest above my shoulders.

I stiffened, but kept my smile in place. "Well, I'm looking for two tabs," I told him.

"I'll do you one better," he said, moving forward and opening a drawer in the coffee table and taking out an orange prescription bottle. He handed it to me. "Here are four for the price of two. A getting-to-know-you present."

I stared down at the pill bottle in my hand and all at once felt like I might throw up. "Is there a bathroom around here I could use?"

"Oh, sure," he said. He pointed to a door on the opposite wall.

"Thanks," I said, leaving the pill bottle on the table. "I'll be right back."

I shut the door and pulled the chain on the light bulb hanging low and bare from the ceiling.

My hands found the linoleum edges of the sink as I doubled over with my eyes closed. "Breathe," I whispered. I gripped the sink tighter and opened my eyes, bringing them up to the mirror.

The mirror was disproportionately large for the small bathroom—the whole top half of my body was visible.

I looked into my eyes and allowed them to go big. This was a step I knew I would probably have to take, but I didn't expect it to feel like this. I was about to buy drugs in a bar from a stranger. More than that, somehow I was about to owe him a favor.

I straightened my spine and started combing my hair back. Copying my motions from earlier—flinging my hair over and sticking out my chest—I realized with a jolt that I had unconsciously slid into position as the girl in the picture. I gulped and slowly, deliberately this time, did it again.

And just like that, I was wearing a fake face. Inside, my guts may have been churning like a hurricane, but even I could tell that the mask was convincing. Pale hair tossed carelessly around my face, shoulders relaxed, eyes narrowed: I belonged in that back room, flirting with an E dealer, getting what I needed from him.

I almost laughed out loud. I was the glowing girl and it had taken nothing at all. I just had to decide to put it on.

Eyes still on my reflection, I knocked the door open sideways with my hip and rejoined Trev on the couch.

"Everything OK?"

"Yeah," I said, grinning and picking up the orange bottle. I slipped it in my purse. "Of course. Thank you so much for this. What do I owe you—aside from my everlasting gratitude?"

"For just two? Thirty. For the four, that plus your good will."

I got up. "It was a pleasure to meet you, Trev."

"All mine, believe me."

I turned to leave and then realized I needed one more question answered.

"I'm really the only dork who says 'doses'? That's sad. I need to stop hanging out with Mason so much."

If I hadn't been looking for it, I might not have noticed the flinch. "Mason?" he said.

"Yeah, you know him, right? He mentioned he had a friend at the Fish Hook, but when I saw Simone, I just got the number from her."

He fidgeted a lighter out of his pocket and started playing with it. "I know *a* Mason. He's a friend of yours?"

"Sure," I replied innocently. "That's where I picked up the apparently outdated slang. I guess he's just trying to add to his mystique."

He laughed a little, but it sounded hollow compared to before.

"Anyway, I know he was dry," I went on. "Some sort of drama with supply. Hasn't affected you, has it?"

I had gone too far. Trev stood up and stuck out his hand, "It was really nice to meet you, Kendall. But unfortunately I have to get back to the coal mine." I shook it and then followed him into the bar with a shrug. He had given me a lot more information than I would have expected. Couldn't win them all.

Trev gave me a distracted high five and then left me alone. I let myself out from behind the bar and squeezed and dodged my way back outside into the cool lamplight.

Gilly was still waiting across the street, playing with his phone. He didn't see me until I was right in front of him.

"Did you get what you needed?" he asked tightly.

I let out a breath. "I think so," I said, running my hand through my hair and casting a look back toward the bar. "I know who in our class regularly buys ecstasy. Whatever that gets me . . ."

"Did he tell you anything about this Mason guy? Kendall? Earth-to-Kendall. What are you looking at?"

A bulky but gracefully tapered silhouette was lighting a cigarette to the side of the entrance to the Fish Hook. As he leaned forward to offer a light to a small blond chick, his chocolate colored curls and black leather jacket came into view.

I drew a raggedy breath.

It couldn't be. That would just be too unfair.

He straightened up, tossing the lighter to a buddy and I saw his snub nose and pouting red lips. It was definitely him.

"Oh shit," I said, as he laughed at something the girl said. "That sucks."

"What?" Gilly's voice was way too loud. "Wait. Is that Grant Powers?"

"Shut up," I hissed, but it was too late. At the sound of his name Grant looked up and peered across the street. He exhaled and half-waved at me with a cocky grin.

I turned my back quickly. "Is he still looking?"

"Yeah, he's looking. And he's coming over here."

"No, no, no," I moaned. I felt Gilly put his hand on my elbow. He wrapped his long fingers around it and squeezed.

I looked up at him. He was standing in front of me, looking down with a mixture of compassion and exasperation on his face. All my contempt from earlier drained away, and I hung onto his relatively friendly face like an anchor.

"Hey, Kendall," I heard behind me.

Gilly tightened his grip and I . . . just . . . reacted. I went up on my toes and pulled Gilly's ear to my mouth. "Don't stop me," I whispered. Then, with my hand still buried in his hair, I swerved to the side and kissed him.

CHAPTER ELEVEN

I SMASHED MY LIPS AGAINST HIS AND HELD THEM THERE, WAITING FOR HIM TO RESPOND—OR NOT, I GUESS. But it didn't take long. I'd caught him by surprise and felt his sharp intake of breath, but after what felt like either a light-second or a century, he exhaled and his lips pouted out, softly wrapping around and in between mine, sapping the sensation from every other part of my body. Like a rush of blood to the head, only instead of my head it was my mouth and my fingertips still on his scalp.

It didn't feel the way I would have expected it to feel.

Not that I had ever imagined what kissing Gilly would feel like. But instantly my mind was wiped clear of everything except for was happening on and in my mouth. I don't think I was even conscious that it was Gilly I was kissing, just that I *was* kissing.

His hand dropped from my elbow down to my waist and pulled me closer to him. I grabbed and pulled on the front of his shirt. He took his mouth off of mine to breathe. In the space of that breath, he gasped, "What . . . ?"

That was enough to break the spell. I was out of the fog and pressed face-to-face with Michael Gilbert, breathing heavily. We were in a discordant rhythm, me inhaling his exhale and vice versa. I let go of his shirt, but it took a few seconds for the fingers on my other hand to get the message to relinquish his hair.

Gilly abruptly let go of my waist.

I took a step back.

He looked anywhere but at me.

I opened my mouth but realized I wasn't sure what to say. "Gilly—"

"Powers went inside. You're covered."

"Good," I answered, trying to catch his eye. "Thanks."

"Let's go find a cab," he said, heading in the direction of the more populated Van Brunt Street.

"Hey, wait," I said, struggling to catch up. He stopped but didn't turn around. I skipped in front of him. "Are we cool?"

"Sure, Barbie."

"Jesus, Gilly," I exploded. "Stop fucking calling me that!"

He cracked up. He started laughing so hard he had to sit on the curb. Unsure whether this was a good sign or bad, I decided to keep my distance and stay standing on the street.

He eventually ran out of laughter and looked up at me, eyes wide.

"What the hell was that about?" I asked, annoyed. It felt like he was laughing at an inside joke with himself, one I didn't get.

He sobered up. "Nothing," he told me, looking away.

"OK," I said, reaching out to touch his shoulder. "So are we cool?"

He shrugged me off. "We're fine. Now let's go find that cab."

We walked to the corner without talking, but I kept sneaking glances at him and catching him doing the same. We had passed some sort of boundary that lived between girls like me and boys like him, and I didn't have a map of the new terrain.

No cabs were in sight. I checked my phone—11:45—and stopped suddenly.

"I just realized I have no idea where you live," I said, turning to Gilly. "Do you have a curfew? Am I getting you in trouble?"

He snorted. "I think my parents would be really excited if I didn't get home until dawn; don't worry about it. But I live in Windsor Terrace, a little south of you. I see you on the train some mornings."

We resumed strolling toward the F train. "That's convenient," I said. "Actually, it's a relief. I wouldn't want to take the train by myself after midnight and I don't see any cabs."

"You can do battle with angry henchwomen, go into seedy bars to do drug deals, but you don't want to take the subway at night. Weird."

"Hey, you wouldn't either if you'd been trained the way I have," I said. He grabbed my elbow and pulled me out of the splash as a car barreled through a puddle down the street. "Thanks. If you were a girl, you'd know."

"What exactly?"

I sighed. "Every girl I know was given the exact same instructions from their parents about the subway: Don't ride it after eleven unless you're with a boy."

"Unless you're with a *boy*? Isn't that sort of what they're trying to prevent?"

I shook my head. *What an innocent.* "There are boys and there are attackers. Not the same thing."

His forehead wrinkled. "Isn't that kind of sexist? Girls need boys to keep them safe?"

I shrugged. "I don't make the rules. I just follow them." Gilly scowled so hard I could almost hear it. I laughed. "I am a very good girl, you know."

"I can see that," he said flatly.

"Oh, hey, a cab!" I ran out into the street to hail it. I motioned toward Gilly, but he was standing with his arms crossed. I turned back to the cab as the driver rolled down the window.

"Tenth and Sixth please. Get in the cab, Gilly," I said, bouncing in. "I'm sorry I assaulted you. I'm not a good girl. It's like you said in the nurse's office: I'm a bad, bad girl." I pouted at him and was pleased when his stern expression cracked into a smile.

"You do genuinely annoy me," he said, as he got into the car. "I want to make that clear."

"So you spent all night helping me under protest? You want that noted for the record?"

He turned toward me and stuck out his tongue. "I told you," he said. "I'm writing a book."

When the cab pulled up to my house, I quickly thrust a twenty-dollar bill at Gilly and hopped out. I ran up to my stoop and then stopped. Whirling around, I said, "We're not telling anyone this happened, right? This is not a *thing*."

He grunted. "Like it would be great for either of our reputations at this point."

I scrunched up my nose and gave him the finger. He smirked and blew me an ironic kiss. "Go ahead," he said to the visibly annoyed driver and the car sped around the block.

As I tiptoed up to my bedroom, I could feel the bravado and adrenaline of the last couple of hours drip away, slowly, but inevitably, like honey off a spoon. Five minutes later, I was in my bra and underwear in front of the bathroom mirror, staring blankly at myself, not sure which girl I was looking at.

I wasn't sure what to expect in the way of fallout after the flare-up between my mother and me.

We didn't fight a lot. Oh, we *argued*. We argued a lot, and sometimes those arguments got heated. But there was no *argument* in what happened between us on the stairs—no rational reasoning at all. There was just *irrational reaction, anger, irrational reaction, anger.*

When I came downstairs Saturday morning, my mom was already at the table with a bowl of Cheerios, a cup of coffee, and the newspaper.

"Morning," she said, placidly, not looking up from the paper.

"Morning," I answered back. I made my way to the Keurig. After putting in my pod and my cup, I turned back to my mother.

I felt uneasy. "We're OK, right?" I asked.

My mother looked up, peering at me over the rims of her reading glasses. "Of course we are," she told me and went back to reading. "Everything's fine," she said. "We'll just forget about it."

I nodded. That was the most conflict resolution that ever happened in my house, so I'm not sure why I had expected any sort of closure. But, even though she said everything was fine, I couldn't shake a queasy twinge in the pit of my stomach. I wished my mom would look at me, but she just kept reading. I took my coffee back up to my room.

I had a suspects list. Sure, none of the suspects were talking to me, but if I could bullshit my way through last night's meeting with Trev, a complete stranger, I could find a way to interrogate people I'd known since before we all became bitches. So I did what I always did:

My homework.

I started a new document on my laptop and made a list of each Howell student Trev had mentioned.

Immediately, I eliminated the boys. Grant and his friends had no reason to humiliate me more than I had already humiliated myself. Lucas was new last year and we had been nothing but friendly: No history there. Lemon was a sweetie. Dave was an unpleasant X factor, but I had had little to no contact with him for all of high school. And this felt personal. Which meant, it felt like a girl.

Danica, Simone, Ellie, and Audrey.

Danica was a hippie type who I had run against for student council vice president last year. She had campaigned against using animal products in the cafeteria. She had a decent argument: It was cost-efficient and promoted health, and those who didn't want to abstain could go out to eat anyway. I destroyed her in a landslide. Could it have been her?

I tapped my fingers against the space bar. The fight hadn't gotten mean. She had shaken my hand afterward, and I had even asked her to present a proposal for Meatless Mondays in the cafeteria. It got voted down, but I think she appreciated the thought. I eliminated Danica.

Simone. I thought a second and crossed her out. If she had framed me, she wouldn't have put me in touch with Trev.

Audrey. My heart sped up, but I forced it to slow down. Obviously, Audrey was the most likely person to want to harm me. She had motive. She had been in the back room at the Fish Hook, so she had opportunity. She even knew my Facebook password.

But . . . Audrey hated drugs. Audrey hated *all* drugs. She wouldn't have wanted to touch them. I was surprised she had even gone into that back room. She couldn't have known what Grant and Ellie were there for.

Eventually, I zeroed in on the likeliest suspect: Ellie Kurtz. Ellie was technically my friend, but she had always been a little bit my enemy, too. She wanted to be closer to Audrey. I had fallen, and if Ellie had seen an opportunity to keep me down, she would have taken it.

I highlighted her name on the screen and bolded it. Pleased, I closed the document and turned to my *actual* homework.

But suddenly, just as I opened my history textbook, my mind landed on Gilly. I flashed back to him grabbing my waist and a swift cramp raced across my stomach, like a somehow pleasurable electric shock.

Great. That's just what I needed.

I gave up on homework and went to Hulu on my laptop, turning on a rerun of *America's Next Top Model*. I tried willing the image of Gilly's mouth out of my head, but it wouldn't leave. I could still feel the ghost of the kiss, the way his teeth had nipped my lips in surprise.

Anyway, I reminded myself, it wasn't even me who had kissed him. I was still the girl in the picture when that happened. I had had her sheen, her patina of glamour, coating my skin like an especially potent body glitter. The glitter smudged a little when I saw Grant.

Grant. Fucking *Grant.*

I shut the laptop, lay down, and clamped my eyes shut.

Audrey had never told me why she broke up with Grant, and that was out of character. Audrey was a girl who valued articulation. She insisted on expressing herself and being understood. Instead, I found out my best friend had dumped her boyfriend practically by default.

It was maybe a month after the warehouse party. I was waiting for Audrey by her locker when Grant walked toward us.

"Hey—" I started to call out, when Audrey shot me a freezing look.

"Don't do that," she warned.

Grant rolled his eyes and moved sideways to talk with Pete Morrison.

"Why not?" I asked, trying to catch his eye, puzzled and secretly frightened. I had started to depend on his funny faces and gentle body checks when he passed me in the hallway. I didn't want to lose this small bright spot, this secret way I had of feeling special.

Audrey shrugged slightly. "I broke up with him."

"What?" I turned to stare at her. "When? Why?"

Audrey set her mouth and again just shrugged. Still in shock at this sudden fault line in my foundation, I looked back at Grant and felt my throat close. He was looking back at me and smiling. He wasn't looking at Audrey. He grinned like he was opening a present.

Perhaps unsurprisingly, I didn't sleep well that weekend. Monday morning, I was slumped against my locker, mainlining coffee, when Simone's impossibly spiky crocodile heels clicked to a stop in front of me. She slid easily into a graceful side-saddle-esque sitting position and cocked her head to the left.

"Good morning," she said lightly.

Simone and I had never hung out before. The longest conversation we'd ever had was last week. "Morning," I answered.

Simone hadn't been looking me, but when I answered, she did, and, to my surprise, she looked as unsure as I felt.

"Is it OK if I sit here?" she asked. I nodded. She tipped her head in acknowledgment and scooted so that her back was against the locker bank, sitting right next to me, but far enough away that there was no danger of touching. When nine o'clock came, she unfolded herself and stood up. Without saying anything, she offered me her hand. I took it and she pulled me up.

"Thanks."

"No problem." Simone turned and went to class, with me still staring after her.

At lunch I decided to do an experiment. I got a salad from the cafeteria and sat down to eat it in front of her locker. A few minutes later, the door to the hallway opened and Simone stepped through. She stopped when she saw me. I didn't know her face well enough to read what she was thinking, but after a second she smiled briefly and sat back next to me, pulling a peanut butter and jelly sandwich out of her locker.

"I usually eat lunch alone," she told me. "I like having time to myself."

"Oh. Sorry. I can go?"

"No, I don't mind." She put down her sandwich and looked me straight in the eyes. "I just don't want you be disappointed in my lack of, well, girl talk. It's not my forte."

I recalled Audrey's glib jabs about Ellie's party, her fake compassion and tears. I shuddered. "Good," I said quietly.

A rubber band snapped into the locker dangerously close to my head, glinting. I picked it up and saw that it had been decorated with red and silver twist ties, braided sort of like a lanyard. I looked in the direction it had come from, and saw a corner of hallway occupied by Gilly and his friends. I picked it up and smiled in spite of myself.

Simone was looking over her shoulder with disgust on her face.

But when she saw me holding the rubber band, she chortled, "Oh, come on. Not really?"

I dropped it. "What? I don't know what you're talking about."

She looked behind her again, shaking her head at Gilly. "Colin Creevey over there actually, *finally* made a move? Like . . . a *moderately successful* move? That's sort of astounding."

Unaccountably blushing, I shook my head. "What do you mean, 'finally'?"

"You're kidding, right? No adolescent boy who acts like he hates a pretty girl as much as he did last year isn't totally nursing, like, an everlasting gobstopper of a boner for her."

Gilly was watching us, an agitated look now on his face. Simone bared her teeth at him and hissed like a cat. He scowled and looked away. Simone turned back to me.

"You're healing fast," she observed. "I'd offer to help you with makeup, but I think you're actually kind of rocking the look."

I laughed.

"So, Kitty called," she went on. "Said you stopped by the Fish Hook."

I stiffened and looked at her closely. She was looking back at me, just as closely. There was a staring contest that I lost.

"Are you going to tell me what's going on, then?" she asked mildly.

I looked around at the still-crowded hallway. "Not here."

She finished her sandwich and fished *The Great Gatsby*, our English class book, out of her backpack. "Meet me after school then. I'll give you a ride home."

At three o'clock, Simone led us out the back door of Howell and down a few blocks, eventually stopping at a gargantuan, immaculate, vintage bronze Cadillac.

I gaped at her. "*This* is your car?"

She shrugged nonchalantly but ran her fingers lovingly over the hood as she unlocked the door.

"I inherited it," she said, once we were both in the car. "Well, my great-uncle Myron died and no one wanted it, so I appropriated it."

"No one wanted this?" I asked, sinking into the velvety upholstery.

"It was a junker sitting in an unused corner of a field in Woodstock," she said. "I spent some time up there a couple of years ago. Fixed it up."

My face grew warm as I realized she was talking about her mysterious disappearance in tenth grade. But she didn't seem embarrassed as she pulled out, cool and in control, switching gears with a deft hand.

"So. Talk."

And, with an ease that I couldn't remember feeling in years, I talked to a girl. I didn't worry about how I was sounding or coming off. I just told her a true story and she listened.

Simone parked in front of my house. "You realize that sounds like bullshit, don't you?" She pressed a button and I heard my door unlock.

I was aghast. "It's the truth, I swear."

"Come on, Kendall. I've been going to Howell for as long as you have." She nodded toward my house and, in shock, I opened the car and stepped out.

I started to say, "Simone, I promise—" when she cut me off with a sharp, "Oh please, Ken. You're never going to convince me that Michael Gilbert was of any use to anyone." She raised an eyebrow at me, smiled, and shut the door.

I watched her speed down the street, a gasp of incredulous laughter exploding from my chest.

CHAPTER TWELVE

SIMONE AND I STARTED DRINKING COFFEE TOGETHER IN THE MORNING AND EATING LUNCH TOGETHER EVERY AFTERNOON. It was as simple as that. There was no flattery involved, there were no insinuations, no probing questions, no gossip. I got the feeling Simone wouldn't have known how to do that even if she wanted to. We talked about Jane Austen and *Supernatural*. I told her about applying to YATS, and she told me about the soldering iron she had bought over the summer to experiment with making jewelry out of scrap metal from her dad's industrial plumbing company. Just like that, we were friends.

I didn't know it could be easy. And, I knew with a lot of girls, including me a year ago, it wouldn't be. I tried to push that thought down.

I spent the week trying to track down Ellie's summer activities. According to her parents (I called pretending to be in the admissions office at Brown University, their alma mater), she had spent the summer taking tickets at the Film Forum, a fancy repertory and independent movie theater in the Village. I got my Facebook account back and checked her photos: no cinder-block offices or green Priuses. Just BMWs in the Hamptons and shots of her and Audrey on the beach.

I stalked her in the halls and snuck glances into the lockers and backpacks of everyone on Trev's list, but I didn't find anything. I watched everyone who had ever held a grudge against me, but no one was acting stranger than anyone else.

Ellie was still my most likely suspect. But I had nothing to go on and no way to get at her.

By Friday afternoon, I was near despair. I was never going to find Mason's stolen stash. I could kiss YATS good-bye.

And then Ellie finally did something out of the ordinary.

I was in the library, desperately doing math homework in case I had to argue my way back into YATS after experiencing total disgrace, when Ellie and Pete walked in together.

Ellie didn't like Pete.

They started walking in my direction. I grabbed my books and hid behind the stacks with the dictionaries.

They stopped on the other side of the shelves. "This is not my problem, Pete," said Ellie, in a low voice. "If Grant wants her at this party so badly, he's going to have to convince her to go him-self, because I'm not doing it."

"You guys are both such hypocrites," hissed Pete. "You've done ecstasy and Audrey doesn't refuse to hang out with you." My head shot up. I pressed my ear against the stacks.

"No, I haven't *done* ecstasy, I *did* ecstasy: singular, one time, once," Ellie answered harshly. "And I didn't expect Audrey to hold my hand while I did it. Just because I'm more considerate of Audrey's feelings than her boyfriend is doesn't make me a hypocrite, and it certainly doesn't make Audrey one. It just makes Grant an asshole."

I snorted and then clapped my hands over my mouth, but they didn't hear me.

"Ellie, come on. You know Audrey will go to the party if you ask her to go with you."

"You're wrong." Ellie sounded tired. "I can't get her to do anything. And I don't have any particular reason to want her to go to a party so that Grant can show her off while rolling, so he's just going to have to deal with it himself." She paused. "Let go of my arm, Pete."

"Look, the address is 179 Cranberry Street. It's tonight. A whole bunch of us will be rolling. You should come. And bring Audrey."

"Where did you even get it from? I thought the guy at the Fish Hook was dry all summer."

"He was. He just re-upped, like, last week. We're getting it at the party. Think about it, OK? Everyone is going, plus lots of NYU and Columbia kids. It's the first big party of the year. I know Audrey doesn't like it when Grant rolls, but do you really want to miss out on all the gossip of the first party of the year? You know you girls love to be at the center of the gossip."

"Fine. I'll think about it. Now, let go of me."

Several hours later, I found myself in front of a brownstone while Simone rearranged my hair, combing the strands back and forth with her sharp, immaculately clean nails.

I slapped her hands away. "What are you doing?" I asked.

She looked at me as if I were a child. "Just a crisscross part. Because I thought it would look nice. Do friends not do that?"

I sighed. "Sorry for snapping," I said. "I haven't been to a party for a while."

"Are you nervous?"

"No," I scoffed. "I've been to a million parties."

"That is true," she said. "What was the last one you went to without Audrey?" She took her hands away and smoothed the complicated cowl neck on her black, angora mini dress.

"Why do I feel like I should be insulted by that?"

"You shouldn't. I just imagine that to be a very specific dynamic."

"I don't know," I said, flashing back to St. Patrick's Day two years ago, when Audrey insisted on both of us wearing these huge, foam leprechaun hats all night.

"We totally should have brought Nerf guns," Audrey had whispered to me giddily, laughing eyes scanning the rowdy crowd. "We could have filled them with Lucky Charms."

"Wouldn't whiskey be more appropriate?" I had asked.

She grinned wickedly. "Exactly. Idiot boys would be lining up to try and get totaled with us and we'd dash their dreams."

"She was fun, you know," I said suddenly. I glanced over at Simone. "Audrey, I mean."

"She looks fun," she said smoothly. Simone looked over at me and her face softened. "'Audrey fun' isn't the only way, you know."

I relaxed a little and managed to smile. "Oh, teach me, Master Simone."

Simone stuck her tongue out at me in a rare moment of pure, unconsidered silliness. "I *am* the master," she said, laughing. "You are about to get a unique glimpse into the famed Simone Moody party maneuver. I ninja myself into places: No one's ever there to see me enter or leave."

I must have had a look on my face, because she added, "I didn't mean that in a bad way. I *like* being this way. I observe, I partake when I want, and I'm out when I want." She looked at me, hard. "Don't feel bad for me. I decide. It's all about me."

"Should I stand far away from you?"

She rolled her eyes and grabbed me by the elbow, hurrying us up the stairs. "Come on, Ken."

Jerry opened the door.

"Hi," I said, taking a surprised step back. But Jerry looked pleased to see me and stepped to the side, motioning us in with a gallant hand gesture.

"Hey, welcome, glad you came," Jerry said gruffly, closing the door. "Who's your friend?"

Simone put her hand out, curled like a cat's paw. "Simone Moody," she purred. Jerry took her hand with a grin.

I inwardly rolled my eyes. "Simone, this is Jerry. I know him from, um, from . . ."

But Simone wasn't listening to me. She produced a shiny brass zippo from out of nowhere and lit Jerry's cigarette for him, checking out his ass while he bent over the flame.

I *outwardly* rolled my eyes. "Where are the drinks?"

Jerry pointed me toward the back of the room and I pushed my way through to the kitchen. When I finally got there, some tall blond kid was blocking all the booze.

"Excuse me," I said impatiently. "Other people want to drink. Very badly."

The checked fabric of his shirt shifted as the boy stood up straighter. "What can I get you?" he asked, and I recognized the voice.

I groaned. "Oh, for fuck's sake."

Mason turned around, grinning.

"What are you doing here?" I asked.

"It's my party. Want a whiskey sour?"

He busied himself with a solo cup and a whiskey bottle, while I stared. "This is your house?" I asked.

"Well. No. It's my father's," he answered, dropping a maraschino cherry in the cup. "It's one of my father's houses. I'm borrowing it. Here you go."

I wasn't going to drink anything he gave me, but hoping to end this interaction, I took it. He caught my arm. An involuntary tickle rippled up my spine and I pulled out of his grasp.

He put his hands up. "Sorry," he said. "Didn't mean to offend."

I wished fervently that I was already drunk enough to vomit all over him.

I gave him my brightest, sweetest smile. "No worries." Then I thrust upward and my drink dripped down his face, staining his blond hair a brownish pink.

I stood there, frozen, waiting to see what he would do, anticipating that moment when he would clap his hands, turn stony, and move in for the kill. Get scary.

Instead, he stood there calmly, catching errant drops with his tongue. He pushed his hair to the side and squeegeed it into the sink. "Nice aim," he commented pleasantly, as if commending a good spike in a volleyball game. He wiped his lips, sending alcoholic droplets playfully in my direction.

I recoiled and backed away, colliding with a hard body and

bony hand that yanked me backward by the elbow; Jo reared up in my face.

"What the hell was that?" she asked sharply, looking from me to Mason and looming over everything like an Amazon: tall, jacked, and buzzing for a fight. With her burning eyes and thick curtain of dark hair, it was like being interrogated by Wonder Woman.

"Relax, Jo," said Mason, voice rasping over a chuckle. I narrowed my eyes at him, annoyed—I didn't know whether he was laughing out of awkwardness or actual amusement, but either way I didn't think getting antagonized by my former assailant was funny. But he ignored me and continued to grin, wiping his face with a paper towel as he said, "We're just being silly."

She took a step and turned to him with an affronted look. I tried to step away, but she maintained an iron grip on my arm, giving me a front seat view of her enraged face. She was really pretty, I realized. I mean, I found her so frightening that I hadn't considered her that way before, but all of those strangely narrow features, combined with that hair and pale, papery skin, fell together in an unsettlingly beautiful way. Like a Digger wasp: When its stinger is out, it's easy to forget that its iridescent blue wings are gorgeous.

"You're just being silly," she repeated in a low voice, dripping with venom. "You're being silly with the girl who, weeks ago, was an ant you asked me to drown."

"Jo," he said firmly, his face hardening.

She cut him off, shaking her head in disgust. "Enjoy playtime with Princess Peach, you hypocrite. I hope your new agenda works out for you. Because I'm done."

With a hard glance at me, Jo stomped out of the kitchen.

Mason stared after her, his face blank. Eventually, he sighed and shook his head. After taking a sip of his own drink, he seemed to remember I was there and refocused on me. "Do you want to get some air?" he asked, moving closer to me, watching me intently. "Come get some air with me. Let's talk."

What I wanted was to do the opposite of what Mason asked me to do.

He stepped even closer. "Come on, Kendall," he said softly. "I didn't *want* someone to steal my property, you know. I wish I didn't need your help. I'd *like* to let you out of this if I *can*."

His voice was dripping with melted butter. I looked into his cool, blue eyes and knew it was a probably a trick, maybe even a trap, but I couldn't be *sure*—at least not sure enough to know that there wasn't a chance to wheedle my way out of this.

And I couldn't stop that pancakes-with-syrup tone from seeping into my shoulders, relaxing the muscles there.

And so, almost involuntarily, as if that arctic gaze of his was pulling puppet strings, I gulped, nodded, and followed him out into the mild, still summery night.

There were two or three smokers hanging out on the stoop, farther down on the steps. We sat.

"So," he asked, "You having fun yet?"

He sounded chummy—intimate and apparently genuinely curious. I stared at him, emotional whiplash raising my body temperature. "I'm not here for fun," I hissed. "I'm not having fun, Mason."

He raised his eyebrows. "You're on the case, huh?"

"Go fuck yourself. I don't have a choice."

Again, he chuckled. We sat for a moment in silence, sipping our drinks. The strangeness of the moment was not lost on me: it was like the Big Bad Wolf slinking back to Grandmother's house looking for a belly rub and Little Red Riding Hood just giving up.

I snuck a look at Mason and found he was staring back at me. He seemed content to sit in silence and watch me hate him. And, I had to admit, there was a pleasure in being able to openly loathe someone. I was used to having to hide my hate, be nice.

Someone tumbled out of the doorway behind me and Mason's face went strange.

"What is it?" I said, turning around to see Grant, rosy-cheeked and laughing with Pete. He looked around and noticed Mason.

An odd sort of shadow flickered over Grant—nothing anyone who didn't know him would notice, probably. He didn't ever stop smiling. But for a moment, it was like someone hit pause on every muscle in his face. He didn't take his eyes off of Mason.

"Hey, man," he said. "Great party."

Mason nodded, toasting him with his drink, but didn't answer.

Grant came down the stairs. "So, when did you get back into town?"

Mason continued drinking, past the point where it was time to answer. Grant swung one foot down a step, still graceful even when drunk and rejected. That's when he noticed me.

"Little Kendall Evans!" he exclaimed, happy to see me, with just a hint—maybe more—of mocking in his voice. "You are stalking me!"

I opened my mouth, but Mason beat me to it.

In the politest, most even tone of voice *ever*, he said, "Please, get bent, Grant."

Grant did a double take and I held my breath, worried I would break in two if I let go of my laughter.

"What was that?" he asked, looking genuinely not sure if he'd heard right.

Still smiling with extreme pleasantry, Mason said, "Go. Get. Bent. *Go fuck yourself.*"

As Grant startled backward and went back upstairs, throwing a concerned, wounded look in Mason's direction, I started gasping like a goldfish, hyperventilating with laughter while Mason calmly sipped his drink, looking at me with a small smile hanging around his lips.

I struggled to compose myself. Mason was my enemy, but I couldn't deny that he had made my night.

CHAPTER THIRTEEN

ELLIE AND AUDREY NEVER SHOWED UP AT THE PARTY. Simone got bored with Jerry and offered to drive me home.

"This really is a beautiful car," I said, sliding into the passenger seat.

Simone smiled wide enough to show teeth. "It is the best car in the world," she said, absently caressing the steering wheel with her index finger. "I remember when I found it. It was right after that snowstorm two years ago. The snow was actually worse upstate, believe it or not."

She switched on her turn signal, moving onto the bridge.

"My grandfather's place is on a field, leading up to woods on three sides. It was piled three feet high before we got out there with shovels, and even then, we just dug a few tunnels: to the garage, to the shed, the driveway out to the main road." She paused and narrowed her eyes. After a second of thought, she said, "I hadn't spoken to anyone for about three days at that point. I had been feeling nauseated for a week and for some reason I couldn't get enough of the cold. It was the only thing that would stop me feeling sick; it kind of ate through any other symptoms, you know? So, after my grandfather went inside, instead of walking in the clear spots, I walked in the snow. Walked around the yard in circles. For hours. I stayed out there until the sun started to go down.

"When it was getting dark, my grandfather came out on the porch and yelled at me to come inside. I still didn't want to walk in the paths, or backtrack in my footsteps, so I went the long way around. And I literally walked smack into this car. It had sunk into the mud earlier that year and was totally submerged. I would have just ignored it maybe, but the sun was setting and happened to catch the paint where the snow had fallen away."

She snuck a glance at me. "It's a good thing I'm not as short as you, I would have drowned. I can't believe I didn't catch pneumonia. Anyway, I've spruced the car up since then, but I almost wish I hadn't. The sunset on the rust was . . . pretty."

I had a million questions, but I only had the guts to ask the easiest. "Where did you learn how to fix cars?"

She shrugged carelessly. "A lot of the old guys up there had worked at the repair shop. Pop, too. I'm good at mechanical things."

We drove the rest of the way in silence and I watched Simone. Watching her drive was like watching a ballet, her arms moving in sure, centered arcs from the wheel to the gearshift, her hips turning with the beat of the motor underneath them, every little motion of her fingertips carefully and skillfully calculated, to a technical, but somehow beautiful effect. An image of her, enraged, slamming a chair through a glass window with a piercing, guttural war cry came unbidden into my head. I remembered how very little I knew about Simone.

On Monday morning, I woke up to a voice mail from a blocked number.

"Hey, Kendall." It was Mason's voice. "It was great seeing you the other night. You have been a lovely blackmailee. The terms have changed. Come by when you get out of school."

I played it for Simone at lunch. She listened, frowning.

She handed it back to me. "What do you think?" I asked.

"I'm not sure. I don't really care for his tone, but I don't know. What do you think?"

"Maybe it's a good thing? Maybe he found the thief and doesn't need me anymore? That could happen, right?"

Simone looked up and stiffened. "Can I help you?" she asked imperiously. I whirled around to see Gilly.

He ignored her and turned to me. "Kendall, can I talk to you alone, please?"

I avoided Simone's glare and followed him to the hallway, where he stopped and said, "I thought I should tell you that I'm going to call the cops and tell them about the whole thing."

"Goddamn it, Gilly! Why?"

"Have you found the drugs yet?"

I looked down. "No."

"Were you just talking about having to go see Mason?"

"You were eavesdropping? That's attractive."

He nodded. "Right. So that's that. I was trying to stay out of your business, but you're not safe. We're calling the cops now."

"*We* are not doing anything, Gilly. This has nothing to do with you."

"But it has something to do with *her*?" He motioned to somebody behind me.

"Ahem," said Simone. Swallowing a curse, I turned around.

Simone was also slouching against the lockers. But her arms were crossed and she was definitely not smiling.

The two stared each other down like gunfighters outside a saloon at high noon. She narrowed her eyes; he clenched his fists. The other students filling the hallway were so many tumbleweeds.

I turned back to Gilly. "We're friends," I told him, keeping my voice down.

He rolled his eyes. "Whatever. If she gets to help you, I get to help you."

"Calling the police is not helping me."

"Let me come with you to talk to Mason and I won't call the police."

I sighed, nodded, and walked over to Simone, who was looking at Gilly's retreating back distastefully.

"So, can you give me a ride to your building after school?"

"Fine."

I took a breath. "I have to bring Gilly."

"Jesus, Kendall!" Simone threw up her hands and walked away.

Simone hadn't gotten over her annoyance at having to include Gilly, but at the end of the day she set her teeth and unlocked her car door for him anyway. Gilly scowled as he slid into the backseat, muttering some unintelligible bitchery, and slammed the door hard behind him. Simone rolled her eyes at me and let me into the passenger side.

"So, last time I saw him there it was around 4:30," I said, awkwardly breaking the silence.

"Well, that's barely enough time to prepare," Simone said, pounding the gas pedal.

"Prepare how?"

Gilly broke in. "Set my number on speed-dial and then keep your ringer on silent, with your phone in your pocket, so you can text me if something goes wrong. It's 917-"

"She already did that with my number," Simone interrupted tersely. I elbowed her in the ribs. She shot me a death glare, but said, "Though I guess it won't hurt. Go ahead."

After entering his number in my phone and handing it back, Gilly grumbled. "What was *your* big plan, Simone?"

"Nothing that concerns you."

"OK, you know what? Let's just have some quiet time," I said, turning on the radio. "Listen to some music."

When we got to Simone's apartment, she kicked off her heels and motioned for me to do the same with my Keds, disappearing down the hall to her room. I turned to make sure Gilly was behaving but found that he had automatically taken his shoes off already. Curious, I held back and watched as he made the turn to Simone's room just a fraction of a second before I did.

Inside, Simone was laying out a pair of narrow black pants with a big silver button and a red and black corset top.

"Is this for me?" I asked, fingering the lush velvet of the pants.

"Yes," she said, pulling a crate of shoes out from apparently nowhere. "Put it on. You"— this to Gilly—"wait outside. Kendall, what size shoe are you?"

"Six-and-a-half," I said, quickly unbuckling my pants. Simone rummaged to the bottom of the crate and pulled out slightly worn silver flats.

"These should work for you. My feet grew like crazy two years ago," she said. Turning and seeing Gilly still standing there, Simone snapped, "I thought you were gone already! Go away so Kendall can change."

Gilly opened his mouth, looking furious, but I guess he couldn't think of anything to say, because he eventually shut it and left the room with a long-suffering look in my direction.

I changed into the clothes Simone picked out for me. The pants were tight and sleek. I ran my hands down them, feeling the firmness of my thighs, while Simone tilted my head forward and shook out my hair, ripping a comb through it.

While she worked on me, I took in her room, which was weird in a kind of spectacular way: somehow both Spartan and Roman. It had a military tidiness and a crisp minimalism: no movie posters, no visible shelves, no stuffed animals, nothing. There were several armoires and cupboards, but they all had doors and all the doors were shut, and her desk was an old-fashioned rolltop. Much of the room was white: the walls, the ceiling, the armoires, the desk, the curtains. Even the floorboards had been painted white.

Her bed was a gigantic, bronze four-poster mounted on a black circular platform and hung with a shining, sheer black canopy. Beyond its folds, I saw silver satin pillows and a sumptuous velvet bedspread in gold. The same metallic colors had been neatly painted onto the moldings lining the bleached furniture. She had strung gold, silver, and bronze PVC bars in intricate patterns high up on the walls, near the ceiling.

Other than the pipes, there were only two pieces of wall decoration, stuck side by side in the very center of the wall perpendicular to her bed: one was a black-and-white photograph of a boy wearing a yarmulke and a fringed scarf, reading from a scroll—the Torah, I guess. The other was a yellowed piece of paper with four Chinese characters printed in red ink, in a red border. They were in identical black frames.

Simone let my hair go. "OK, now throw your head back."

I did as she said. She stepped back and surveyed me. "Dress for the job you want, or in this case, the one you've been blackmailed into," she told me. "I think this will help. Take a look." She called out to Gilly, "You can come in."

I turned to the mirror and gaped. I still looked like a high school student, but somehow Simone had managed to make me look as sophisticated and adult as it was possible to be in that stage of the human condition.

"And this is your contribution, Simone?" scoffed Gilly. "Make her look like you. Yeah, that will give her credibility."

"You will literally never, ever understand girls, huh? That must be sad for you. Good luck with that V card."

They glared at each other and I was about to yell at them to knock it off, when I looked closer. Simone was clenching her fists so tightly her knuckles had gone white. Gilly's forehead and collarbone above his T-shirt were both shiny with sweat.

They were scared, I realized. They were trying so hard to be helpful because they were scared.

I turned back to the mirror. Was I scared? I reached down into the pocket of my crumpled jeans for my cell phone and checked the time. 4:25. I slid it into the pocket of Simone's pants.

"I'm going to go down there," I heard myself say. Feeling slightly disconnected, like I was floating, I moved toward the door. "I'll be back soon."

I searched myself for fear in the elevator and again as I pushed open the doors that led to the basement stairs. *I'd better be scared*, I told myself, the light getting dimmer the farther I went down. I knew that staying scared meant staying smart. Using my cell phone for light, I concentrated on finding the right door.

Once I did, I took a deep breath and wished so hard for an empty room that I actually expected one. What I did not expect was to push open the door to the secret office and find Mason alone, headphones on, bare feet tucked up underneath him on the couch, playing *God of War* on a PlayStation.

"Um, got a minute?" I asked, after standing awkwardly in the doorway, waiting for him to notice me.

He looked up and smiled at me, pulling off his headphones. He put down the controller and motioned me in.

"Sit down," he said. He swung his legs off the couch to make room for me next to him.

I looked at the soft dent in the fabric where his feet had been and felt something twist in my chest. *Fear*, I finally identified, as if it were something happening to someone else.

I willed myself to calm down, ordering my circulatory system to pump blood at a normal rate. I raised my eyes to his. "I think I'd rather stand if it's all the same to you."

Mason met my gaze with his own. "Jerry, I ordered a pizza at the corner. Would you go pick it up?" I hadn't even noticed Jerry, but there he was, leaning against the far wall with his eyes closed, like he was napping.

Jerry looked from him to me. "Now?" he asked, hesitating.

"Yes, please," answered Mason, still looking right at me.

I felt Jerry waiting for my reaction. Remembering how I looked in Simone's clothes, I threw my hair back and my hip forward, jamming myself into the girl in the photograph. I nodded.

"OK," he said, throwing his jacket on.

The door shut behind him and Mason said, "I wasn't sure you would come."

My head snapped back to him. "What would you have done if I hadn't?" I asked, suddenly suspicious.

"I probably would have called the TA at YATS," he said, putting his feet back up on the coffee table. "But I wouldn't have enjoyed it." He looked up at me and tilted his head. "Kendall, come on, sit down. You were so friendly on Friday. Why be nervous now?"

"I'm not nervous," I lied. "And I wasn't friendly on Friday. I threw a drink in your face."

He laughed. "That was great."

"You must have a weird fucking social life."

Mason nodded. "I do. That's actually why I asked you here. Please sit down, Kendall. I know you haven't found the thief. I'm not mad about that—we re-upped, so there's no supply issue. I've got time to find the idiot. Sit down and talk with me."

I pulled out the desk chair and sat.

Mason scooted down the couch so he was closer to me. "Jo's very angry at me."

I snorted before I could stop myself. "OK. I'm sorry?"

"Yeah, me too. She's been in my life for a long time. I tried to talk to her this weekend, but she wasn't letting it go. I think we're kind of broken now."

I stared at him, but he didn't say anything else. "That's a really sad story," I said eventually. "What does it have to do with me?"

"I'm getting to that." He pulled a pink cell phone out of his pocket and started fiddling around with it, twisting it between his palms. "She was my childhood friend, but she also helped me with my business."

"Yeah, I know," I snapped, pointing to my just-barely-healed black eye. "Remember?"

He looked confused and then laughed. "Oh, no. Not *that*. I'm not Scarface, dude, I don't need a full-time goon on payroll. Even if I did, Jerry would be better for that gig, don't you think? Though it would have been harder for Jerry to fit in at Howell. No, Jo is my—well, she liked to say courier, but really she was my delivery girl. But Jo quit and I'm out a delivery girl. And it's a busy season."

It was slowly dawning on me what he was saying, but I couldn't quite grasp at the truth of it. I didn't want to believe it. I wouldn't believe it. So I did what I do when I don't want to believe what I'm being told, whether it's the truth or a lie, and played dumb.

I asked, "What do you want from me?"

He laughed again. "I want what every guy wants." He flipped the phone out of his hands, sending it twisting through the air. I caught it neatly in my lap.

"I need a new gal Friday," he said. "I need a new Jo."

CHAPTER FOURTEEN

I TURNED THE PHONE AROUND IN MY HAND AND SAW THE BARBIE LOGO—BARBIE, AGAIN—SCRAWLED ACROSS THE BACK. "What's this?" I asked.

"Your new work phone," Mason answered, pulling out his own, nondescript, black-cased phone. He punched at it a few times and the cell in my hand beeped. "That's my number, but don't save it under my name."

I stared at the screen in my hand, my fingers hovering over the unfamiliar digits. "I don't want this." I thrust it back toward him.

Mason shook his head, pulling his hands away. "Sorry, kiddo. You don't really have a choice. I told you the terms of your blackmail had changed. The *fact* of your blackmail hasn't. And, seriously, I think you're going to be really good at this once you get used to the idea. Hey, Jerry's back. Yay."

Jerry brushed by me and dropped a large pepperoni pizza onto the coffee table. I ignored him and thrust the phone back at Mason.

"No! *No!*"

Jerry looked at me, startled, and I realized that I was shouting.

Mason reached out his hands. But he didn't take the phone. He twined his long fingers around mine, locking the phone in my grasp.

"Your reputation is still bad enough that I can wreck you, Kendall," he said gently. The bottom fell out of my stomach. I pulled my fingers away from his and, when they were free, I was still clutching the phone.

He smiled. "Don't worry, kiddo. I'm not going to ask you to do anything you're not entirely capable of doing."

"And what's that?" I whispered.

"I think you're capable of anything you put your mind to." I tried to put every ounce of rage I had ever felt toward anybody into the glare I gave Mason, but he looked me in the eye and said, "I mean it as a compliment!"

Jerry brushed past me and I felt him put a surreptitiously sympathetic hand on my back. I counted the steps he took back to his chair by the wall and at the end—*eleven*—was calm enough to say, "Just tell me."

"It will be very easy for you. You'll pick up a few doses at a time from me and I'll text you addresses and first names. You'll deliver the product, collect the money, and then stay for a little while to socialize. That part is important. That's how we don't get caught. That's why I need someone like you."

I felt sick. "You deliver to Howell kids."

He hesitated. "I did. I'm phasing that out. It has to be one of the Howell kids who stole from me, so I don't feel like doing business with them right now. It's mostly going to be to former prep schoolers who stayed in the city to go to college You know the landscape and you'll pass."

"How long do I have to do this for?"

"You don't give me any trouble, you'll be out in Texas by January. Gives me enough time to find a replacement."

I cast about desperately for an ejector seat. "If I find the thief in the meantime, will you let me stop earlier?" I asked, feeling feverish.

He cocked his head to the side. "That's an interesting question." He paused a moment. "You've got a deal." He stuck out his hand.

I recoiled. "No thanks."

"Oh, come on. Don't be like that. This will be fun!"

"Not for *me*."

"We'll see. Want some pizza?"

If I ate anything, I knew I would throw up. I shook my head. He nodded. "I understand. Go back up to Simone's apartment."

I started to leave but stopped at the doorway. "How did you know my friend lived here?"

He walked over to the pizza box. "Because I live here. Sometimes, anyway." He looked up at me. "I'm glad she's made some friends. She's had a rough couple of years. We'll talk soon."

Mason turned back to the pizza box and I momentarily locked eyes with Jerry. He gave me a small shrug. There was no help to be had there.

I felt like Alice trying to scramble back up the rabbit hole, only to keep sliding back down.

Simone's front door was still unlocked, so I let myself in.

I took off Simone's shoes and carried them down the hallway. The silence was suspicious until I made it to her bedroom and saw Simone and Gilly sitting as far away from each other as possible. They had each chosen a corner and were facing in opposite directions, noses stuck in separate textbooks. They were so bent on ignoring each other that I had to rap on the doorframe to alert them to my return.

"Do you guys want to tell me what your deal is?" I asked once they had looked up, losing patience. "This is just weird now."

They exchanged a quick, intense glance. "How'd it go?" Simone asked, ignoring my question.

"Not great," I said. Frustration broke in a wave over my head and I kicked the door so many times that I lost my balance and fell down with a yell.

Simone and Gilly looked at each other again. "What happened?" Simone started to ask, shooting an alarmed glance at the newly scuffed woodwork, but was interrupted by a door slamming.

"Sugar, you left the door open," called out a musical southern voice. "Daddy would have hit the ceiling if he'd gotten home first." I heard heels getting kicked off and quick footsteps down the hall to her room. "Have you eaten yet, baby girl? I picked up some entrées at the Whole Foods buffet." Simone's mom collided with me in her hurry to get to her daughter. She squealed and gave me a little hug. "Oooh, I'm sorry, darling, I didn't see you. You must be Kendall! Simone's told me about her new girlfriend. I'm Lorraine Moody."

I don't know what I had expected exactly from Simone's mother, but this wasn't it. She was a small, curvy Chinese woman dressed all in white and beige, down to the pearls in her ears and around her neck. The only exception was a red paper flower clipping back her long, wavy hair. She looked young and her eyes danced.

I looked from her to Simone. Simone actually looked a lot like her, but the bizzarro version, with the firm set of her mouth and blunt eyes. I turned back to Lorraine.

"Yeah, that's me. It's nice to meet you." I stuck out my hand, but she had completely lost interest in me. She was gazing past me. Finally, she clapped her hands together in delight and rushed forward.

"Mikey," she cried, throwing her arms around him. He had stood up when she came into the room and cautiously returned the hug.

"Oh, Mikey, let me look at you." She stepped back and put her hands on his face, turning it first to the left and then to the right. "You look so handsome. Didn't I tell you your skin would clear up by high school?"

"Hi, Lorraine," said Gilly, smiling sheepishly. "It's good to see you."

"Good? Honey, it's *divine* seeing you back in this apartment." She finally let him go and stepped away with clasped hands. "To hell with Whole Foods, I'm making you fried chicken." She kissed him on the cheek. Then she turned to Simone and kissed her on both cheeks, throwing both of her arms around her daughter's shoulders in a squeeze, and practically skipped out of the room.

I turned to Simone and Gilly, who were both innocently looking into the middle distance. Gilly in particular had the expression of a dog that had just peed on the rug and was hoping that you wouldn't notice.

"Should I be expecting an explanation?" I asked, crossing my arms. "Or is that *unreasonable* of me?"

Simone sighed. "Look, we were friends when we were kids."

"Apparently, really *good* friends!"

"When we were *kids*," she countered. "We haven't spoken since seventh grade."

"Because Simi is a traitor and weak of will," muttered Gilly.

Simone hissed back, "Because *Mikey* is a jealous, stunted little—"

"Kids." Lorraine poked her head back in the room. "Are all three of you going to be here for dinner? Mikey, I'm not letting you out of my sight, I already texted your mom, but Kendall, I don't have your parents' numbers."

All three of us started protesting at the same time, but Lorraine was only looking at me, so I managed to force out, "That's really nice of you, Mrs. Moody, but I have to get home."

I really did. I needed to lie down and be catatonic. She must have seen the distress on my face, because she made a genteel "say no more" gesture and left the room with a smile.

Simone, however, turned to me with what I think would have been a hurt expression had her features been accustomed to arranging themselves into something stronger than mild irritation.

Meanwhile, Gilly grabbed my arm. "Don't leave me here. I'm begging you."

I shook him off. "I'm not in the mood," I snapped. "Thanks for asking, Simone, but it did *not* go well with Mason."

"What happened?"

Without warning, my lungs hollowed out.

I sat down on the bed, breathing too hard to stand. "I need some water," I gasped.

"Here," came Simone's voice as she handed me a mug, I guess from her bedside table.

I swallowed the lukewarm water and started to count. *One, two,* breathe in, *three, four,* breath out. *Five, six,* breathe in, *seven, eight,* breathe out.

Gilly yanked on his own hair. "What *happened* down there?" he asked.

I looked down at my hands. I got nervous sometimes. Counting helped. Breathing helped. My hands became steady even though they had no reason to be.

"Everything got worse," I told them.

I was trapped in the girl in the photograph.

Even after all that, I had no choice but to go to school the next day.

I spent all day with the pink phone in my back pocket. Gilly had launched a ferocious attempt to talk me out of it the night before, but Simone took pity on me once I started babbling about Texas. I guessed if anyone could understand a need to leave Howell, it would be her. She literally put her hand over Gilly's mouth and hustled me out the door, telling me to try to get some sleep.

That didn't happen. The new day was long and fuzzy. All I knew was there was a Barbie phone in my back pocket that could go off at any time and turn me into a criminal.

My last class of the day was PE. After changing, I walked into the gym and stopped short when I saw the volleyball net set up. I realized with a surprised pang that team tryouts were coming up.

I snuck a look at the equipment cage, outfitted with a brand-new lock. Coach Guerin emerged with a net bag of game balls and caught sight of me. With a cough and a quick, but not quick enough, glance in my direction, she protected the view and entered the combination right up against her chest.

"Ahh, memories," a voice whispered behind me. I whirled around and saw Ellie laughing behind her hand.

Fuck her.

I smiled brightly at her and strode over to the right back position of the court. My position.

There was an awkward pause until, with a shrug, Coach Guerin blew the whistle. "OK, seniors, you see the net. You know what to do." Quietly, people jostled into positions until they were full, with a few hanging around the other side of the net before slowly, resignedly, walking over to my team.

"Evans," said the coach and tossed me the ball. I rolled the white rubbery sphere around my wrists, feeling the familiar waxy vinyl against my fingertips. I flipped the ball up in the air, caught it between the heels of my hands. One more time, a little higher.

I flipped the ball in the air again, wound my arm back, and jumped, slamming the ball in a hard, fast beeline over the net; landed on the polished floor with two feet, a palm, and a grunt. I smiled when I heard Ellie shriek as she dodged the careening ball.

If I found the thief before Mason sent me on a delivery, I was free. Ellie was still my prime suspect. And I knew for a fact Ellie had a meddling mother and a strict father—she didn't get along with them. She never kept anything at home that she wanted to keep secret.

So, when everyone else went down to the gym locker rooms at the end of the period, I peeled off from the pack and headed to the lockers proper.

Ellie's locker was two down from mine. I crouched in front of the combination lock and held it to my ear.

Around the same time that a mania for séances swept the eighth grade, it became equally in vogue to learn how to pick locks. Not sure why. Maybe we had all seen *The Italian Job* one too many times at sleepovers. But whatever it was, one afternoon a bunch of girls trucked on down to the spy store on Sullivan Street and bought lock-picking kits, although they could never get them to work. I didn't buy one, but I did go with them. I joked that the only lock I ever needed to pick was my locker combination, which, despite my usual ease with numbers, I was constantly forgetting. The guy behind the counter smiled and called me over. He leaned over and said, "That's really not too difficult with a standard school-issued lock." And then he showed me how.

I held my breath and started moving the dial slowly to the right, digit by digit until, at 48, I heard a faint click. I started moving the dial to the left, slowly, slowly, slowly, until—22, click. My fingers shaking a little now, I went to the right again, slowly, slowly, slowly—

"What are you doing?"

My hand slipped off the lock. Still crouched on the floor, I turned and saw Ellie, Audrey, and Alexis all freshly showered and standing behind me, Ellie with her hand on her hip and a shocked expression on her face. All the concentration and focus I had felt a moment before shattered and crashed to the ground.

"Are you trying to break into my locker?" she said, looking appalled and also gleeful. "Oh my god! What is your problem, Kendall?"

I flushed and moved away, collecting my wits. "Is that your locker?" I asked, injecting sarcasm into my tone, the only weapon I could think to use against Ellie. "I'm sorry, I got mixed up. You know, I've been using up that Plan B pretty quickly, not getting enough sleep. My attention to detail has suffered. I guess I just forgot." Her face didn't change. I switched tactics, putting my hands up. "Look, I honestly thought it was mine. I'm brain dead from running around upstairs. Didn't drink any water."

This last part was said in a reasonable tone and was a pretty believable lie, so I stepped away toward my own locker, hoping the encounter was over.

"You aren't going to at least change your shirt, Kendall?" asked

Audrey, ostentatiously stepping away from me. "Don't you think you should?"

Even Alexis, who had been looking a little uncomfortable up until then, choked on a laugh at Audrey's tone, which was like a needle hidden in a silk scarf.

Last period was now a good five minutes over and the hallway was packed. I looked down at my sweaty, shiny limbs and felt a sting of shame, knowing I smelled. I chose not to respond and just bent over my own locker.

Ellie snorted and said, "Hey, what's one more bodily fluid to leak around Howell?"

I went rigid. It was like the first day of school when Audrey made that comment about me being a slut and I couldn't breathe. Except *this* time, I felt my hands clench into fists on their own accord and a literal shiver of rage race down my spine.

Still facing the lockers, I said in my loudest and clearest voice, "I hope it's not getting you too worked up, Ellie. I know how the showers in the girls' locker room affect you." I turned to look at her then and cocked my head in Audrey's direction. Ellie turned bright red and walked quickly out of the hallway, Audrey looking quizzically after her.

As I watched her walk away, my heart sank a little. That was shitty of me—too shitty even for *me*, to just shrug, tell myself Ellie deserved what she got, and forget about it. I didn't care if she had a crush on Audrey or not, although after years of watching her ob-sessively shadow Audrey, I was pretty sure she did. Ellie was not a nice girl, but on a karmic level, was that something I just shouldn't mock? Did I want to sink *that* low?

I needed to find a way to crack Ellie. But I wasn't going to find it that day.

The Barbie phone went off.

CHAPTER FIFTEEN

Twenty-four hours later, I was standing on a deserted waterfront shaking like a flat-chested freshman in the locker room.

The Fish Hook looked different in the light. It was just a drab chunk of concrete with a door in the middle. There was nothing here to be scared of.

There is nothing to be scared of here. There is nothing to be scared of. This was the mantra I'd been repeating in my head since I'd left Mason's office that afternoon and all the way on the long walk from the F train. I compulsively reached my hand back to cover the bulge in my bag, confirming for about the eightieth time that the bottle hadn't somehow ripped a hole through the canvas and rolled down a gutter. Or, you know, to the nearest police station. The nearest police station with drug-sniffing/human-tracking dogs. But the medium-size orange bottle was still there.

I took a deep breath, stuffed my hands in my pockets, and crossed the street to the bar.

It was empty, except for a fat blond cat playing with a catnip toy on the bouncer's stand, and infinitely quieter than it had been the last time I was there. Trev was alone behind the bar, slouching and yawning over a laptop. I put my hand on the cat's head, rubbing its ear. At its meow, Trev looked up and his eyes widened.

"Miss Kendall," he said, standing up, quickly replacing the surprise on his face with a smile. "What can I do for you?"

I looked closer and saw his eyes shifting back and forth, from me to the door to the bar. For some reason, just me being there was setting him on edge.

I gave the cat one last tickle on the neck and decided to press what little advantage I had. I slung my bag onto the bar and reached for the zipper. "Actually," I said, "it's what I can do for you." I took out the bottle and set it in front of him.

Trev took a moment to respond. I thought I saw a question form on his lips, but then he smiled, straightened his shoulders, and sauntered over. He reached for the bottle and popped the cap, counting the tablets.

"All here," he said cheerfully, pulling out bills and handing them to me. "Thank you kindly, Mademoiselle."

I shrugged, pocketing it. "Don't thank me, thank Mason."

"I guess you two have become close," said Trev. "That's a shame. Do you want a drink?"

"Please." Actually, I had to stay for a drink. Mason's rules were that I had to socialize with buyers. It was good for not getting caught, he said, but I suspected that it was equally good for business.

To my surprise—and a little bit not—Trev put a glass in front of me and poured a double shot of bourbon in it, smirking a little. I smiled, thinking he didn't know who he was dealing with, and drank the whole thing down in two gulps.

"You're in high school, right?" he asked, sounding wary.

"Unfortunately."

"True that. Another?"

I looked at the clock. According to the rules, I was supposed to stay in dorms and other places with sign-ins for at least an hour. Everywhere else I had to hang out, but it didn't have to be for as long. I didn't know how long I had to stay in an empty bar on a dead-end street.

"I don't know if I should," I answered honestly. I *did* still have homework to do.

"Would the boss-man not like it?" he asked teasingly, leaning toward me. "Is he very protective of the schoolgirl?"

He was getting closer than I liked. It couldn't hurt to let people believe Mason would protect me. "I don't think he thinks I need protection." I leaned into his face, my lips coming very close to the valley between his nose and his cheekbone. "And I don't, do I?"

Trev smiled again, hollowly this time. "I don't see why you would. Sweet, pretty, helpful kid—who'd want to hurt you?"

"Who indeed," I answered. He looked away first and I grinned at the small victory. "I think I will have another drink, if you don't mind."

"You got it, kid."

I watched him pour the drink. He'd been nice to me. Trev was a little sleazy, but he wasn't going to purposefully hurt anybody. I suddenly felt guilty. I was having too much fun here.

"You know what, don't worry about it," I heard myself say. I collected my things and stood up.

"You sure?" he asked, still holding the bottle. "It's no trouble."

"Yeah, I should get going," I said, looking at him. Not really having anything else to say, I tapped my fingertips on the bar by way of good-bye and left. The cat had scampered away, too, as if it was as scandalized as Trev to see me there.

Starting that afternoon, I was moving through the world differently than I had before. I had never felt so visible or so much like a ghost.

My new domain was the coffee shop breakroom, the library study carrel, and, above all, the dorm.

I first put my finger on the change when I delivered to Jeff. Jeff, I learned, was a regular. He opened the door, wafting marijuana smoke and Nelly music into the hallway. He stopped and stared at me, blinking stupidly.

"Hi!" I said brightly, though not entirely able to suppress a sarcastic undertone. "I'm Mason's tutor. Ready for chemistry prep?"

I continued to stand there with my pasted-on smile while he looked down the hall in both directions and then beckoned me in.

He shut the door. "You're not Jo," he drawled. Not in a southern way—just a lazy way.

Jeff was wearing boxer shorts that were hitting the danger zone in terms of looseness, a white tank, and a pristine Lakers hat. His body lived in that middle ground of sturdy, beefy, stocky, all those adjectives that sounded way worse when applied to girls. He also had a really stupid-looking face.

"No, I'm not," I said, looking for a clean spot to sit and eventually perching on the windowsill. "I'm Kendall."

"But, you're still . . ." Jeff struggled to find the question. "Mason still . . . I mean, you have—"

"Yes, I have your doses," I broke in. "Mason gave them to me and I'm bringing them to you. Not Jo."

Jeff looked relieved. "Oh. OK, cool."

I swung the bag around to my front, unzipped it, and pulled out the doses. "Sixty even," I said.

He fumbled at his hip and then seemed to realize that he wasn't wearing any pants. I rolled my eyes, thereby spotting a full-to-bursting, expensive-looking leather wallet on the desk to my left.

"May I?" I asked, gesturing to the wallet. Without waiting

for him to locate the hand motions that indicate acquiescence, I opened it and had to stifle a gasp.

Jeff only had hundreds. He had eight of them. And a platinum card to boot.

I looked at him, astonished. Why would a college kid need *this* much cash?

"You don't have anything smaller?" I asked.

He grinned proudly. "I know, right?"

I felt my expression sour. "No, seriously. I don't have change. I'm not pizza delivery."

Jeff seemed more relaxed now that I'd seen his money. He kicked a pile of clothing off his bed—showing surprising aerobic ability—and crashed onto it, reaching behind the headboard for a pair of jeans.

He handed me a crumpled fold of twenties. "Thanks," I said, quickly counting the bills. It was all there. I stuck the wad in my back pocket and pulled my bio textbook out of my bag.

"What are you doing?"

I looked up at him, surprised. "My homework."

"Yeah, but . . . why?"

"Didn't Jo stay a little after dropping off?" I asked.

"Yeah, but . . . she didn't do homework."

"Oh no? What did Jo do?"

He smiled slyly. "Jo would party with us."

I drew in an exasperated breath and sighed it out. I didn't want to party.

I shut my book and Jeff perked right up. "Come with me," I said to him, smiling.

"Hell, yeah," he answered. He climbed into track pants and while he had his back turned I grabbed an apparently untouched copy of *Middlemarch* off of his desk.

Jeff followed me down the hall and kept going toward the elevator for a few steps before realizing I had stopped in the common room and was settling onto the couch with my textbook.

"I thought we were going to get drinks. What are we doing here?" he asked, perplexed.

"I'm studying," I told him. "You should probably try it if you don't want Daddy to cut you off after you flunk out."

Mason said I had to hang out with the buyers. He didn't say I had to make it fun for them. And honestly, I would have rather treated Ellie to a mani-pedi than done *anything* else to make Jeff's life *more* fun.

Jeff pouted, but he did as he was told—did what *I* told *him* to do.

It hit me that now, in this new role, I could tell people what to do. I was used to following behind Audrey, but now *I* was the queen of whatever room I was in, or at least the girl in the photograph was.

I finally got a break on Saturday. My parents were visiting friends in New Haven and I was looking forward to a day of zoning out in front of the TV, with no one bothering me.

I got off to a bad start when the doorbell rang at ten in the morning, jolting my eyes open. I trudged down the stairs in my PJs as the bell rang again and again and again.

I didn't recognize the man looking at me through the glass sidebar of the door. Well-brought-up city girl that I was, I opened the door as narrowly as I could and kept my hand on the handle.

"Can I help you?" I asked.

He was handsome in a well-scrubbed, bland way. And he smiled a pleasant smile as he stuck out his hand.

And his badge.

"Good morning! Is this the Evans residence?"

I took his hand and shook it automatically, unable to take my eyes off of the silver oval, even though it was reflecting the sun too fiercely to read any of the numbers.

"Can I help you?" I asked again, forcing myself to look at him. I added in the highest voice I could manage, "My parents aren't home." I opened my eyes wide and slouched for good measure.

The cop leaned in. "Are you Kendall?" he asked, with a conspiratorial wink in his voice. I absolutely didn't trust this.

"What's this about?"

"May I come in?"

He was still shaking my hand. "Not without a warrant," I told him.

He nodded and then all the expression drained out of his face. I squealed in sudden pain as his grip tightened on my hand.

"What are you—?" He jerked me out of the doorway and had me stumbling barefoot down the steps before I could even finish the question. I heard the door slamming shut behind me, the collision of wood on wood violent and splintering, from the momentum of my wrist being wrenched away from the knob.

I opened my mouth to scream for help, but he stopped short and shook his head, waving his badge in front of my face. My mind raced past the twenty hits of ecstasy I had just sold, and that was only from yesterday. I snapped it shut.

He unlocked the back door to an unmarked Crown Victoria and tossed me inside before climbing in the passenger seat. The driver peered at me in the rearview mirror through thick horn-rimmed glasses. "Hi," he said with a jerky little nod.

The car peeled off in silence.

"Am I being arrested?" I blurted out. I went on, trying hard to dull the edge of desperation spiking my voice. "Because my mother is an attorney and if she finds out I'm being questioned without a guardian or lawyer present, you're headed for a bitch of a countersuit."

"Relax," said Glasses. "We're just going to have a conversation."

I crossed my legs, bare except for blue mesh shorts with the Howell Hawks logo on the butt, then opted to tuck them up against my chest instead—I was wearing a bra, thank god, but the gray T-shirt was pretty threadbare, with an ever-expanding hole in the armpit.

The car swerved. Since I wasn't wearing a seatbelt, I got thrown forward and caught myself on the armrests of the front seat.

"Come on, kid," said Glasses, laughing. "Buckle up. Safety first."

I took a deep breath and opened my eyes. A large gold medallion was dangling in my face. I snatched it—NYU, 1st Place, State Swimming Championships. What was this doing in an NYPD car?

Suddenly I remembered. The photo of the green Prius on my Facebook—it had a medal just like this one hanging over its dash.

"Where did you get that police badge? At Ricky's Halloween Store?" I asked, still holding the medal. The fake cop smiled and nodded. He took it out and tapped it, making a puny, hollow sound. Plastic.

I went cold. "Have I done something to piss off Mason?"

He laughed so hard he hit the brakes. So that was a *no*.

A couple of minutes later, the car pulled into a parking garage.

Fake Cop got out and hit a button. An aluminum wall slowly descended, closing off the exit.

Glasses craned around in his seat. He considered me, a wrinkle forming in his forehead. "How old are you?" he asked.

"Eleven."

"Ha."

I stayed where I was until he opened the door and tugged me out by the T-shirt.

Glasses led me over the freezing cement floor to a kitchen in the back, where Fake Cop was sitting on the counter, doing something on his phone. He pulled out a rickety wicker chair, sat me on it, and joined Fake Cop above me on the counter.

"We have a proposition for you," said Glasses, rubbing his hands together.

I pulled my feet up to the chair and hugged my knees, protecting my body—and trying to cover the fact that I was shaking. "I don't know anything," I whispered. "I don't even know who you are."

Fake Cop jerked his thumb at Glasses and then himself: "Rockford. Vin."

I swallowed, trying to remove the lump in my throat. "And you're not cops."

It wasn't a question, so Vin didn't bother to answer it. "We were wondering how happy you were with Mason," he said.

I shook my head in confusion. "Excuse me? Am I happy with Mason? That's your question?"

Rockford nodded.

"I'm going to need you to be more specific," I finally managed.

Vin slid off of the counter. "We saw you at the Fish Hook the other night. You charmed the pants of Trev. Talked to Jerry—he's an old friend. And we can tell you from experience, Mason will just screw you over. Joey here *tried* to warn Jerry. You're just a kid, obviously, but you have a certain . . . potential."

"I really don't," I said, scooting my chair back and away from them. I stood up, putting myself behind the chair. "I'm just a high school girl. I don't know anything about Mason's drugs."

"Who said anything about drugs?" Rockford asked quietly, advancing. For a small, nerdy-looking guy, he moved with a scary grace, like a big cat.

"I mean, everyone knows Mason supplies Trev," I said, stumbling, "That doesn't mean that I have anything to do with it."

Vin looked at Rockford. "Jerry was right, then."

"Fuck me," said Rockford quietly. He turned to me and, in one swift motion, had me backed up against the wall.

"You listen to me," he said. "Mason's not the only one with an interest in that supply line. If you know anything about its production and distribution, you are going to tell me. Now."

I started breathing hard. I shut my eyes and counted the pulses from my blood throbbing through my skull. *One, two, three. One, two, three.*

A landline rang out and Vin rolled his eyes. "Be right back," he said to Rockford and left the room.

Rockford turned to watch him leave and I reflexively took the opportunity to push him off me. He raised his eyebrows and, acting on pure instinct, I stood up straight and flung my hair to side, swinging into the girl in the picture.

We looked at each other in silence for a couple of moments. "Huh," said Rockford thoughtfully, pacing the room.

After a lap, he turned back toward me, now handling a rather large pocketknife with nimble fingers.

He didn't advance or threaten me. Rockford simply moved back and forth around the room, snapping the knife in and out, like a particularly shiny yo-yo. My heart thumped in my chest and I looked around wildly, all my swagger leaking away. I did a double take. There was a back door—and it looked like it might have been left open.

Rockford began to advance, looking at me curiously. I smiled at him, the exoskeleton of the girl in the photograph flickering in and out around me, and, before I lost my nerve, swung my instep into his groin, in perfect penalty-kick form.

Surprised, he dropped the knife, which I caught. And then I ran like hell.

CHAPTER SIXTEEN

IT'S A VERY STRANGE EXPERIENCE TO FIND YOURSELF ON A BUSY CITY STREET WITH NO SHOES, NO WALLET, AND NO CELL PHONE. Like being on Outward Bound, where they leave you in the woods with just a knife—which item, in fact, I actually had.

I ran about ten blocks—dodging garbage can overflow, cars, weird looks—before I had to pause to catch my breath and realized that there was no one chasing after me. I leaned on my bare, sweating knees and panted, trying to be rational. They had a car: If they wanted me back in that garage, I'd already be there.

I straightened up and quickly realized I was still clutching the knife. I hid it as carefully as I could, sticking it in my waistband, and looked around. I had run into the no-man's-land under the Brooklyn-Queens Expressway, the dividing line between a world of warehouses, gas stations, and always-startling urban slaughterhouses, and a world of—well, of *my* world. I ducked past a truck to cross to the sunny side of the street, trying to ignore the pain in my beat-up soles, and found a street sign: Twenty-Fifth Street and Third Avenue. I was about a mile and a half away from my house.

That's kind of a hike in the best of circumstances. Barefoot, dressed in booty shorts and a see-through T? That's an odyssey.

But with my feet really starting to hurt and the sky turning a potent gray, I had no choice but to move through the streets as quickly as possible.

My heart was slowing down finally when, still a good ten or twelve blocks away from home, the air shifted with an audible snap and I was drenched within seconds.

This wasn't a little early fall sprinkle. This was the kind of rain that seems to come down in fully formed sheets. The hard kind that waves horizontally in the wind.

I ducked under the awning of a deli and hugged myself, teeth chattering. It wasn't a perfect solution—my feet and legs were still getting splashed with the blowback from cars slamming the gutter—but at least I had a moment to rest.

"Hey, girl! What are you doing there?" I spun around to see the deli owner looking at me curiously. He eyes went wide as he took in the sight of the small, underdressed girl taking refuge under his awning. I saw him reach for his phone, and started to back away.

"Kendall?" Another voice called out from behind the owner. He moved out of the way and—of course.

He *would* catch me soaking wet in my PJs.

"Hi," I said, shivering, as Gilly, fully decked out in a camping parka and Timberlands, headed toward me with a sly grin on his face. "You live near here, right? Do you think I could borrow some pants?"

He put down his bags and pulled the parka over his head. "Arms up," he said and dropped it over me, pulling it carefully down around my body so as to drip as little rainwater on me as possible.

"I'm just around the corner," he said and ducked out into the rain. I put the hood up on the parka and, side by side, we tore down the block.

Gilly lived in one of the Victorian houses that sprinkle the older neighborhoods of Brooklyn. It was a peeling, but still kind of grand looking, white three-story, with a peaked attic and a wraparound porch. We clumped up the muddy steps and Gilly swung the unlocked door open for me.

It was warm in the house and smelled like someone was making eggs. The sounds of NPR and a woman laughing filtered through from the back of the house and Gilly twisted the shopping bags around his fingers.

"Why don't you go upstairs?" he said quickly, craning his head to look behind me.

"But I don't even know where your room is." Before the sentence was halfway out of my mouth, Gilly had practically thrown me up the first few stairs, his hand pushing on my soaked back.

"Yeah," he said, not really listening, his eyes darting back and forth. "I just don't—"

"Mikey!" A woman's voice called out, musical and deep. "Did you remember the half-and-half?"

"Yes," he groaned loudly, dashing around the back corner, returning without the shopping bag, and hustling me the rest of the way up to his room.

"What was *that* about?" I asked, annoyed at being handled. "What, are you embarrassed to introduce me to your parents? I do *great* with parents."

He gave me a hard look and handed me a pair of cotton gym shorts.

"Here," he said. "Borrow these. And, no, I'm not *embarrassed*, I just don't want to have to explain the nearly naked wet girl."

I snorted. "Yeah, I can see how you and a near-naked girl would be an anomaly. Or even you and a clothed girl. You and a girl in a snowsuit and goggles."

He folded his arms. "What were you doing out there?"

I suddenly realized that I was shivering. "Do you have a towel?" He picked a folded towel off of a desk chair and handed it to me. "Um . . . can I also have a shirt?"

Gilly moved slowly to his closet and unhooked a big gray hoodie with the Apple power sign on the corner from its hanger. I took it from him and looked at him pointedly.

"What?" he asked, irritably.

"Well, Prince Charming, you could turn around while I change."

"Oh, so we're going to maintain that illusion," he scoffed. But he turned. For the first time, I noticed that he was sopping, too. His T-shirt was plastered to his back. While I was shucking off my shorts and rubbing my legs down with the towel, he stretched his arms out to the right and then the left, twisting his hips. Bent over with a towel, I suddenly zoomed onto the patch of skin between his shirt and his pants. The crease in the center of his back deepened and tightened. He sighed a little as he stretched.

"Are you almost done?"

"Oh. Yeah." I hurriedly pulled on the shorts and, after a quick moment of deliberation, my waterlogged bra. "Done," I said, as the hood of the sweatshirt fell over my ears.

Gilly turned back around.

I gathered up my clothes. "Can I hang these up?"

He shrugged and flopped down on his bed. I hung them over the bar in the closet. I ran my hand over the clothes hung in appealing, orderly rows: lots of plaid button-downs and cartoon characters on T-shirts. All of them were soft and smelled fresh and clean.

I turned and surveyed Gilly's room. The walls were painted a warm honey-brown color with white trim. They were mostly bare, except for a framed reproduction of a painting of red and orange squares—Rothko, I remembered from AP Art History—over the bed, and, above the desk, columns of typewritten paper. They were pinned to the wall with thumbtacks, each slightly overlapping the one underneath. I picked up one at random.

Enter **Helena**. *Cue amber-gel spotlight. Cut sound when* **Helena** *reaches downstage right.*

"Are these stage directions?"

"Some of them. Hey, don't go through my desk, all right?"

Deciding to be the bigger person and refrain from reminding him that he rifled through *my* desk, I moved away with my hands up. I spun in place, taking a visual tour of a stacked shelf of stereo, DVD, and Xbox equipment next to a small television, a turtle tank with a prop pirate ship, a bookshelf arranged by color, an antique safe with empty Red Bull cans piled high on top of it in a tidy triangle. Finally, my survey reached Gilly himself, lying on his bed diagonally with one arm behind his head, and my breath cut off mid-inhale.

While my back was turned, he had taken off his wet clothes and pulled on sweatpants from out of nowhere, but he was still damp, and his black undershirt, the tank top kind, stuck to him. His cheeks were rosy and his skin glittered with raindrops.

"I like your room," I croaked.

Gilly examined me as I stood in front of his bed, wearing his clothes. It was as if he was trying to do one of those optical illusion image searches. He was frowning, but his eyes were soft.

"Can I ask you something?" he said.

I stepped closer to the bed and touched the covers. His comforter had a design of blue and darker blue checks, made of that nubby cotton that all boys' comforters seem to be made of.

I sat down on the floor instead and nodded. Gilly propped himself up on one elbow and angled himself toward me. I braced myself for a barrage of questions about my deliveries that week and a lecture about going to the cops.

"Why would you sleep with that guy?" I must have looked confused, because he added quickly, "With Grant Powers, I mean."

I wasn't prepared for that. I looked down and picked at the throw rug. Slowly, head bent, I said, "He and Audrey were broken up. I didn't know they were getting back together."

"That's not what I meant. Why *that* guy?"

I looked up. Gilly was looking at me with plaintive, burning eyes and his mouth hung open slightly, like a little kid the first time he realizes that you can just ask "why?" forever—you'll never reach the end.

Avoiding his eyes, I shrugged. "Boredom? Nymphoman—?"

"Stop it," he cut me off sharply. "I'm asking you. Seriously. *Why?* Did you actually like him?"

The questions caught me in their crosshairs. As I stared at them, I felt something in my chest bend backward and, suddenly, I hurt.

"I liked the way he made me feel," I said. I looked away, ashamed. "For about five minutes, he made me feel like I was the way I was supposed to be. No, not even—" I struggled to put what I was thinking into words. "He made me feel like I was better than what I was supposed to be. Do you know what I mean?"

He didn't answer.

I groped for a way to explain. I resorted to numbers. "Let's say I was a 7. Like, the numeral 7. And I was feeling pretty secure and happy about being a 7. With Grant, it was like I suddenly had an exponent next to that 7 and it had always been there; I'd just never noticed. I had never been 7. I had always been 7 to the power of 10."

Gilly's lips went crooked. "You're such a dork. The jockettes have no idea."

I smiled wryly. "Yeah, well, the whole thing was an illusion. An isolated incident I probably wouldn't think about anymore at all, if it hadn't blown up in such spectacular fashion."

"So you don't like him?"

"No," I said automatically and then stopped, surprised. I continued slowly, gauging the truth of my words as I spoke them. "No. It turns out that nothing that Grant says or does actually means anything. He's pretty simple: He wants what he wants when he wants it. He doesn't get deeper than that."

"But you *did* like him."

"I think . . ." I stopped and tried again. "I think Grant is a good person to play pretend with. I liked someone I made up and he resembled that person enough to make me believe it was him."

Gilly started drumming his fingers erratically on the covers. It was making me nervous, so I changed the subject. "You asked me *that*? You find me barefoot in the rain and you have *no* other questions?"

He smiled and put his arms back behind his head, apparently satisfied with my answers. "Nah. I just figured you got kidnapped by more drug dealers."

"Funnily enough, that's exactly what happened."

He bolted up. "What?"

I fell onto the floor on my back. "Relax, I handled it."

"Tell me *exactly* what happened."

"Fine, Rambo, but I don't know what you think you're going to do about it."

I stayed on my back while I told the story. He looked down at me the whole time, his face a storm cloud.

"So, I just kept running until I was sure they hadn't come after me," I finished. "And then it started raining and then I ran into you. What? Why are you looking at me like that?"

Gilly had an expression on his face like he'd accidentally drunk bad milk. "Are you crazy? Can I call the cops now?"

I sat up. "No," I said firmly, "you can't call the cops. Not after everything I've gone through. Nothing has changed. There are just more . . . complications. But I doubt I'll ever see those guys again. I'm going to find the thief and turn him over to Mason and it will be over."

"Wait—you're still looking for the guy who ripped him off? I thought you were delivering now."

"It's a side deal I made with Mason," I said, slowly. "If I find the thief before Texas, I can stop delivering." I smoothed my forehead, where there was still a ghost of a bump from Jo knocking me to the ground. "I guess I hadn't thought about what would happen to whoever stole it though. Huh."

"Nothing good—are you OK with that?" Gilly sounded tense, but matter-of-fact.

I frowned. "You know that whoever stole it is 100 percent the same person who hacked my profile and got me into this mess, right? I don't owe them anything. Except maybe revenge." I rubbed my bare feet, damp and bruised from the rough pavement of the sidewalks. "I don't know. I'll have to see how it plays out. It's not like I'm behind the wheel here."

"Right," Gilly said, caustically. "Just an innocent bystander."

"What is your problem?" I shouted. He looked toward his door and I lowered my voice. "Whose side are you on? I didn't ask for your help, remember. And, yeah, as it happens, I *am* an innocent bystander. I wasn't the one who *stole* from a *drug dealer* and then basically framed a newly easy target for it."

He put up his hands. "I'm sorry," he said, quietly. "I know you didn't. You don't—I don't think you did anything to deserve all of this."

"Except pin a social 'Kick Me' sign to my ass."

"Either way. Not your fault." He moved onto his stomach and put his hand on my shoulder awkwardly. After a second, he let go.

"Thanks," I muttered, still unsettled. His face was very close to mine. He smiled and reached out a finger, brushing an eyelash off of my cheek. He held it up for me to make a wish. Looking at his eyes like crystals, I blew it away, not wanting to think too hard about the wish.

Suddenly I remembered something. "Oh shit! Shit, shit, shit!" I jumped up and started for the closet to get my clothes.

"What? What happened?"

I pulled my bra off the rack and tucked it under the sweatshirt to put it on, too nervous to be modest. "I left my freaking front door unlocked! It closed behind me, but they dragged me out of there, and it's not like I had a key stashed in my gym shorts."

"But it's still raining."

I pulled my straps on and started digging around his drawers for a pair of socks. "You don't get it. If anything happens to my parents' turntable, I don't even know what they'll do—it won't be the candy-ass 'grounding' I'm getting right now, I'll tell you that much."

Gilly drove me the quarter of a mile or so to my house. I breathed a sigh of relief when I saw that the door had shut firmly enough behind me: a plastic bag that had been hanging from the inside doorknob was still wedged in the jamb from the force of my being yanked across the threshold.

"Looks like it's OK," I said, turning to Gilly. "Thanks for the ride."

He turned and grabbed my shoulders again, shaking me so my head bobbed like a Cabbage Patch Kid's.

"Will you be fucking careful until Monday?" he asked gruffly.

"Uh, sure. OK."

Our faces were very close together. I was breathing in the heat rising off his skin. I made an involuntary move to get closer to the briny, fresh smell of him and his fingers tightened on my shoulder blades through the soft, slightly damp fabric of his sweatshirt.

I lifted my chin toward him and our faces were so close that our lips accidentally touched. It was a soft, gentle brush more than it was a kiss, but it was enough for me to breathe deep and him to startle away. He abruptly let go and leaned over me, pushing open the door. "OK. Get out then."

I stumbled out onto the curb in a daze, my brain screaming to finish the sentence that grazing of lips had started. I turned back to say something—*anything*—that might give me a scrap of that feeling to hold on to, to study, but he was already peeling down the street. I watched him round the corner, feeling like I had an overfilled water balloon in my chest.

In my first stroke of good luck all month, no one had broken into the house. I went up to my room and stripped out of the borrowed clothes, running a hot shower in the bathroom. It was just when I was feeling some of the tension melt off of my shoulders that I realized I had left Rockford's knife under my shorts, which were still lying in a heap of damp clothing on Gilly's bedroom floor.

CHAPTER SEVENTEEN

WHEN I GOT UP MONDAY MORNING I FELT STRANGE. Different. I moved through my routine quickly and easily—dress, brush teeth, sneak past sleeping parents, grab banana, check for keys, check for cell phone, leave just as my mom yells for me to wake up—but something was definitely different.

I didn't find a seat on the subway that morning, but for once I didn't care. Bumps in the track swung my body around the pole, but instead of exhausted, morning motion sickness, I felt strength and energy radiate through me. I zigged back and forth, testing my center of gravity, zinging with pure physical joy.

I felt high.

I couldn't focus at all. Not on what anyone was saying. All morning, my brain kept playing over the images from the weekend. The way it felt when Vin yanked me through my front door. The look on Rockford's face when I kicked him in the balls. The weight of the knife falling into my hand. The crackle in the air before the sky opened over my head.

The sharp nip of Gilly's teeth behind his lips the moment I

barely touched them with mine.

This was a high. Maybe just an adrenaline high, but a high nonetheless.

And, like any junkie, I wanted my next fix. But, for the first time since the nurse's office, Gilly just wasn't there. I had gotten used to seeing him out of the corner of my eye, but he wasn't in any of the usual spots I associated with Gilly: the desk by the door, the alcove corner next to the stairs, the floor in front of his locker—he was just *nowhere*. It didn't make sense.

A pressure had built up and, at Howell anyway, it had nowhere to go without him there. So it was with a mixture of nervousness and relief that I finally saw him opening his locker after last period.

I loitered in the senior hallway, trying to catch his eye, but Gilly kept his gaze steadily on the floor.

I stepped closer to him, standing right behind him when he knelt to zip his backpack. He fumbled with the straps, his hands too fidgety to work properly, but he had a rod-straight spine and staunchly refused to even crane his neck around.

"Gilly," I said, nerve endings buzzing.

He froze. I moved forward. "Should we . . . ?" I swallowed, not sure why I felt such a charge around someone I hadn't even kissed on purpose. "Should we talk?"

Gilly rose slowly, like an old person, weighted down and careful. "I . . ." he cleared his throat. "I can't today, Kendall. I'm sorry."

Without turning to look even in my direction, he shouldered his bag and bolted out the double doors.

I was left standing alone, staring after him, wondering whether or not I had actually been rejected by Michael Gilbert and, more, why that should hurt so much?

What did I want from him? Why did I want him?

My high from the morning contracted until it was nothing more than a glowing ember of anxiety sitting firmly in my chest.

The next day after school was when I started to feel watched.

I made the right turn from Howell to the F train like always and everything was perfectly normal. But about halfway down the block, my eye dragged to the left, drawn to something just outside my vision. I stopped and turned my head as slowly as I could. There was nothing there.

I kept on walking, trying to put it out of my mind.

It didn't go away.

For the rest of the week, every time I left school, it was as though someone was standing very close behind me, casting the tiniest of shadows, but I couldn't catch them at it.

On Friday, the train was crowded and any number of people could have been looking at me. I turned my head this way and that, scanning the faces, catching an eye here and there, but no one registered. I exited the train frowning, feeling like I was either missing something or going crazy.

I turned a corner and bent to tie my shoe. And then I heard it.

A scrape of rubber on pavement. One scrape, two, and then it stopped. I stood up slowly and started walking, careful not to turn around. Scrape, scrape, scrape: paced like a heartbeat.

I walked past my block to the Bank of America without turning around, and I didn't turn around in the lobby, either, just pressed myself against the wall and waited.

I counted slowly to ten and inched closer to the double doors leading outside. The sidewalk outside was empty.

He couldn't be gone. I couldn't just be making it up. I stood still, with the linoleum pressing against my back, waiting to see . . . something, *anything*, to prove I wasn't hallucinating on top of everything else.

Just when I was about to give up, there it was: a tiny flick of white at the edge of the right-hand glass door.

I straightened up and clenched my fists, pumping my muscles. I wanted to feel strong. I turned left out of the building, took five steps and then, with as close to a prayer as I get, I spun on my heels and launched to the right, slamming into a hard, sharp chest. I looked up and sucked in my breath.

It was Rockford.

"You!" I gasped, staring into his dark little eyes behind the owlish frames.

"And you," he answered. Then he moved so precisely, so gracefully, that I was pinned up against the alley wall next to the bank before I even registered his hands on my hip and shoulder.

Rockford held me to the brick while I panted and looked for escape. He had left enough space between us to be able to react quickly if I made a move, but not enough space for me to get enough momentum to kick him again.

"Not so sassy now, are you, Evans?" Rockford asked, looking at me like I was a bug.

"Don't you remember?" I answered, working hard to catch my breath. "I'm just a little high school girl."

He chuckled a little grudgingly. "Right," he said in a gruff tone. "I forgot. You're completely innocent."

"That's right, officer." I smiled up at him. "Now why don't you let go of me before I scream."

He loosened his grip, but didn't quite let go. "First we have to have a talk."

I struggled against his hand, but he was too strong. Finally, I gave up and looked at him. "Why are you following me?" I asked.

"Because I wanted to see how you spend your time. Get a feel for who you are."

"*Why*?" I squeaked. "I really *am* just a high school girl. I'm *no one.*"

He smile faded and his voice got soft, but serious. "You need to keep your head down and stay out of my way," he said, looking at me intensely. I could feel the heat rising out of his pores. "I'm not sure what you're angling for here. I don't know how you got involved with Mason. But, believe me when I say that you are not up for this. Stay away from Mason, stay away from his drugs. Don't go looking for any more trouble—and by that, I mean his drugs. You *will* find it."

I drew a shaky breath and he squeezed my shoulder. "I'm warning you," he told me. "I'll be watching." He let go. I reflexively grabbed my shoulder and rubbed the smarting skin.

And by the time I looked up again, he was gone.

When I got home, I took out my laptop and made a list of everything I knew about Rockford. There was very little.

Name: Joey Rockford. Occupation: student at NYU. Associations: rivals with Mason, friendly with Jerry, partners with Vin. Interested in Mason's drug supply.

Interested in me.

But for what? In the warehouse, he seemed to want me to be a courier, until I mentioned Mason's stolen stash. That's when he pulled out the knife—when I mentioned the stolen stash.

I closed my eyes and tried to find the solution to the equation. The variables swirled around until they fit together.

He was warning me away from the stolen stash, following me to see what I knew.

My eyes flew open. Rockford had the stash. *Rockford* was the thief.

No, he wasn't the hacker—he didn't know me from a hole in the ground, so there's no reason he would bother. He must have been working with someone else from Howell, but he could *lead* me to the hacker.

And I could lead Mason to his thief. I could be free.

And, I realized, pulling my laptop closer, that list of what I knew about Rockford wasn't quite complete. I knew where he had driven me when Vin yanked me out of my parents' house in my PJs. I could *definitely* retrace my steps to that warehouse.

It was lucky for me that I had just made a friend with a car.

"You want me to do what, precisely?" asked Simone, at lunch on Monday.

"Stake out a warehouse with me?"

Simone chewed her sandwich. "To what end?" she asked carefully.

"I think he might have taken Mason's stash. If I can confirm that, Mason will let me out of the deal. I can't keep doing this."

She nodded thoughtfully. "No, I don't think you should. It's dangerous."

I agreed. But not for the reasons she thought.

Mason was right. I was good at this. And I was getting too

good.

At first, even just doing deliveries had taken some getting used to. I had never considered myself a saint, but I had always been, essentially, a good girl. I was not accustomed to committing crimes.

But I *had* been in a popular girl entourage. I'd had to learn how to be unobtrusive. How to read a room. How to project confidence where I felt none. To ignore unsavory behavior. To always observe the world around me but keep those observations to myself.

It turned out that that skill set was transferable.

That surprised me, but more than that, it frightened me. An incident over the weekend had made me worried that I had reached a point of no return.

It happened on Saturday night. I was still reeling from my encounter with Rockford when Mason handed me a folded piece of paper instead of a pill bottle.

A lump of anticipation formed in my chest. "I'm done?"

He laughed. "Not quite, Kendall. It's just a different kind of delivery." I raised my eyebrows. "It's not even illegal,. I promise!"

"And this isn't something you can do yourself?"

"No," he said shortly and pulled out a laminated card and handed it to me. "I don't think you'll need this, but in case they don't let you in without ID." It was a fake ID. The name was mine. The photo was the girl in the picture. It said I was twenty-two.

"I'm going to a bar? Is it the Fish Hook? Because Trev's not gonna card me."

He shook his head. "I need you to go to TY Bar in the Four Seasons Hotel to deliver that piece of paper to a guy named Leon Cohn." He pulled out his phone and showed me a picture of a thin guy, about thirty, with a slightly receding hairline, but expressive features and an attractive, confident smile.

I unfolded the piece of paper. It was scrawled with an address, 1286 Brook Trail, Cold Spring, NY 10516.

I frowned. "You went to the trouble of getting me a fake ID so that I could deliver an address? Couldn't you just, I don't know, text it?"

He smiled wryly and walked over to the couch, unzipping his backpack and pulling out a giant freezer bag of unmarked prescription bottles—full ones. It was the most pills I'd ever seen at one time, outside of the documentary they'd shown in tenth grade health about the dangers of indiscriminately going through your grandparents' medicine closet. He moved to the desk and opened the large bottom door, gauging the space.

Finally, he looked back up at me. "I'm a criminal, Kendall. I don't put important things where a subpoena could get at them."

I put the note in my pocket. "Fine. When will he be there?"

"Eight-thirty." I nodded and started to leave. "And Kendall?" I looked back. He had thrown the bag in the drawer and was looking down at it, like it was a hurt kitten he was nursing. "I'm sending you instead of going myself for a couple of reasons, but one of the most important is that I want it to look *normal*. Just a guy and a girl flirting at a bar. So look like you belong at the Four Seasons. Do you know what I mean?"

I had affluent parents and friends with absurdly affluent parents. I knew what he meant.

I nodded. He looked away from his pills for long enough to smile grimly at me. "I know you do," he said. "I know you won't disappoint."

At 8:15, I slid onto a leather stool and set the clutch Ellie had gotten me for my last birthday on the bar.

I leaned forward and smoothed back my hair—straightened and sprayed glossy—to smile at the bartender. "Just a cranberry juice, please."

I sipped the juice slowly, as if nursing a drink, and waited for Leon Cohn.

He was right on time.

Impeccably dressed in an expensive gray pinstripe, Leon entered the room and stopped at the edge of the bar.

In person, Leon Cohn was more magnetic than he had seemed in his picture. He was comfortable to look at—the visual equivalent of ocean sounds. But at the same time, I felt like I could forget his face in an hour. It occurred to me that that could be a very useful quality to possess.

Leon looked casually down the length of the room.

Scratch that, I corrected myself. *It's not as casual as it looks.*

He stroked his lapel a little too rhythmically. His fingers on the polished bar were a little too stiff. He didn't know what—or who—he was looking for and it was making him nervous.

Eventually his gray-blue eyes fell on me.

The bartender came up to him. "What can I get you, sir?"

"Do you have Widow Jane?" The bartended nodded. "Neat, please."

When the bartender moved away, I leaned toward Cohn. "What's Widow Jane?" I asked. If he was already antsy, it made sense to put him in a position where he felt like he had an answer, an advantage.

He looked at me and smiled, an indulgent, curious smile. "Do you like bourbon?"

"I do!"

He cocked his head to the side. "Really?" he asked.

I matched his incredulous pose. "And why is that so surprising?"

The bartender brought his drink. Leon nodded a thank you, shot me a quick, sweeping glance, and returned his eyes to his own drink. "Most girls who like bourbon don't drink vodka cranberries," he told me, amusement flickering over his face. "Especially when they're alone at a bar."

I smiled. This guy wasn't dumb, at least. "So, you think I don't like bourbon and that I'm just trying to impress you by my manly taste in liquor."

He leaned in, enjoying this, relaxing and joining in my game. "Aren't you?"

I smiled a little and looked away, shrugging.

The bartender returned. "Do you want to start a tab, sir?"

Cohn glanced around the bar and sighed. "I might as well." He pulled out a Visa Black card and put it on the bar, right where anyone could see the name: Leon Cohn.

I sat back, taking my time. "Are you waiting for someone?" He nodded, taking a sip. "Who? A date?"

He laughed again. "Not quite. I'm waiting for . . . a *business associate*, I guess."

I smiled at him. "That's nice."

"Is it?" He took a long swig of bourbon. "Personally, I have my doubts."

I didn't respond. He looked at me and his gloomy expression softened into a smile. "Are *you* waiting for a date?" I shook my head. "A *business associate* then, too?"

"That's right." I put a finger on his card. "Luckily for me, it turns out he's pleasant company."

He followed my finger to where it tapped his name. He looked up, surprised. "You?"

I nodded, still smiling. "I'm supposed to be meeting Leon Cohn. It's nice to meet him."

He looked taken aback but recovered himself. "You have the advantage over me. I don't know your name."

"I'm Kendall Evans."

He raised his eyebrows. He was still smiling at me, but when he spoke, his voice had a heavy overlay of sarcasm. "So, you're young Mr. Frye's . . . what? *Partner*?"

"Not exactly. But, I did bring a message from him." I pulled Mason's note out of my clutch and handed it to him.

He took it. After reading, he looked back at me. His face was grim. "What?" I asked.

Cohn shook his head. "I'm just not sure this is a good idea." He reread the address. "There's a lot of risk in me even being here. I don't really know anything about this kid." He looked at me. "Who am I dealing with? Really."

I smiled, keeping the muscles in my face as relaxed as possible. "Right now? Me."

"Ha. And who are you again?"

He was teasing, but he was genuinely troubled. Suddenly I felt bad for him. "I'm Kendall Evans," I told him again, injecting as much kindness into my voice as I could. "I'm younger than I look, but I'm smarter than you think. And, for whatever it's worth, Mason knows what he's doing. I don't know what you two are doing together, but if Mason's planning it, you can be sure it's not going to be sloppy."

We made eye contact and he smiled again. He finished off his shot. "Tell him I'll be there."

I smiled back, but felt uneasy. Why had I said all that? Because he looked upset? Why should I care? "He'll be glad."

What had I just facilitated?

He looked at me, his eyes scanning mine sharply. "Well he did send you instead of coming himself. It's smarter if he and I aren't seen together somewhere where people will be able to identify me. You're right. He's not sloppy." He gulped the rest of his whiskey and then said into his glass, so quietly I almost didn't hear him, "Anyway, I don't really have a choice at this point."

I left first.

I strode straight out of the Four Seasons, my head held high. Several men and at least a couple of women sent loaded glances my way. I wasn't sure what they were looking at until I passed a mirror on my way out and stopped short.

I was the girl in the photograph. That wasn't the weird part, though. I had gotten used to seeing myself in that disguise. What was strange was that I didn't remember putting her on.

In fact, I *knew* I hadn't.

Mason went to that meeting in Cold Spring. He never told me

what it was about, but he came back from it in a strange mood. He was exalted, triumphant, but there was a razor-sharp edge to his eyes—to his voice, to his gestures, to *him*—that made me . . . uncomfortable.

He brought up Leon only once. It was apropos of nothing and days later. I was just dropping off the day's take, counting out the cash, when he asked me, "So what did you think of young Mr. Cohn?"

I was taken aback by the phrasing. "That's exactly what he called you," I told him. "'Young Mr. Frye.'"

That seemed to tickle Mason. "Really?" he said, smothering a laugh. "That's pretty funny. Did you like him?"

"I did, actually," I said, surprising myself with the answer. "He seemed sharp, but not cruel."

"Is that so?" Mason seemed less amused now. "Sharp, but not cruel, huh? Seems like a lucky combination."

I had had a similar thought, that he had a fortunate combination of traits, so I nodded. "Pretty lucky guy, I would say."

Mason snatched the cash off the table, which wasn't like him. "I don't need you anymore today," he told me and turned away.

I wasn't sure what I had done that day in the Four Seasons, but I knew I had done it very well, and that alarmed me. Back in the cafeteria, Simone finished her sandwich. "I only have to drive you?

I don't have to do any tailing or anything like that?"

"No. I can do that."

"Good," she said, standing up. "I'd be terrible at that." As I watched her saunter down to the trash, hips swinging over leopard-print heels, her hair tucked into a netted silver bun cover she got god knows where, I had to agree. She turned her head and called across the cafeteria, "But you really do have to learn how to drive."

She was looking over her shoulder at me, so she didn't see Gilly until she smacked straight into his chest.

"Why does Kendall have to learn how to drive?" he asked, looking past her to me.

I felt something throb across my abdomen and sat up straight, trying to push the ache down and away.

Simone's heels had collapsed to the side with the collision. She put her hand out to the wall and straightened herself. "No reason," she snapped. "Next time watch where you're going."

Gilly briefly rolled his eyes and then refocused on me. "Do you need a ride somewhere?" he asked me. The throb redoubled in strength.

Simone answered before I could. "I've got it," she said.

Gilly swallowed, nodded, and turned to walk away.

"You could come with us," I called out. It was more of a whisper than a yell, but Gilly stopped in his tracks.

Simone turned to me and folded her arms. I just shrugged. She pointedly raised an eyebrow, but didn't make a verbal objection.

Gilly still hadn't turned around.

"I mean if you want to. It would be OK with me. You *could* come . . ." I trailed off.

Gilly finally faced us, smiling wider than I had ever seen him.

With my newly full schedule, we didn't have a lot of time to just hang out in a parked car in front of a warehouse. So it was lucky that Simone, Gilly, and I were staking it out for only a third time when we caught a break.

Simone was in the process of lighting a cigarette when she leaned forward, her fingers clenching the steering wheel, cigarette dropped on the floor unnoticed. "Someone's here," she said, nodding toward a beige sedan pulling into the warehouse driveway.

"It's him," I said, sitting up and buckling my seatbelt, readying for action. "That's the car they drove me here in."

Gilly was in the backseat. He leaned forward, peering through the window. Suddenly he snapped, "I *hate* this. This guy attacked Kendall, literally assaulted her, and we're just sitting here, *not* getting him arrested. This is bullshit."

Simone glared at his reflection in her rearview mirror. "Actually, what's bullshit is that you're under the impression it's up to you what Kendall does or how she conducts her life. You didn't have to come with us."

He shot a glance at me. "Kendall wanted me here, so I'm here," he said quietly. "Right?"

I shrugged, but I didn't answer. The truth was I *had* wanted him with me, but not to advise me. Just to *feed* me—feed the energy that had been aggregating, the buzz that had been growing every time I saw him, or saw him see me. But there was no unselfish way to say that.

Luckily, Rockford came out of the warehouse carrying a grubby messenger bag he hadn't gone in with and I didn't have to answer. It was bulky—bulky enough to be holding a bag of pills.

"Quiet," I said to no one in particular. "We want to see what he does."

Simone turned on her engine. As Rockford started his, I nervously looked at her. She was watching him intently. "I thought you didn't want to tail anyone," I said. "I'll do anything that happens on foot, but are you OK with this?"

She shrugged, frowning with concentration. "In for a penny, in for a pound, I guess. As long as I'm in a car, I'm all right."

Rockford pulled out.

"Do you know how to do this?" Gilly asked. "Follow someone?"

Simone put her foot on the gas. "We'll find out, I guess."

We followed Rockford from a distance of about three cars. We wound our way through the shortcuts of downtown Brooklyn and eventually over the bridge, almost losing him in the maze of intersections on the other side. We drove in silence, with the radio off, too afraid to even breathe loudly, as if he would somehow hear us creeping up behind him.

Eventually, Rockford rolled up next to a guard station, showed some sort of ID, and drove into a fenced-off parking lot.

"Shit," said Simone, squinting through the windshield at the lot. "That looks like a City Hall lot. We're not going to get in there. What now?"

I craned my head out the passenger window. This area looked familiar to me, but I didn't know when I would ever have been so near to government buildings.

"OK, you guys park," I said, unbuckling my seatbelt. "Send me a drop pin when you do. I'm going on foot."

Simone looked like she was going to object, but then she saw the storm clouds gathering on Gilly's face. She narrowed her eyes and nodded, keeping the car running.

I nodded back at her and quickly hopped out while she lit what was sure to be the first of many more cigarettes. "Good luck," she told me.

"Wait," said Gilly, struggling out of his seatbelt. "Unlock my door, Simone."

"No," she said, and pulled out.

I zipped up my sweatshirt and threw the hood over my head before sprinting across the street and pinning myself against the guard box's blind side, just in time for Rockford to stroll out of the lot and turn right. Crossing my arms and turtling my head further into the hood, I followed, stepping as softly as I could. Once, he turned around and I dropped to my knee, pretending to tie my shoe. Peering out from inside my hood, I watched him look around, shrug, and keep going. He walked briskly to a crosswalk and I leaned against a tree to watch him as he crossed the street and headed up the steps to 1 Police Plaza.

That was why this area had seemed familiar. Back when I was little and my mom was an assistant district attorney, sometimes she would have to take me to court and stash me with the nearest clerk. I had been here before.

This was NYPD headquarters.

For a moment, I was too shocked to do anything. My brain was yelling at me to move, but I couldn't process it. Finally, adrenaline kicked in and I dashed into the street just as the light turned red, making it across just in time to see Rockford stride confidently through the front door.

I hurried after him and got in line for the security checkpoint, not knowing what else to do. But Rockford didn't do the same. He went straight to the head of the line and pulled out his wallet. He opened it and showed it to the guard.

There was a badge there. Not the shitty, plastic one Vin had used to trick me out of the house. A real one. Real gold-plated metal, with a real NYPD seal.

"No fucking way," I whispered.

The guard waved Rockford through with a back clap. "How's tricks, Detective?"

"No *way*," I said again, louder this time. People in line turned to look. I quickly pulled the drawstring on my hood. I walked out of there as quickly as I could without running until I made it back outside to fresh air.

Rockford was a cop.

CHAPTER EIGHTEEN

ALL DAY AT SCHOOL THE NEXT DAY, I STARTED AT LOUD NOISES, INSTINCTIVELY POSITIONING MY BODY IN A DEFENSIVE STANCE. Every whisper or dumbass comment from my classmates, even the ones *not* directed at me, was like someone using my own hand to slap my face and saying, "Stop hitting yourself. Why are you hitting yourself?"

Finally, the clock struck three. I grabbed my bag and bolted down to the lockers. I wanted out of that building, preferably before anyone else had the chance to talk to me. An odd feeling, like something was boiling, had started in my head and I wanted to be alone in case it exploded.

I ran down to my locker and began shoving books in as fast as I could. The hallway was still empty.

"Yes," I breathed. I stood up, turned, and walked smack into Ellie Kurtz.

"Sorry," I muttered and dodged around her, still heading toward the door.

Behind me, she said with a quiet, nasty laugh, "What, does the two-for-one special at the liquor store end at 3:15?"

And pop goes the weasel.

I dropped my bag off of my shoulder, pivoted, and launched myself at Ellie, knocking her to the ground.

When I caught my breath, I was lying on top of the wriggling Ellie, hands burning from the fall on the rough carpet, kicking at her ankles to keep her down. She managed to get a slap in and the shock rolled me to my side, scratching and pulling at her hair, until our flailing, interlocking limbs blossomed into a full-out girl fight of smacking wrists and shirt-pulling, our legs tangling in the struggle, both of us horizontal on the floor.

Someone grabbed my free arm and yanked me to my feet. I stood over Ellie, still scrambling upright, listening to the yelling that had taken over the hallway. It wasn't until I was led through the double doors toward the administrative offices that I realized the yelling had mostly been me.

Some middle school teacher I didn't know dumped me in a chair outside the principal's office and turned to Ms. Lowery. "She started a fight in the hallway," he said, jutting his finger in my direction. "Can I leave her with you?"

Principal Meyers walked in but stopped short when he saw me. I reached up to smooth my hair down.

"What happened?" he asked, sounding exhausted.

"Uh . . . I think I just got suspended."

"*What?*"

I told the story, from Ellie's comment to getting dumped in his office, mechanically, factually. It didn't take long: It was a pretty simple story.

He shook his head, not in negation but in confusion. "Ellie Kurtz said something snide, so you knocked her down? That's it? That's all you have to say about it?"

I shrugged and nodded.

He sat back, dumbfounded. "What were you thinking? What is happening inside your head?"

A significant upswing in serotonin and endorphins. "That's rhetorical, right?"

"I am sincerely and seriously disappointed in you," he said, on the knife-edge of yelling. "You are most definitely suspended. We're going to have to start talking about a disciplinary plan going forward. And I should let you know that I will be giving your parents a list of counselors who have worked with Howell students in the past—"

I listened to him in a state of beatific calm, literally feeling my muscles soften. I rotated my head, kneading the kinks out of my neck. I hadn't felt this at ease in months.

"Are you hearing me, Kendall? Kendall!"

I stopped rolling my head and composed my features into a serious position. I nodded. "Yes sir," I said, the words sounding strange in my mouth. Had I ever called someone "sir" before?

He shook his head and reached for the phone, putting it on speaker. I heard my mother's voice mail click on. Principal Meyers sighed and started to dial my father's number.

"He has an appointment from 2:45 to 3:30 on Wednesdays," I said helpfully. "You should probably try him at 3:45."

He looked at me with narrowed eyes. "Don't think I'll forget," he said acidly. "Go home now, Ms. Evans. I'll see you back here in my office at 8:45 a.m. on Tuesday morning."

I felt a corner of my brain scream in horror: *a three-day suspension.* Had that ever happened to anyone in my class?

While that one neurological nook panicked, the rest of me was able to say, "I understand. Have a good weekend." Then I calmly picked up my backpack, got out of my chair, and walked through the hallway and out the door into the fresh, mildly windy fall afternoon. I took a deep breath.

Punching Ellie had given release to something I hadn't acknowledged before: I was angry. And not just at Mason or my hacker or Grant. I was mad at the world and had been since getting caught in that gym.

What really killed me about this whole mess was that everything I was, everything I had ever been—athlete, honor student, class officer, friend; smart, social, responsible, funny—had been wiped out the second I had sex. Not just for Audrey, not just for my classmates—for *everyone*. My teachers, my coaches, even my parents. All I was to them now was trouble, and what did my society-appointed caretakers assume was at the root? Had to be the sex.

The Barbie phone went off; the dorm at Columbia. *Great*, I thought. An encounter with Jeff was the perfect complement to my mood of righteous indignation.

Because it wasn't just about sex in and of itself, I corrected myself, as I rode the subway uptown. After all, no one threw the book at Grant because he wasn't a virgin. So what made me so special?

Outside, as I walked to the dorm, a light rain dotting my white tank top, some unconscious lock in my brain snapped open and images started leaking out in a slow, steady stream.

Grant holding my face in both of his hands, forehead pressing into mine, everything blacked out except for the bones in his cheeks and nose and brow, shadowed, seemingly outlined in glowing red, like campfire coals.

Black curls falling between my lips as he bent his head to fold his mouth around my collarbone.

Scraping my finger along his ribcage and the sweat and dust accumulating under my nail like clay. Marveling that instead of being gross, there was something primal and profound about having access to particles and chemicals from someone else's body.

After signing in as K. Evans in the dorm lobby, I rode the elevator to the seventh floor and made my way to Jeff's room. I knocked on 7A, but there was no answer.

I checked the phone again and frowned. I had misread it and was going to a new room, down the hall from Jeff. I shivered as the rain dried on my skin, leaving it cold, and made my way down the hall.

Grant wasn't the first person I had had sex with. That would have been Naya's cousin, at her sixteenth birthday party. All I remembered feeling was intense relief that I was getting it over with, with someone safe, and that it didn't hurt too much. My brain was working so hard that afterward I couldn't even remember what it had physically felt like. I don't think I had been paying attention to my body at all.

It wasn't like that with Grant.

I knocked on the door. Grant opened it, and my skin went from chilled to searing.

He smiled like he was expecting me. "Hey you," he said.

For a second I was sure I was hallucinating. I closed my eyes, but when I opened them again, Grant was still there.

"What are you . . . ?" I asked, standing uncertainly in the hallway. Could he read what I had just been thinking about on the lines of my face?

He put his hand on my shoulder and reeled me into his room. "You're at the right place, don't worry," he said, sounding pleased. "I heard you were doing this and wanted to pick up some E anyway, so . . . come on in. I mean, I'm surprised, duh, but it's nice to see you."

Grant Powers's room even smelled like boy. All the bedding was green or brown and downy soft.

I heard the door shut behind me. I willed myself to turn around, to simply trade pills for money, to be as icy as I had been with Jeff or any of the others. But I couldn't. I no longer felt icy. I was burning up. Trying to shake it off, I reached down into my pockets, noticing as I looked down that I had been clenching my fists so tightly that my nails had left tiny crescent moons in my palms.

He sat on the comforter, stretching out his legs and rotated his ankle, the one he sprained sophomore year during basketball season. It still bothered him, but only when he was preoccupied.

"I wanted to talk to you," he said simply, a smile hovering around his lips but not quite landing. He looked down for a moment, turning his head away, unaware as ever that his neck was maybe the most beautiful part of his body. I looked at the long, delicate muscles there, feeling strangely empty.

I put the pills on his desk. "Let's get this over with," I said.

Pouting a little, but his eyes lighting up at the sight of the pill bottle, Grant shot me a quick look and then handed me a few bills.

I reached out for the money, but he caught my hand before I could withdraw it and didn't let go.

I avoided his eyes. This I had not signed up for. "What did you want to talk to me about, Grant? It's been kind of a long day."

"You're not even gonna sit next to me?" he said, scooting over with a dare in his bright, dark eyes. "Come on, Skipper. Please?"

Against my will, I smiled at the sound of my old nickname. Grant had called me that since I was fourteen years old. It was his own personal nickname for me, devised after he heard my mom call me Ken Doll at the sports banquet at the end of eighth grade, when high school athletes welcomed the incoming ninth-graders. I sat down on the other side of his bed.

"You totally screwed me over," I said suddenly, surprising myself. He turned to look at me. "You do realize that, right? How completely you just abandoned me?"

He grimaced and looked down. "What did you want me to do about it?" he asked sulkily. "I can't control Audrey. You know that."

"You could have taken some responsibility!"

"How do you know I didn't? How do you know what I said to her?"

Because I know you and you don't have it in you. It was on the tip of my tongue, but suddenly I didn't want to go over it with him. What was the point?

I stood up. "I'm going to leave now."

"Wait," he said, struggling to his feet. "I wanted to talk to you about Simone."

"What?" My hand on the doorknob, I stopped and turned around. "Simone? What about Simone?"

He shoved his hands in his pockets. "I want you to know that I had nothing to do with what happened," he said, pleadingly. "I know I'm an asshole and all that, but it's important to me that you know that it wasn't my fault. That it wasn't me."

My stomach turning, I said slowly, "Why would I think that?"

He raked his hand through his hair, making the curls stand on end. "OK, yes, they got those capsules from me. But I thought it was just a rave drug. I really didn't know. The thing with Simone wasn't anyone's fault, you know? I didn't find out until later that the liquid doses did that. It got a little out of control, *maybe*, and she freaked out. I mean, you were there—we were just using it to party. Shit, those doses weren't even *for* me."

He seemed to be waiting for me to respond. When I didn't, he sighed and shrugged. "Look, I know you and Simone are close now. Trev told me about it after I saw you at Mason's party. I wanted to make sure you weren't mad at me for *that*, at least." He shut his eyes briefly and then opened them. "Things aren't simple here. Me and Audrey. You and me."

"There is no 'you and me,'" I croaked, feeling like I was choking. I cleared my throat. "Never call Mason again."

I opened the door and slammed it shut behind me, running all the way down the stairs, into the rain, pure and cold.

CHAPTER EIGHTEEN

Two years ago, Simone Moody went crazy. Then she disappeared. And when she came back, she was different.

It wasn't wholesale personality change. I had never known her that well, but she had always been sarcastic and wry. She had always been poised, the only one of us who could walk a whole hallway in heels with a book on her head during Howell's ill-advised decorum unit in eighth grade health. When she came back to school, she was still all of those things, with one big difference, so subtle I had never thought of it until now, lying on my bed, staring at the ceiling, trying to fit the pieces Grant had given me into the puzzle of Simone Moody.

In the last two years, I had never seen Simone back down from any position, laugh at any joke, ask how she looked, apologize, or be embarrassed. Simone no longer cared what anyone else thought of her. Everything she did, she did because she wanted to.

I dialed the phone. She picked up on the fourth ring. "Try and get whatever shrink they make you see give you Klonopin," she said. "It's supposed to be very relaxing and if anyone needs to mellow the hell out, it's you."

I smiled a little. "Hey, you busy tonight?"

"It's Wednesday, Kendall. I'm clubbing."

I hesitated. "Could you come over? There's something I want to talk to you about."

She sighed. "It's like having a pet. I'll be over in a bit." She hung up.

I spent the next hour pacing the floor, compulsively lining my belongings up in rows, trying to figure out what I wanted to ask her. I felt that I knew the question, but somehow there was caution tape around it in my head: *Dangerous. Do not enter. Do not go there.*

I was still trying to figure it out when Simone knocked on my door.

"Hey," I said, surprised. "You're here."

"Your dad was getting in just as I got here," she said, looking confused. "He said he was glad that you were rebuilding friendships with young women, because at this stage of psychosexual development, it's important to have a homosocial support network. I told him I was happy to help?"

"That was probably the right answer," I said wearily.

"So what's the 911?" she said, spinning my desk chair backward and straddling it. "Has someone slipped a stolen diamond in your coat pocket? Anonymously sent you top secret missile plans?"

I drew a deep breath. "I ran into Grant."

Her face remained impassive. "And?"

"He wanted to talk to me," I said awkwardly. "About you."

Simone's eyes narrowed. "Really," she said in a clipped, tight tone of voice. "And what did Grant Powers have to say about me?"

"Why did you go away sophomore year?" I blurted out.

At first, Simone didn't seem to react. Her face motionless, she surveyed me without an ounce of discernable emotion. Finally, she unfolded her legs from behind the chair and, standing up, said, in a breathtakingly even, dismissive tone, "If you already know, then why ask?"

She turned to go and I ran ahead and blocked the door. "I really don't know," I said fiercely. "He was very vague. But if Grant Powers feels guilty enough about something that happened to you to apologize to *me* . . ." I found I couldn't finish the sentence.

Simone still looked calm. So calm, it was scaring me. "There must have been rumors," she said, staring me dead in the eyes.

"Honestly, it was so weird, most of the theories ended up being more like Simone fan fiction, less like gossip." She looked thoughtful at this and sat down on my bed.

Simone looked at me appraisingly. "I don't really talk about this," she said matter-of-factly. She didn't sound angry anymore. "It's not something I need to talk about. Does it matter to you to know?" Scared, I nodded.

She nodded back at me. "You're going to feel bad and there's nothing you can do about it," she said. "But since you want to know, I was doing what I thought was ecstasy with Pete Morrison and Burke Kenneally at the party that happened over Thanksgiving break at Grant's house. I think you were there."

I nodded, remembering climbing up onto the roof with Grant, Audrey, and Ellie. Ellie slipped on the ladder and I caught her. Mellower then, Ellie laughed for about fifteen minutes, clutching my shoulders and cracking me up as she slipped into a flawless impression of a boozy Joan Rivers, trashing everyone's outfits, mine included, too funny for anyone to get mad.

"I was, but I don't remember seeing you," I said.

"That's because I was mostly in Grant's room with Pete and Burke," she continued evenly. "The ecstasy was in tabs and we all swallowed one. Then they started laughing. They had emptied a capsule into my drink and the tab I had swallowed was an aspirin. They had run out of the tab ecstasy and just had liquid left. They said they didn't want me to miss out and apologized for tricking me. I think I laughed." She paused. "And six hours later I woke up in Grant's bed not wearing anything."

I felt like someone had popped a balloon in my ribcage. "You don't mean . . ."

She shrugged a little. "I don't really know exactly what happened. Pete and Burke were gone; I was alone in the room. But when I was getting dressed, I found a used condom on the floor, so—"

"Oh, I'm going to throw up," I whispered. I held my stomach and tried to steady it through sheer willpower. Simone waited patiently until I looked up and nodded at her. "Sorry," I said. "I won't interrupt you again."

Simone took a cigarette out of her purse. "I'm going to smoke if that's OK," she said.

I nodded and she laid a soot-stained, empty lip balm tin decorated with enameled roses out on my bedspread—a travel ashtray. Even when her hands shook slightly as she lit the cigarette, I couldn't help but admire the endless style of Simone Moody.

"Thank you," she said, her shoulders lowering, visibly relaxing. She smiled tightly. "I'm just not used to it. Seeing people react, I mean."

"You didn't tell your parents?"

She smiled wryly. "Eventually. Right when it happened, I was kind of numb. I acted very . . . mechanically. Methodically. Like I was going down a checklist in my head of how someone should act in this situation. I even"—she smiled again here, shaking her head—"I even stopped at the pharmacy on my way home to get the morning-after pill. Stood there in line at the counter like a big girl and asked for it like it was the most natural thing in the world, like I was at Starbucks or something."

"You didn't go to the police?" I ventured.

She put her cigarette back in her mouth and shook her head silently. She was quiet for a moment and then sighed. "I didn't know what to do," she said simply. "I didn't know if it . . . counted."

"Counted as what?"

Simone looked me in the eyes. "As rape."

I winced and she snorted. "See?" she said, pointing at me. "Even hearing the word is so . . . stark. Strange. It didn't seem violent enough to me for it to count. For it to make sense for me to feel that bad. I mean," she ticked it off on her fingers, "one: These weren't strangers; two: I was voluntarily under the influence of alcohol and drugs, even though it wasn't quite the incarnation of the drug I had purposefully taken; three: Maybe I had seemed totally OK and awake, maybe it wasn't their fault, maybe this was just what grown-up drunk sex was. What did I know?" She flicked ash into her jar.

"Of course, now I know that just the fact that they put a drug I didn't consent to taking in my drink would almost definitely translate into actionable assault charges," she continued steadily. "And I wish I had gone and gotten a rape kit immediately. If only to scare the shit out of those disgusting, fucking creeps. But honestly, I don't think they would have been convicted."

"What!?" I sat bolt upright. "But it definitely would be assault. I've been watching *Law & Order* with my mom for over a decade. Believe me, it's assault."

She turned slightly to face me, smiling a sad, patronizing smile. "Technically, maybe; by the letter of the law, it was assault and sexual misconduct. But think about it. Two rich boys with excellent lawyers go in front of the jury and say, 'Oh, she was just drunk and now feels stupid about it; she was taking the ecstasy all on her own.' I wouldn't be able to deny it. I'd just end up looking like the slut I'm sure they would somehow make clear everyone already thought I was anyway. Just now I'd be a vindictive one." I looked at her, appalled, and she shrugged. "I'm not saying it was the right move not to go all SVU on their asses. Just . . . I couldn't face it. I handled it another way."

I shook my head. "How did they get away with it? I can't believe it."

"And that is the point," said Simone, stubbing out her cigarette. "Think about how you would have reacted if you had heard this story after it happened. Two years ago. What *you* would have thought."

I blanched. "It wouldn't have made a difference," I said quickly. "Drugged is drugged."

Simone pursed her lips and looked at me so sternly I had to look away. Miserable, I lay down on the bed, if only to avoid her gaze.

I would never have believed that that thing, that horrible thing I had been training my whole life to avoid, could have happened like that. So casually. Almost as a joke. Like snapping a girl's bra strap in seventh grade. Sure it was bad behavior, but nothing to get worked up about. Just boys being boys. Just spoiled, funny Pete and Burke being their normal, entitled selves.

I felt like I was rotting from the inside out as I pictured Simone steeling herself to walk back into school, knowing what she knew, not able to acknowledge it. Passing by a smirking Pete or Burke and wondering what everyone knew. If they were laughing.

"You had to go away," I said. "I see." My voice broke a little at the end.

If she had told me two years ago, I'd have blamed her. For being drunk. For liking sex. When had the world become so sneaky? Good and bad was supposed to be easily quantifiable. People doing bad, stupid shit to each other was a given, but everyone should at least be able to agree on what was bad and stupid. Instead, everything was blurry, seen through a scratched school bus window while your seatmate got carsick all over you.

I sat up finally. Simone was waiting for me, her mouth tight, but her eyes dry and clear. I quickly wiped my eyes.

She took a deep breath and said, "So that's the story of how I got my car."

I nodded solemnly and she burst out laughing, a hoarse, wild laugh. It was contagious.

Obviously, Simone calmed down first. Frowning, she said, "I hope Powers doesn't shoot his big, slobbery mouth off about this.

I'd rather not do this once a week."

I nodded. "The last thing I'll say about it is my mom is a lawyer," I ventured. I pictured my mom hearing this story, how her face would turn to stone and her eyes would blaze with focused rage.

It suddenly hit me that I hadn't had an honest conversation—or really much conversation at all—with my mom in weeks and weeks. If I was being honest, maybe it had been longer.

I shoved that away. "If you ever want to talk to her . . . I bet the statute of limitations hasn't run out."

"Forget it. I've dealt with it. I'm done with it."

I frowned. "You know, that *is* weird."

"What is?"

I stood up and paced to my desk, then back across and over to the window. "Why would Grant drag this up now? I mean, he said he just found out, but that's probably a lie. Even so, why would he come to me with it now, two years later? What does he care what I think about him or it?"

"He wants to make sure you still know what a sensitive, evolved man he is." She shook her head. "All's fair in love and ass-tapping, right?"

"But, my ass has pretty much been thoroughly tapped, no? I mean, mission accomplished, right?"

Sneering, she said, "Trev likes you. So does Jerry. Cool people talking up his former second-string groupie must have made him even more insecure than usual. No offense," she added, inclining her head.

A tiny light bulb exploded in my head. "Mason," I said, sitting down heavily.

"What about him?"

My foot was at the threshold when Mason said, "You want a shot before you go? You're having a hell of a week I'm betting."

"You said Pete and Burke had bought those capsules from Trev, right?" Blood was pounding through my veins, thunderously loud.

Before I could reach the door, my nerve endings started to bubble and fizz.

"Actually, no," she said, sighing. "Poor Trev. Somehow I can't help liking the dope. But, anyway, he only sold us the tabs, not the capsules. I'm not sure where the guys got the capsules."

. . . the room flickered. As quickly as the colors had brightened, the world started turning black from the outside in, tunneling my vision until it disappeared completely.

"Kendall, are you OK? You look . . . *gray*."

I had passed out in that basement and wiry arms had caught me. Long, tapered arms, rigid with muscle, softened by golden hairs. Mason's arms.

And then I woke up twelve hours later on stone steps, with no memories and a note: *Hi Kendall. Don't be mad.*

Suddenly Simone was in my face. "Hey," she said, shaking me a little. "What's wrong?"

I didn't find out until later that the liquid doses did that.

The doses. *The fucking "doses." Liquid doses, designed to do that.*

"Kendall? Wake up!"

I looked at her, my eyes wide. "Grant got the liquid doses from Mason. Mason sells those drugs. And I've been delivering them."

CHAPTER NINETEEN

"WELL, FUCK," SAID SIMONE, PACING MY ROOM AND LIGHTING HER THIRD CIGARETTE. She paused for a moment and then started pacing again, shaking her head. "Fuck."

"Do you have to chain-smoke?" I whisper-moaned, face in my hands. "I'm getting a headache."

"No, Kendall, this is really very bad," she continued, yanking the window open. "You realize what this means, right? You've been working on behalf of a roofie dealer, protecting his interests, fraternizing. . . . I'm going to fucking smoke."

"I can't remember if I sold anyone capsules," I whispered. Everything had been in unmarked pill bottles. I hadn't known to check for tablets versus capsules. "Oh god. Oh god, *did* I?"

At my wail, Simone collected herself. "I'm not angry at you," she said, leaning against the desk. "You are not the enemy. *They* are the enemy." She kicked the desk. "But, god, look at how I'm looked at! Look at how *you're* looked at. I know exactly how people see me Kendall and it's why I didn't go to the police. It's why they got away with it." She balled up her fist. "This is the way it is, and girls like you and me are going to continue to participate in the system, because celibacy is the only alternative, and we're human beings with desires and that's not fucking fair either. It's fucking criminal." She laughed, sounding manic. "There oughta be a law, right?"

I stared at her. "That's it? You just accept it?"

Her eyes narrowed. "I've had to."

Hearing Simone say those words sent a shudder through my body. I made a decision.

"Unless I finally take Gilly's advice and go to the police," I said.

She looked at me. "Do you have enough to take to the police?"

I could go to Rockford, but without hard evidence he might just tell me to stay out of it again. I needed to show him I had access to the drugs. I thought back to the office, to the new stock I had seen Mason lock in the desk. There was just a combination lock on it now—I could pick it. I had my phone, filled with addresses and names. I nodded.

"What about YATS? I doubt Howell's going to rat you out for the suspension, but selling drugs. . . . That's a different story."

I thought about how much I had already done to keep that dream. Lying, spying, breaking and entering. Selling drugs. I thought about how much I had wanted to escape my life, how desperate I was for a new one. Well, I'd certainly gotten a new life now.

Then I thought about why I had needed to escape my old life, what had gotten me excommunicated in the first place: I was a slut. I had called *myself* a slut just before Jo knocked my lights out.

And people thought Simone was a slut, and so Burke and Pete got away with rape.

I stood up and paced. Maybe we were sluts. But thinking of that as a bad thing sent me down a criminal wormhole and Simone to the woods.

I stood up and looked at Simone. "We are not worthless because we wanted to have sex," I told her. "I'm going to Rockford."

Simone didn't answer. But she did stub out her cigarette, walk over, and hug me.

She didn't quite know how to do it. Her arms tangled around my neck and she conscientiously kept her mouth away from my hair. But she hugged me, tight. And said, "Thank you."

Later that night, a few hours after Simone left, I found my mom sitting alone in the kitchen with yet another glass of wine.

"Where's Dad?" I asked, standing in the doorway. Silently, she pointed to the chair across from her. I took it and she grabbed an empty wine glass from the counter behind her, filled it with the sauvignon blanc and pushed it toward me.

I accepted carefully, scanning her face for red flags but finding nothing but slight circles under her eyes. "Thank you," I said finally.

Only when I was mid-sip did she speak. "I fixed your suspension," she told me, her voice neutral.

"Really? How?"

She smiled wryly. "It may have escaped your notice, Kendall, but some people find me quite intimidating. I called your principal this morning. After calling two members of the board who owe me favors."

"Wow . . . I mean . . . thanks. Thank you, Mom. That's amazing."

She definitely looked tired, but, watching her sip wine, it occurred to me that only I would be able to tell that. Any stranger would just see the straight spine, the sleek golden bob, the implausibly dewy skin; to a stranger, she was simply not to be fucked with.

"Thanks, Mom," I repeated, not sure what else there was to say.

She laughed a short, ugly laugh. "Yeah, well. It's my job, right?"

I stiffened. "Are you mad at me?"

She opened her mouth and then pressed it shut, laughing that same unfamiliar laugh.

"What?" I asked, getting more nervous the longer she laughed.

Mom got up. "I don't know, Kendall. I know that I'm sorry."

"For what?"

She looked at me with the look she used to smoke out liars.

"For messing up. Apparently I no longer know my daughter and she seems to be just fine with that. So I've failed. So don't thank me. I did what I do; I defended my client. Just not my daughter."

She walked out of the kitchen, leaving me alone with my shock and my wine.

Instead of going to school the next day, I simply cut and took the train to the Upper West Side. It didn't matter anymore what I did. It didn't matter how many suspensions I weaseled my way out of. I was going to be disgraced no matter what.

The office door was locked. I knew it would be. But, as Simone had said, in for a penny, in for a pound.

I had done my homework last night, even stooping to consult a site called TheArtofManliness.com. I reviewed the notes in my head and studied the door.

Luckily it opened away from me. I stepped away from the door and raised my right leg, bringing my knee in close to my hip, balancing myself with outstretched elbows. I pulled my knee in a little closer and then kicked straight out, right next to the lock. The wood splintered but didn't break.

Maybe I'm just not manly enough to kick down a door. I pulled my leg back up, and shot it forward again, into the door.

"What are you doing here?" slurred a familiar male voice. I lost my balance and twisted to the ground onto my knees, straining a muscle in my groin.

"Simone's home sick and I came up to see her during my free period," I lied, turning around. "Hey, Jerry."

Jerry looked ragged. His eyes were wide with fatigue and the hair around his temples was sweaty and disheveled. Pale and shaky, he nodded dismissively, and moved past me toward the door, unlocking it without commenting on the battered lock. He flung himself sideways onto the couch, stretched his arms out over his head, and sighed.

"What are you doing here?" I asked sitting down on the metal chair he'd deposited me in our first time together in this office.

"Napping," he grumbled, with his eyes still shut.

He was way too tall for that couch. His feet were dangling off the edge. "Why don't you nap in your own apartment?" I asked, studying him. Was he drunk? At eleven in the morning?

"It's quieter here." He opened his eyes and took a second focusing them on me. When he finally seemed to see me, he asked, his voice harsh, "How have your deliveries been going?"

"They've been going fine."

"No one's been giving you any trouble?"

Did he care? "No. Or nothing I haven't been able to handle."

I got up and dragged my chair closer to the couch. He nodded briefly and his eyes seemed to shut of their own accord.

I took a chance. "Mind if I ask you a question?"

Jerry opened one eye. "If I answer, will you go away and let me sleep?"

"For sure." He nodded. "Why were you talking to Vin and Rockford about me?"

Jerry sat up, rubbing his eyes. He glared at me. "You had to bring that up?"

"Um, they kidnapped me. Forgive me for being curious."

Jerry pulled out a cigarette with a resigned look on his face. "Me talking to Rockford wasn't anything sinister," he said, putting it in his mouth. "We're friendly. They go to Columbia, too. We hung out some last semester."

I raised my eyebrows. "Does Mason know about that?"

He laughed as he shook out a match. "He introduced us."

I paused while I digested that information. How long had Rockford been after Mason?

"But why did you tell them about me?" I asked. The factors didn't add up. "I understand how you know them, but why would you think they would be interested in a high school girl being blackmailed by Mason? Unless . . ."

I stopped talking. Jerry was looking at me through wary eyes. I looked down at his fingers and saw that they were fidgeting around his cigarette.

Unless he knew that Rockford was looking for some way into Mason's routine, Jerry would have had no reason to mention me.

So there were two options: Either Jerry believed himself to be helping a rival dealer, and was therefore secretly working against Mason, or . . .

Jerry knew that Rockford was a cop.

"How did you start working for Mason?" I asked, trying to sound casual.

Jerry exhaled. "Mason knew I needed money. What's your excuse?"

I recoiled. "You know why I'm doing this. I'm being blackmailed. I don't have a choice!"

He looked at me blankly and then laughed. "Oh, right. You won't get to go to Space Camp. How terrifying." He smiled at me in a way that seemed fond. "I'm glad Rockford hasn't been bothering you anymore. Getting involved with him raises the stakes a little bit."

"To what?"

"*Freedom.*" He practically spat out the word and suddenly I understood. Jerry had to talk to Rockford or he would be arrested. He would go to jail.

We avoided each other's gaze for a minute and then Jerry got up.

"I'm clearly not going to get a nap here," he said. He walked to the door and glanced down at the scuffed-up lock. "Will you listen to a bit of advice?"

"OK."

"Go back to being a good girl."

I lifted my head, but he wouldn't meet my eyes.

He turned to leave but stopped. With his back still to me, he said, "Or, if you don't, learn to kick down a door correctly. JV soccer isn't the same as breaking and entering. You're not big enough. Just use a crowbar."

He left.

"Thanks for the advice," I called out to his back.

He didn't answer. Maybe it was because he knew it was too late.

CHAPTER TWENTY

As soon as Jerry's footsteps faded, I sprang into action. It was an old combination lock. Maybe it was Mason's from high school. For whatever reason, it was the fastest I had ever picked a lock.

The mechanism clicked open and I ripped it off. The bag was still there, sealed up and pristine. It looked like even more capsules up close.

And they were *all* capsules. No tabs.

I only needed a few. In fact, it was probably better if I took just a couple, or even one, so Mason wouldn't catch on that any were missing before I had a chance to go to the police.

But I looked at piles upon piles of little, white capsules and knew that each one equaled one Simone.

I took them all.

I went straight to 1 Police Plaza, before I could change my mind. Sweat trickling down my cleavage, I walked up to the nearest uniform and said, "I need to talk to a Detective Joey Rockford."

The cop looked me over as if he wasn't quite sure what he was seeing. "Why do you need to talk to Detective Rockford? Are you reporting a crime? Because he might not be the right guy for you to talk to."

"I'm not exactly reporting a crime." I could feel the weight of the capsules in my backpack like an anvil. "I have information regarding one of his ongoing investigations."

He smiled indulgently. "And how does a little girl like you end up even knowing what one of our detectives is investigating?"

He meant it kindly, affectionately even. Sometimes I looked older than I was, but mostly I looked younger, and I'm sure I was so pale I was almost green. But something about being called a little girl made me stand up straighter and speak more clearly. "I need to see Detective Joey Rockford," I said firmly, looking the officer in the eye. "If you tell him Kendall Evans has information about Mason Frye, I think he'll want to see me."

Sixty seconds later, I was sitting alone in an interview room. Rockford was making me wait.

After five minutes, I started looking carefully at the mirror on the wall to my right. He was probably behind there, I decided. He was watching me. He wanted to see how I would act.

I decided that if he wanted a show, I would give him one. I shook off my cardigan and leaned back in my chair, sliding into the girl in the photograph like a glass slipper. I bent over my backpack and removed a single capsule. I put it on the table, waited a beat, and then put my feet up next to it.

Rockford opened the door and sat in the chair across the table from me. He looked much more like an adult than the last few times I'd seen him. Maybe it was because he was wearing a tie. Then again, maybe it was because he didn't have me pushed up against a wall.

He spoke first. "Miss Evans," he said, his voice even and cordial. "I'm impressed that you even knew to come here. I need to know who you've told about turning yourself in."

"I've told one friend who has had no involvement with Mason whatsoever," I lied. "I don't intend to tell you their name. I don't want them involved."

"As long as none of our mutual acquaintances know, that's fine." He picked up the pill on the table. "Now, tell me about these."

I had intended to cooperate. That was why I had taken such risks and gone to him. But at the command in his voice, the dismissal of my risks, the idea that I was turning *myself* in—suddenly I felt angry and in no mood to cooperate.

I crossed my arms across my chest. "First, why don't you tell me what a cop is doing abducting teenage girls from their homes and threatening them with knives?"

He stiffened and his eyes flickered to the back corner of the room. I turned my head and noticed a small black box hanging from the ceiling. I looked back at Rockford and he had his finger up, warning me to wait. He got up and went back to the door, where he flipped a switch. An ambient noise I hadn't even noticed before ceased.

Rockford sat back down, looking tired. "Obviously I was undercover, OK? Which you already knew, because you're not an idiot. It was never my intention to 'abduct' you, but I was very close to wrapping up my case against Vincent Rainier—Vin, as you know him—and when Jerry mentioned you, he had the idea. Rainier was a long-standing, if rather small-time, rival of your pal Mason's, as you may have also figured out. I took Rainier into custody yesterday, in fact."

I absorbed that information—which I had *not* figured out—and he rubbed his forehead, like he was in pain. "You're the one who came to me, Kendall," he said. "Cut the shit and tell me what you have."

I contemplated his face for a moment: his intense, annoyed, but underneath it all, eager face. I didn't like him having the upper hand. I didn't want to be the one to squirm. "Did you make detective fairly recently, Rockford?" I asked, probing. "You're pretty young. Young enough to pass for college-age anyway. You must be ambitious."

"Stop it," he said flatly.

"Stop what?"

"Stop trying to throw me off by psychoanalyzing me. Your little mean-girl mind games aren't going to work here."

"They're *not*? Oh *no*. Whatever shall I do?"

"Tell me where you got this pill and get on with your life."

I leaned forward, this time invading *his* space. He moved backward. "I think I have a better idea. Since my mean-girl tricks are powerless in the face of your big strong copness, why don't I just call my mother, the former District Attorney turned high-powered litigator, and tell her all about the time you threw me around an empty warehouse in nothing but my underwear, undercover or not? See if she thinks that's something we should discuss in a room where the tape recorders are on."

"If you didn't come here to show me that pill, then why are you here?" He looked me in the eye. "What do you want?"

His glare jolted me back into the reason I was there. "I want to help you nail Mason Frye," I told him. "And I want you to stop treating me like a little girl."

Somebody knocked on the door. "Come in," called Rockford, not taking his eyes off my face.

"There's a call for you, Rockford. She said it's urgent."

"Fine. Give me a minute. I'll be right there." The other cop left the room and shut the door behind him. Rockford pocketed the pill. "I'm going to take this call," he said. "When I get back, let's have an honest conversation, OK? I won't try and fuck you over and you don't try and fuck me over. We share what we know. Deal?"

I hesitated but nodded. "If you're serious. But I'm going to need something in writing that I'm not going to be charged with anything. I am not an accessory to Mason."

"You *are* a lawyer's daughter, aren't you," he said, getting up.

After he left, my phone beeped. I pulled it out of my pocket and frowned when I saw the text was from a restricted number.

Hey Kendall, read the text. *What are you up to?*

I don't have this number in my phone, I typed back. *Who is this?*

What's your favorite scary movie?

Despite the situation, I smiled at the reference. *Is this Gilly? Why is your number restricted?*

Not Gilly, ridiculous name that that is. It's your friendly neighborhood ghostface. So what is your favorite scary movie?

I rolled my eyes. *It's* The Breakfast Club. *I'm busy, Gilly.*

I don't think that's really your favorite scary movie. Anyway it shouldn't be. Take a look at this.

A video was attached to the text. I pressed play.

At first I wasn't sure what I was watching. The video was blurry and loud and all I could tell for sure was that there were people moving around a room. Then one of the people stepped out of the frame and I could see the bed.

I knew that bed. I had been in that bed. It was Grant's bed.

A girl in a white tank top and black underwear was on her side facing away from the camera. A male voice—Burke, I recognized, out of the corner of my mind—laughed and said, "Dude, she is *trashed*," rolling her onto her back. A hand reached into the frame and pulled black hair out of the girl's face.

It was Simone.

She mumbled something and her eyes fluttered open. "I'm here," she said softly.

"Sure you are, cutie pie," said Pete, putting the phone on the dresser and joining her on the bed. "We're all here." The video cut out.

A new text popped up at the top of my screen. *Seen enough? That's just a trailer. Want to see the feature presentation? We'll invite everyone.*

I clutched my stomach, willing myself not to vomit in the interview room. When my abdominal muscles stopped contracting, I pulled myself together and typed, *What do you want?*

Leave the police station, go to the Upper West Side, and bring me back my fucking doses.

I swallowed. *And if I don't?*

Then the uncut version of this video hits every screen at Howell.

I put the phone down. It was too late. I was in a goddamn interrogation room at NYPD headquarters. I had shown Rockford that I knew where the pills came from.

And in doing so I had fucked over Simone.

My breath started to come faster and faster as I contemplated the space the pill had occupied on the table. Rockford was taking a long time on his call.

I picked my phone back up and pressed play. Again Simone was rolled to her back and her hair pulled away from her beautiful face. She tried to focus her eyes and whispered, "I'm here."

I couldn't do it.

I couldn't be the one responsible for making that incident—*no, say the word*—that *rape* define her forever. I couldn't be the one to shame her.

Panic breathed new life into my body as I stood and picked up my backpack. I looked at the mirrored wall and listened closely, straining to hear any ambient noise, any monitor picking up my movements. There was nothing.

I zipped the compartment securing the rest of the drugs, opened the unlocked interrogation room door, and left the station.

Mason was waiting for me. He had never been waiting for me before. He was always playing video games, or scrolling through his phone, or even occasionally doing what looked like homework. He never seemed concerned about when, or even if, I was going to show up.

Not this time. He was alone, sitting in one of the metal chairs with his arms folded. There was a second chair set out in front of him. When I hesitated in the doorway, he motioned toward it.

"Sit, Kendall."

I looked behind me. If I sat in that chair, I would have my back to the door. I didn't like that.

"Sit down," he said again. "Shut the door."

I swallowed hard and straightened my shoulders. Jamming my hip to the side and tossing my hair, I scrambled into the girl in the picture. I shut the door and sat down, facing Mason.

He spoke first. "I was hoping not to have to use that video. You didn't leave me any choice."

"What are you going to do with it?"

"That depends on you. If you stay with me, I won't do anything with it. If you leave, or go to the police, I'll send it to every email address on the Howell listserv."

I shook my head, confused. "You want me to keep making your deliveries? Why? Why not just destroy my future and be done with it? Wasn't that the plan all along?"

Mason thought a moment before answering. "Would you believe me if I said I liked your spirit?"

I laughed out loud, a completely mirthless laugh, and he smiled briefly. "There really doesn't seem to be any point to fucking with me anymore," I told him.

"I'm not," he insisted, leaning forward. "I think you're a great find. I got lucky."

I felt my lip curl up of its own accord. "There's no luck involved here, just *criminality*."

"Oh? No luck?" he moved in closer. "You took the shot, didn't you? You didn't have to."

I drew in my breath. "What do you mean?"

"It would have been much harder to blackmail you if you hadn't taken it. You were a good girl before Grant and that gym, Kendall. Even if I had pulled the trigger on the TA, you might have been believed over him. But no one believes a bad girl. If you'd said no to that shot, you might never have seen me again." He smiled. "That's when I knew you and I were fate."

I needed to scream. Screaming wouldn't help. I felt stupider than I had in years.

"But, but . . . I was about to turn you *in*," I managed finally. "I don't want to work for you anymore, to the point that I'm willing to let you get me thrown out of YATS or even high school. I don't *like* you."

"That's *why* I like you."

I felt nauseated. "You're kind of disgusting, aren't you?"

This time he laughed. "You see, this is why we're going to make a good team. Jo *liked* me too much. That's why I had to replace her with someone who understood me a little better. Someone like you."

"You said she quit."

"I lied. She wasn't useful to me anymore. Her loving me made her mushy and weak. I needed someone sharp with a good stockpile of misanthropy—just general *loathing*—to work with. Jo's aggressive, sure, and that's been helpful, but she doesn't have any subtlety to her. She can't seduce or lie. She can do angry, but she can't do mean. And once you get past her muscles, she's not scary. She's not ruthless, just in love. I needed someone willing to burn shit down. I needed a mean girl. And then I found you."

"I'm not—" My voice croaked a little. I cleared my throat. "I'm not any of those things."

He cocked his head at me. "You were willing to burn down your own life on principle. And now that you know what kind of people I deal with, you'll be more than happy to rip them to shreds if it seems necessary. Even if it *doesn't* seem necessary. Cultivating fear in my clients is useful. You can do that."

I pulled off my backpack and pulled out the liquid capsules. "I won't deliver these. Under any circumstances."

He looked at me closely. "Not even to protect Simone? Every college admissions counselor she deals with will see the video. And that video gets pretty gnarly. I've watched it a few times. Believe me, you don't want to be responsible for that getting out in the world."

I swallowed. "I'll keep delivering the tabs," I said in a rush. "But not the capsules."

He thought a moment and nodded. "I can live with that. For now."

"And this is only until YATS."

Mason leaned forward again and picked up my wrist. He ran his fingernail all around the bone, and then started stroking the palm. "Kendall," he said. "This doesn't end with you going to YATS anymore. This ends with you either by my side or in jail."

I forced myself to stare him down. "We'll see about that."

Mason grinned. "You are the best. I like you so much."

CHAPTER TWENTY-ONE

After the fifth call from an unfamiliar Manhattan phone number that night, I shut off my phone.

Fifteen minutes later, at dinner, the landline started ringing. I made sure to grab it before either of my parents did.

"Hello," I said, wishing fervently for a telemarketer.

"Hello, this is Detective Joe Rockford from the NYPD major crimes division. Who I am—?"

"Wrong number," I broke in and hung up. The phone immediately started ringing again and I surreptitiously yanked the cord out of its socket, before answering it again.

"Hello," I said into the silent receiver. "Hello?" I put the phone back in its cradle and turned to my parents. "They hung up," I explained, returning to the table.

My mother didn't answer. In fact, she hadn't spoken to me since our conversation about my suspension. Not really anyway. She said, "excuse me," and "pass the salt," even a polite "good morning," but nothing that would have alerted a casual viewer to the fact that she was my mother.

"Kendall?"

"Yeah, dad," I said turning to my father.

He smiled at me. "How's student council going?" he asked.

My fork clattered to the floor. I bent to pick it up, my face burning. I hadn't even run this year and my father had no idea. Why should he? I had been out of the house every afternoon on my deliveries anyway.

When I resurfaced, I did something I had never done before.

"It's going fine," I lied, looking my father straight in the eyes.

My mother didn't even bother to look at me and so the deception stayed where it was.

The worst thing is I slept well that night. I found it frighteningly easy to fall in line with my mother, to become impersonal. In fact, it was an enormous relief for me to be blank, detached, unemotional—and that in itself was a terrifying realization.

So I went to school, still on autopilot, and easily lied to Simone.

"How'd it go?" she asked, leaning against my locker before homeroom.

I bit the inside of my cheek, trying to inject some life into my face.

"Mason was there," I said, avoiding looking directly at her. "I'll have to try later this week."

"Oh."

My breath caught in my throat and my answer came out strangled. "It will be OK," I said quietly. "I promise."

I finally looked up at her and she was frowning. She opened her mouth, but before she could, Ms. Arnold, the art teacher, stepped between us.

"Simone," she said excitedly, "I was wondering if you'd be interested in entering that PVC sculpture you've been working on into the National Art Awards this year? I know you don't like contests, but—"

I nodded at Simone from behind the teacher's shoulder and hurried away to class, trying to feel empty. Empty was better than how I felt when I thought of that video.

The day inched along.

"Kendall?"

I looked up blearily and Gilly had materialized in front of me. I was in AP Bio, but I could have been on Mars. I would have preferred to be on Mars.

"Are you ok?" he asked.

He was too close to me. It was reminding me of too many things, things I couldn't think about without breaking down, my hands in his hair and rainstorms and him pulling me out of the way when a cab splashed by. "What do you mean?" I asked warily.

"You got *suspended*?

"Oh, that." I was relieved. And I was reminded of one more thing: He didn't know about Simone's rape, about me taking the pills, about the video. Gilly was *clean*. Gilly was *safe*.

He sat down next to me. "I've been texting you. You haven't texted back." A brittle quality crept into his voice. "You've been pretending you don't see me when you pass me in the halls."

Gilly was safe, but only because of the things he didn't know about me, about the world I was living in. *Maybe it should stay that way*, I thought.

I made my voice hard. "Maybe I just *don't* see you when I pass you in the halls," I said. "Did you think of that, *Mikey*?"

He was sitting close to me—close enough for me to hear a catch in his breathing.

Dr. Forrester stopped in front of us. "You were late, Mr. Gilbert. Ms. Evans almost had to do this lab by herself."

I clenched my fist. I couldn't be near Gilly with all of his gazing and questions. "I don't need a partner, Dr. Forrester," I said. "I can do it by myself."

He folded his arms. "Really, Kendall? Tell me, what lab are we doing today?" I didn't have the answer. "Page 138, Ms. Evans. You're working with a partner—with this partner, in fact."

Gilly finished setting up the microscope. "Here," he said, his voice gruff. "You look. I won't do this by myself."

"You go first."

He pressed his lips together but stood and peered in the microscope.

"I even called Simi," he whispered. "You should have checked in with me."

"You're not responsible for me or my well-being, Gilly. You should stop caring. Remember that week you decided you didn't have time to talk to me anymore? Go back to that."

"No, but I *am* responsible." His voice was just one level under a shriek. Kids turned to look at him and he sat back down. "You confided in *me*, remember," he said in a lower voice, making notes on the lab work sheet. "I am involved, whether you like it or not." He threw down the pencil. "Your turn."

Standing heavily, I leaned over his arm to peer into the eyepiece, not really looking at the cells on the slide. He shifted a little out of my way, tapping his toe like a malfunctioning metronome.

"Am I making you nervous, Gilly?" I asked blandly.

He laughed, short and breathless. "You always make me nervous."

"That's probably smart." I gave up on the slide and dragged the lab notebook to me, checking off the same boxes he had on the data sheet. "If I took down Ellie Kurtz, I can certainly kick a stage manager's ass."

He caught my wrist and held it. Leaning down, he put his mouth next to my ear and said in a low, harsh tone, "Always. You have always made me nervous." He drew in some air and blew it out shakily, sending warm ripples across my earlobe and down my collar.

A sweet electric shock shot through my lower back. I wasn't prepared, and the rush was enough to buckle my knees into the lab stool, whacking it against the table with a cringe-worthy linoleum squeak.

I looked up at Gilly, ready to tell him to knock this off once and for all, but was stumped by his face. It was absent of any and all nervous or pissed-off tics. He was just looking hard at me, his silver eyes clear and locked on mine. His mouth, that unbelievably—like, literally, would not have believed it if you had told me a month earlier—gorgeous mouth, was straight and set.

Adjusting his fingers more comfortably on my wrist, circling it with more decision, he started, "I . . ." He shrugged and then simply told me, "I don't want you to pretend I don't exist. I care."

Helplessly, I curled my fingers so the tips touched his. His mouth tightened.

At that moment, Simone's dejected, angry face popped into my head. *Girls like you and me are just going to keep participating in the system,* she had said. *No recourse at all.*

It had infuriated me at the time, but she was right. I couldn't seem to let go of Gilly's hand, because it felt too good. Was it me? Was I the problem? Was I helpless?

"I know," I said, cutting him off as he opened his mouth again. Forcing myself, I unwound my fingers from his. "I know you do."

I looked away.

The bell rang. I scooped up my bag and my books in one gesture and left, counting my breaths on my way down the stairs, trying to shake the reverberation of Gilly out of my hand.

Simone's words kept sounding in my head: *No recourse. Only alternative.*

Girls like you and me.

I stopped dead on the stairs. Girls like me. Well, who was that? If I believed Mason, I wasn't the kind of girl without recourse, without resources. I could make my own rules. I craned my head up and saw Gilly shuffling through the hallway above me. I turned and loitered there.

His steps slowed down as he approached. When it became clear that I was waiting, they stopped altogether.

He was clutching his messenger bag much harder than it needed to be clutched.

I moved up a step. Snatching his hand, I jumped back down the stairs, looked both ways down the empty hallway, and pressed my fingers into Gilly's chest.

"What are you doing?" he asked, his voice cracking.

I met his eyes and dropped my bag. "Taking something," I said, backing him into a corner.

Gilly froze and then rushed me, grabbing the back of my shirt and crushing his mouth against mine. A small bonfire exploded in my chest and my mind went blank for a second. Or a century.

My cell phone went off, the pink one, and I broke away.

He cleared his throat. "Do you . . . do you need to answer that?"

I thought about it for a minute. "Yes," I said. I had made a deal after all.

"Are you going to then?"

I looked at the boy in front of me and thought of the boy waiting for me in a shady basement. They both thought they knew what kind of girl I was—namely, the kind they wanted me to be.

Gilly spoke again. "Don't go," he said quietly. "Come over to my house. Don't go to Mason. Be with me."

A line from *The Wizard of Oz* flickered through my head: *Are you a good witch or a bad witch?*

Are you a good girl or a bad girl?

"Mikey! I didn't know a guest was joining us tonight," said Gilly's mom as she opened the door. She was a tall, athletic woman with bronze-colored hair. She looked nothing like her son.

"Oh," I said awkwardly. "I'm sorry. Gi—Mikey invited me."

"You must be Kendall," she said warmly, ushering me in. "I'm Donna. I'm afraid we already ordered food, but I'm about to set out some ice cream sundaes. Friday night tradition—we do dessert first. We call it Friday Sundaes." I laughed and she smiled. "Let me just go get the restaurant on the phone," she said. "Mikey, set another plate at the table. Does Chinese work for you?" I nodded and she hurried out, Gilly trailing after her with a reluctant look back at me, still in the foyer.

This was the kind of house where all the lights were left on, all the time. It was environmentally and economically irresponsible. At least that was the party line in my house, where reading or table lamps were used more often than overhead lights. But here, even the shadows glowed and I could see into all of the corners.

A tiny sprite of a girl with golden-red curls wandered into the hallway and stared at me with blatant tween rudeness. She looked familiar. *What was her name?* I tried to remember.

Eventually she bailed me out. "I'm Sarah," she told me, sounding bored.

I tried to smile at Gilly's little sister. "I'm Kendall," I said.

"I know who you are," she said. She appraised me. "Why are you hanging out with my brother?"

"Why shouldn't I?"

She gnawed on her pinky nail. "No reason, I guess. Just . . . I mean, he's such a loser."

I smiled genuinely this time. Sarah Gilbert looked like she might be trouble. "You're at Howell, right? What grade are you in again?"

"Seventh."

I looked at the small, pretty girl in front of me, from her not-quite-tamed red curls to her enormous, scornful eyes. "I could do worse than your brother," I told her.

Gilly reentered the room and scrambled in between his sister and me. "Sarah, go away," he commanded.

"Fine," she sighed, stalking off. "It's dessert anyway."

Gilly exhaled slowly. "I didn't really think this through."

"No?" I asked, turning to face him. "You didn't want the criminal you're sweating to have ice cream with your family?"

The front door opened and a tall, reedy man with dark hair and glasses came in. He put down a briefcase and cordially stuck his hand out at me. "Well, hello," he said. "Are you joining us for our weekly Friday Sundaes, my dear?" Gilly muffled a groan.

He had the kind of New England accent that almost sounds British. "Hi, Mr. Gilbert," I said, slipping a gratified mask over my face. "If it's all right with you, I would love to. Donna was already nice enough to ask me."

Still holding my hand, still smiling, Mr. Gilbert asked, "I'm sorry, dear, you are very familiar, but I'm afraid I've forgotten your name. Encroaching senility and all."

"I'm Kendall Evans—Judith Evans's daughter."

He made a delighted guffaw noise. "That's why I know your face so well! You are so like your mother."

I hesitated a moment and then said, "Thank you. I've never really thought I looked all that much like her."

"You do! Even in the way you're holding yourself. I can't wait to let her know that I've seen you again after all this time. Last time, well, you and Mikey here were babies."

Donna called out, "Get in here, guys."

Gilly closed his eyes and seemed to collect himself. "Mom, we're just going to watch a movie, OK?" he called out. "Can we take the ice cream upstairs?"

She looked up and over at Gilly. "Just this once, you can skip the sundaes," she said, with only a moment's hesitation. "Because you have a guest. I'll call you when the food gets here."

I watched in fascination as she walked over, kissed Gilly on both cheeks, and turned around, striding back into the dining room without another word or a look behind. That was not the way my mother would have reacted. *My mother would have wanted answers.*

Like me, I realized.

Gilly grabbed my hand and pulled me up the stairs to his bedroom. As he shut the door behind me, I couldn't help remembering that I had been in this exact position before. Hustled away from his mother and up the stairs, basically tossed inside, and left to stand awkwardly on the wall-to-wall while he locked the door with his back to me.

I spun slowly in place. Gilly's room basically looked the same. If anything, it was actually neater and more organized. It was a comforting room, full of soothing colors, and soft textures, and action figures in their original packaging.

It was a comforting room, but it hurt to look at it. It was hard not to remember the last time I had been here and him brushing an eyelash off of my skin with a gentle finger;, to not remember the way he'd given me his raincoat. It felt like a long time ago.

"What's wrong?"

Gilly was standing in front of his door with the bearing of someone who had no idea what he was doing there or why.

"I'm just giving myself a headache," I answered, looking away.

"You want some aspirin?" He started fumbling with his night-stand drawer and then he stopped, dismayed. "We forgot the ice cream!"

"Shocking. Not like you were in a hurry to get out of there or anything." I slipped off my shoes, kicking them in opposite directions across his room, knowing that would drive Gilly crazy. "What was that about? You must really not want me to spend time with your parents."

He shrugged. "*I* don't like spending time with them."

I studied his face. "I don't think that's true. You have 'Friday Sundaes.'"

He looked uncomfortable. "OK. I don't like spending time with my parents when it's not just us. All right?"

"Why not? Your parents aren't embarrassing as parents go."

"Because it's no one else's business," he snapped. Then he took a deep breath and tried again. "It's like . . . I'm weird."

I laughed before I could stop myself. He scowled and I stopped. "Sorry."

"I'm weird," he continued stonily. "And they're not really weird. And I can't . . . act . . . when they're there. Like I did with your parents. I can't pull it off in front of them. So I just seem weirder."

"Do you really care if you seem weird in front of me? At this point?"

He avoided my eyes and I grew warm. "Where are your movies?" I asked, changing the subject.

"I have a bunch in the cabinet under the TV, but they're mostly old." I went to the cabinet and felt him following me. "We can just watch something on Netflix."

But I had already seen what I wanted. "*North by Northwest*!" I cried, grabbing it out of the cabinet and thrusting it at him. "I want *North by Northwest.*"

Gilly took the DVD, looking at me curiously. "You want to watch this?" he asked. I nodded and launched myself onto his bed, feeling the grin spread across my face.

I had always suspected that I was named after the girl in *North by Northwest*, a cool blond named Eve Kendall. She's not really the lead: that's Roger Thornhill, played by Cary Grant, who gets mistaken for George Kaplan by a bunch of gangsters. But it turns out that George Kaplan doesn't exist—he's an invented character, part of an FBI sting against a criminal mastermind. Thornhill gets involved against his will, coming across Eve Kendall, the gangster's girlfriend, along the way. In the space of a day, she seduces him, betrays him, and then sacrifices herself for the greater good, and Thornhill turns out to have been wrong about everything: Eve Kendall was working for the FBI the whole time.

When I was a little girl, I just loved her poise and her shiny, shiny hair. When I was a bigger girl, I admired her as a brave and skilled player in a game I was just beginning to grasp. She could switch from femme fatale to ingenue at any second and in all that chaos she was the only one who really understood what was going on: the only one with the whole picture.

Anyway, it was my mom's favorite movie growing up.

Gilly slid the DVD into the player and walked back toward his bed, turning off the overhead light. Then he sat down next to me, his legs sprawled across the top of the bedspread, hanging awkwardly over the side of the mattress.

The mischievous patter of the score started up and the credits flashed across the screen. The room was dark except for the desk light Gilly had left on, casting golden shadows on the wall around the TV. I suddenly realized that I had crawled enthusiastically into Gilly's bed, without giving any thought to how that might look, and then remembered how I had attacked him in the hallway.

But that encounter had been an act of defiance, a snap decision. A singular desire fulfilled at my discretion.

I snuck a look at Gilly. What did I want from him now? Did I just want to kiss him? I was pretty sure I could kiss him. Maybe the better question was, what did he want from me?

He caught me looking at him and I swung my eyes back to the movie.

Eve doesn't show up until about forty-five minutes in, so I had a good long while to enjoy the movie's easy charm.

But when she did show up, something occurred to me that had never occurred to me before. Eve had been *sent there* to seduce Thornhill. By her *boyfriend*, presumably with the knowledge of her secret employer, the FBI "good guys." And suddenly Thornhill, despite being played by Cary Grant, seemed . . . stupid. He seemed like a sucker.

On the screen, Eve pressed up against the doorframe and whispered into his ear, "I'm a big girl."

Thornhill replied smugly, "Yes. And in all the right places, too."

Stupid.

And then Gilly's face was right there, his cheekbone grazing against mine. I turned to look at him and saw that he was breathing hard and his eyes were glassy.

"Gilly—?"

Then he was on top of me, pushing me into his pillows, his

mouth moving all over mine and then down my neck. To be honest, my first instinct was to push him off and rewind the movie so I wouldn't have missed anything, say I didn't feel like hooking up anymore. But then he did something that made my insides melt and then fuse back together, like I was being smelted into a slightly finer metal.

He pulled his face back and looked at me, running his fingertips over my nose and down to my chin. Still looking right at me, he said, "Kendall. Goddamn it, Kendall."

I could have kissed him. So I did.

It started out as just a little kiss. I meant to pull away after a decent interval, but my arms just wouldn't unwrap themselves from around his waist. I felt an intense desire for heat, his heat, first rolling up the hem of his shirt to access his hips and then rolling it higher and higher, wanting more and more of his smooth, burning skin, until I'd nudged it off entirely.

In some far away, removed corner of my brain, I was aware of soft, strangled sounds coming out of my throat, muffled by two sets of lips, but I was mostly just focused on his skin, and wanting more of it, so much so that I couldn't even tell you when my shirt came off, or my bra, or my pants.

I had to stop to breathe and found myself tangled up in Gilly's limbs, naked except for underwear he had his hand down the back of. We were both panting and I could feel him through his boxers.

I looked at his face and it looked like he was struggling.

"I have . . . I have condoms," he said softly.

I think I must have nodded, because then he was kissing me ferociously and holding me so hard it seemed like I would break. And that felt really, really good. Until I caught another glimpse of his face.

He was looking at me intently, like he had been looking at me before, only it wasn't quite the same. When I had kissed him, his eyes were shining, but they were focused—focused on me. Now, with all of our clothes off, they were misty, blurry, vague. It disturbed me and I couldn't figure out why. And then I realized that I had seen it before.

That was the look on Trev's face when I leaned toward him on the couch, on Jeff's face when I smiled. And it was the look that Grant gave me before I followed him into that classroom, that first time. That was Thornhill's dumb face in Eve's hotel room, the one he hadn't been invited into but had entered anyway.

I pushed myself off of Gilly.

"What?" he asked, out of breath. "What's wrong?"

That expression didn't even seem human. It was everywhere, but it was just base, predatory instinct. It was evolution—biology. It wasn't anything but cause and effect—no emotion involved.

It was like slamming my hand in a door, but I yanked my legs away and started scrambling through the sheets for my clothes.

"Where are you going?" asked Gilly, sitting up now, sounding scared.

I liked science. My head spun with the scientific method as I pulled on my clothes as quickly as I possibly could. For the first time, I realized that, over and over, I had systematically induced that look and used it to achieve the desired results. And, come to think of it, cold or not, I didn't find anything intrinsically wrong with that.

But something inside me was screaming that I liked the Gilly who gave me his raincoat and blackmailed me into being careful. I didn't want Gilly like this.

"Kendall, what's happening?"

I was fully dressed now, so I stood up. "I'll see you on Monday," I said, avoiding his eyes but trying to make my voice sound as friendly as possible. I stopped before I got to his door and turned back around. "Please, *really*, don't take this personally. I . . . I liked it."

It was only half a lie. I ran.

CHAPTER TWENTY-THREE

At school, I finally had a bright spot, long-awaited, glittering at the end of my day: volleyball tryouts.

It should have been a formality. I would have been a fourth-year varsity veteran and my aim was never anything but fucking deadly. Never. That was especially true this year, when I had adrenaline leaking out of my pores and every single time I stepped up to serve, I sent the other girls flying across the court, grabbing air. I was even impressing myself.

I breezed through the first round of tryouts and then waited contentedly with the others for Coach and her assistant to confer and announce the A group and the B group for the second round, my heart still hammering out a satisfying rhythm against my ribs, blood still thrumming in my ears.

And then somehow, for the first time ever, I was in the B group.

I wasn't going to start. The very first day of gym, coach had hidden the equipment cage combination lock from me, and now she had taken away my starting position. For literally no reason.

And just like that, the second she downgraded me, the second she decided to *shame* me, I found I didn't care anymore what she thought. It was a surprise, but also a comfort, as the hot, sick, liquid feeling of humiliation burned itself pure into sheer, righteous anger. "Fuck that," I whispered, rubbing the tender spot between my thumb and my index finger. "Fuck every little bit of that." I shouldered my backpack and walked from the gym to the senior hallway with my head held high.

And smacked right into Ellie Kurtz.

"Fucking perfect," she muttered and bent to retrieve a book from the floor. When she straightened, I noticed a fading curved scratch above her cheekbone.

"Jesus, was that me?" I hadn't meant to ask.

"This? No, this is from the *other* crazy bitch that attacked me this month," she answered tartly.

I couldn't help snorting. Ellie always had great delivery when it came to insults.

She huffed out a breath and looked me over. "Did I get you anywhere?"

I rolled up my sleeve to show her the constellation of three fingertip-shaped bruises. She leaned in and rolled her eyes. "It's not as good as drawing blood on the face, so I'd say you win. Congratulations, Kendall." She made an ironic curtsy.

I had a sudden urge to apologize to Ellie. I felt my face go soft and I opened my mouth, but Ellie seemed to catch my intention and walled herself off. She took a step back and folded her arms. Her legs went rigid, but bent slightly at the knees, like she was getting ready to run. I shut my mouth.

The door to the hallway opened and Gilly walked in, accompanied by, of all people, Simone. They were arguing, but when he caught sight of me from across the hall, he stopped talking and smiled tentatively. Simone narrowed her eyes and stepped in front of him, blocking my view.

Ellie, she of the sharp eyes, looked from him to me, and this time she was the one to snort. "Not really," she said, turning back to face me. "That's not a thing, is it?"

I shrugged.

She scrunched her face up. "Ew, Kendall. Ew."

"You don't even know him, El."

"It's not about knowing him, Kendall. It's about him being a dirtbag who's obsessed with you."

"What on earth are you talking about?"

Ellie looked frustrated. "You didn't notice how he would follow us around last spring? He was practically stalking you by the end of the year. Remember when we spent that week in the computer lab running simulations at the end of the semester? He kicked that sweet kid Jacob out of his assigned seat every day, just so he could sit next to you and glare."

I laughed and walked past her to my locker. "Oh, sure, totally,"

I said, unlocking it. "Come on. You have to be exaggerating."

"Uh, no, I'm not," she said, whirling around to face me again. "I don't know why I'm even bothering to give you a heads up, but do you know I actually caught him looking through all your Facebook messages one day?"

I froze. "What?"

"I'm not sure where you were, the bathroom or something. I told him to beat it as soon as I saw what he was doing."

I leaned forward and banged my head against the locker.

"Hey, are you OK?" Ellie asked, putting out her arm but not quite reaching my shoulder.

I clutched my stomach as it lurched toward the floor. "No," I gasped, my throat dry, my voice cracked. "I'm going to be sick."

I slammed my locker shut and stood up, swaying on the spot. I turned and saw, behind Ellie (still in fighting stance), Gilly stepping toward me, his face concerned.

"Kendall? What's wrong?"

I stared at him, the world spinning around me. I bolted, only making it to the sink of the nearest bathroom before the burn climbed up my throat and I retched lunch onto the cheap porcelain.

I clutched the edge of the sink, shivering. I looked up at my reflection. Saliva was dripping from my slack lower lip and my skin was dry and beige.

I closed my eyes and saw Grant crouching next to me in the computer lab after his last final, whispering teasingly, "Come on, Skipper. You're not exactly working on your dissertation here."

"Some of us still have to get into college, old man," I'd said, suppressing a giggle.

He'd put his head on my lap and I nearly gasped at the friction of his thick, soft hair against my bare leg. "Please?" he said, his brown eyes twinkling and looking up at me with affection. "It's the only way I want to celebrate."

Like the addict that I was, I'd thirstily nodded and followed him into the empty classroom across the hall—not even bothering to close Facebook.

I opened my eyes and looked at them, red and watery in my reflection. I licked my lips, still a little swollen from kissing, and ran my tongue over the spot Gilly had touched with his fingertip while we sprawled across his bedspread.

I stood up straight and slapped myself sharply across the face.

It was Gilly the whole time.

CHAPTER TWENTY-FOUR

I GOT OUT OF THERE FAST. I don't know if Gilly was waiting for me. I didn't look. Just picked up my backpack and sped out of the building in my gym clothes.

It was a long walk home and hot as July out, but I couldn't stand the idea of going underground. By the time I let myself into my house, dripping with sweat, calves stinging, I had it all pretty much figured out.

Gilly had to have stolen the stash. The surly friend Lemon had brought to Trev had been Gilly, not Drew—no wonder he hadn't wanted to come in with me.

No wonder he'd gloated in the nurse's office.

No wonder he'd wanted me to go to the police with the drugs he stole and not to Mason.

No wonder he was upset by the idea of me giving the thief *up* to Mason.

No wonder a lot of things.

"So you just assume I'm *a hacker and can fix it."*

Dick.

I stripped off my clothes and got into the shower. It had to have happened the night of the warehouse party. I knew there were sales going on there and I now knew Gilly had to have been there.

I closed my eyes and tilted my head under the pounding stream of water. I tossed my hair back and then to the front and side, jamming out my hip and thrusting out my collarbone, moving into position as the girl in the picture. It hit me hard and all at once: *He* was responsible for the girl in the picture. I collapsed into myself and crumpled my face into tissue paper until, finally, for the first time in a long time, tears came.

I cried willfully. It was the kind of crying that's like doing laundry after weeks of near-emergency. It's a chore and it's time-consuming. But your body demands it, and at the end everything is clean.

When biology reached its limit and there was nothing left to expel, I abruptly calmed down. I uncrumpled my face and turned off the shower.

I swiped a clear patch onto the fogged-up mirror and carefully applied a mud mask. No need to abandon my routines simply because yet another boy had turned out to be not at all who he appeared.

I scowled at my reflection. It was my own fault. Why had I latched onto the nearest boy like he was a life raft?

Lying down, feeling the mask sting my skin, I dismissed pure loneliness. Loneliness was part of it, but, with a sinking stomach, I realized that it wasn't all of it. I had acted like the second-tier social climber I always had been, flirting until somebody looked at me and wanted something. So I could feel special. So I could feel worthwhile. So I could feel like I was pretty, wanted, chosen—the way a girl was supposed to be. A *good* girl, anyway.

I jumped up and ran to the bathroom, peeling the mask off with my fingernails, and then washed the whole mess away. I wasn't that girl anymore. I dried my face until it was red and patchy. Gilly had called it from the beginning, back in the nurse's office. I was a bad girl.

I opened my closet and saw tidy rows of colorful cardigans, muted skirts, and lacy camisole tops. Underneath were more rows: scrubbed-up sneakers and buckled shoes with high heels. Folded in a hanging cloth column of shelves were hemmed, well-fitted jeans and cords, no holes or rough edges. I picked up the top pair of bright blue jeans and, dropping my towel, held them up to my waist: not too tight and not too loose.

I dropped the pants on the floor and turned around. Then I changed my mind.

A guttural, athletic noise ripped out of my throat as I tore down the hanging shelves, sideswiped the hangers off the rack, and punted the heels across the room. I yanked the sole remaining garment off its hanger, my shot silk junior prom dress in butter yellow, wrinkled it into a ball, and tossed it high in the air. I grabbed my hair dryer off the shelf and used it as a bat.

The dress sailed across the room, knocking a water glass off the nightstand with a shatter and a splash.

Ten minutes later, I surveyed myself in the mirror and was satisfied with what I saw in a way that I couldn't remember being for years. The black jeans were from two years ago, so they fit tight, but somehow that felt supportive, not constrictive. I had dug out a T-shirt that I had only ever worn to bed, also black, with "This *Is* Rocket Science" in peeling white letters across the chest, bought at the Kennedy Space Center when we visited my grandparents in Orlando three years ago. I pulled on lace-up black converse that Audrey had called "nineties."

I pulled my hair into two long braids, how I had worn it every day until eighth grade, and filled in my lips with burgundy lipstick. I stepped back and nodded at myself in the mirror: "This is you," I said, and then shut the light, leaving my room in shambles.

Bounding down the stairs, I called out, "I'm going to Mikey's! See you later!" I slammed the door behind me, not waiting for a response.

Sarah answered the door and, with nothing more than a deep sigh and a hair toss, motioned me upstairs.

Gilly's door was shut. I knocked.

"I'll be down in a minute," he called out in an annoyed voice.

I opened the door.

"Jesus, Mom," he groaned, face down on his bed with his eyes shut. "Are you kidding me with this?"

"Evening, sugar," I said, shutting the door behind me.

Gilly scrambled off his bed, his eyes wild.

"What are you doing here?" he asked. He squinted. "Is your hair different?"

I sat on his bed, stretching out my legs and propping myself up on my elbows. "Why do you think I'm here?"

Gilly's silver eyes widened as they moved up my legs to my chest. He sucked in his lower lip as he leaned over me.

I let him get an inch from my mouth before I put up a hand and whispered, "Wait."

"What?" he said, almost whispering.

I hauled off and slapped him.

Gilly, startled, tumbled to the floor. I stood up and went over to his desk.

"Where are they?" I said, opening and shuffling through drawers. "Did you flush them? Gilly?" He didn't answer.

"Well?" I asked, moving onto his closet. "You didn't sell them, did you? I'm not sure I can do anything to save you if you did that. Mason is not a good guy."

"I ha—I have them," he said quietly, his voice breaking.

I turned to look at him now. He was still on the floor, his cheek in his hand. He had curled his legs up under himself and his face was pink and spotty.

"You look miserable," I said, turning away and squelching the pang I felt at seeing him look so sad.

"Kendall—"

I slammed his closet door shut. "While I'm here, I'd like the clothes I left and my knife. I dropped it the first time I was here."

I moved to his nightstand and he grabbed my hand from down on the floor.

"Can we talk about this?"

I wrenched my wrist out from his grasp and laughed. "Sure. Let's talk about it. Why don't we start with what I ever did to you?"

He looked away.

I laughed again. *Pathetic.* "Good. Ignore me again. There's the Gilly I always knew and *never gave a shit about*. Where've *you* been?"

"Stop it," he said, standing up and walking away from me.

I darted in front of him. "No, let's talk. I'd really like to know why you decided, having obtained these drugs, that rather than going to the cops yourself, as you've so strenuously argued for me to do, you decided to set me up—to involve me at *all*. What had I ever done to deserve that? To anyone I ever *spoke* to even, let alone you?"

Gilly scowled his trademark scowl and mumbled something, looking away.

"That's just great, Gilly," I said, sneering. "You're right. Why would I even try to elicit a reasonable explanation from the guy who's going to be voted 'Most Antisocial' in his senior yearbook?"

I pushed past him and started scanning his bookshelf for likely hiding places.

"You think you're really nice, don't you?"

I whirled around. He smiled bitterly at me. "You're just so much better than everyone else. Every time Dennis called someone fat or Audrey arbitrarily excluded someone from a table, I saw you flinch and hang your head, like, 'If only we could all just get along.'"

"Your point? I'm getting penalized for having a conscience?"

"What's the point of a conscience? You never said anything! After a one-second-long frown, you always went right back to smiling at whoever had been doing the shit-talking."

"Excuse me, I was just trying to survive high school! All I did was keep my head down."

"Exactly," he practically spat out. "All you did was keep your head down, mindlessly following Audrey and the other jockettes, willfully blind to everyone and everything else. Did you know Grant Powers beat Lemon up in the locker room after gym every single week in ninth grade?"

I drew in a sharp breath. "No."

"It wasn't exactly a secret. Did you know Audrey told Jody Mueller that she had been ranked the least attractive girl in class by the seniors last year? In a totally sympathetic and caring way, of course."

I hadn't, but I could imagine exactly how that scene had played out.

"You were *at the same table*, completely ignoring everything that would offend your little nice-girl sensibilities."

At the reproach in his voice, something snapped and I started literally vibrating with rage.

"I did nothing wrong," I said, expending a huge amount of energy keeping my voice steady. "You've had months to come up with a justification for screwing me over and all you can come up with is I didn't stop events I didn't notice were happening."

He stuck out his lower lip and muttered, "Didn't *care*, you mean." He stepped toward me and started to launch into yet another diatribe, but I cut him off.

"You're pathetic," I told him.

He stopped short, looking like I'd slapped him again.

"All you're mad about is that I didn't notice you. You don't care about Jody. I couldn't have done anything to stop Grant any more than you could have. Your feelings were hurt because I didn't like you back. This whole thing is petty nerd revenge."

He collected himself and made a feeble attempt at a sneer, "Don't flatter yourself."

I felt my lip snarl. "Oh yeah? Then tell me something. That

picture of me you put on Facebook. Why did you have it?"

Gilly slumped over, burying his face in his hands and gulping wetly for air. When he looked up a moment later, his eyes were red and ringed with shiny damp patches.

"I'm sorry," he said, his voice hollow. "God, I wish I could take it back. I got *so* angry, I couldn't think—" His voice cracked here and he started sobbing out loud.

I was alarmed and a little afraid to see him cry. I didn't trust myself to answer coldly, so I didn't answer at all.

He went on. "I was at the warehouse party with Lemon. He knows Trev from judo and he's got this raver girlfriend who wanted to do ecstasy with him. He invited us to the party. I didn't want to be there. But then I saw you." He took a deep breath. "You looked so happy and I wanted to . . . I don't know. I wanted to remember it. I took the picture. Then Powers grabbed you and you . . . you *let him*. And you just kept on letting him. For weeks. Like an idiot. Or," he added quickly, "like someone a lot less smart than you are."

He looked at me pleadingly. "Am I making sense?" he begged.

I shook my head. "No. You're not. It's none of your business what I do. Get to the stash. How did you manage to steal it?"

Gilly continued, "A couple of weeks later. Lemon dragged me to the Fish Hook again, to hang out with Trev. Mason was there. He was trying to get Trev to do something, I'm not sure what, but

Trev didn't want to do it. Mason went really quiet for a minute and then fucking Powers shows up and agrees to it."

"Do what?"

"I don't know," Gilly said wearily. "I was distracted by my sheer hatred of Grant Powers. Anyway, Mason cheered right the hell up and invited us over for a party at his apartment. He drove us over in his car. The Prius, in the picture. Turned out it was Simone's building, which, you know, I knew pretty well at one point. The party was stupid so I was just wandering around and I saw Mason sneak off to the basement. I followed him to that office you described and that's where I found the pills. They had a post-it on them saying they were going to *Grant*."

"Why not just go to the cops?" I asked.

"I don't know. I wanted to scare Mason. The guy was just so smarmy."

I couldn't help but laugh, but there was no joy in it. "Fine, yes. Mason is an asshole. Grant is *also* an asshole. You were having a shitty time at a party. What the *hell* did I have to do with it?"

He looked around the room, as if he would find the answer written on the walls.

"Gilly? *Look at me*." He did, but just barely. "Why me?" I asked again, sternly.

Gilly visibly swallowed and looked away. Finally, he said, "Do you remember what the fall play was freshman year?"

It was not what I expected to come out of his mouth. I was surprised enough to answer. "I don't know. Some Shakespeare comedy, right?"

"*Twelfth Night*," he answered. "Naya got Olivia, one of the leads. I did sound and lighting."

"OK? Who cares? What does Naya have to do with this?"

"Nothing. It was you. You and Audrey and Grant. Grant and Audrey used the auditorium balcony to make out all that semester. *You*—that day you were on lookout."

He practically growled the word "You." I stiffened. "Is this story going somewhere?" I asked.

Gilly's eyes were welling up again. "You don't remember this at all? Really?"

I cast my mind back to freshman year. Grant and Audrey had just started dating, and Audrey, always with her puritanical streak, often wanted me on the sidelines at their dates back then, essentially as a chaperone.

I remembered being in the auditorium, several rows away from them, burying my face in my algebra textbook, trying not to want to listen to them but failing, and grasping at every laugh or scrape on the carpeting.

Did I remember Gilly being there?

Gilly would likely have been in the lighting booth. But that didn't make sense, because the lighting booth was visible from where I was sitting. I would have alerted Audrey and Grant and we would have been gone. Could he have been on the stage?

"Why don't you try out for the plays?" I had asked him. *"I bet you'd be really good."*

His face hardened. "That's not going to happen."

I mentally squinted and a picture of Gilly, shorter and pimply, standing on the dim stage at Howell appeared.

"You were doing a monologue," I ventured. "Why were *you* doing a monologue?"

He just scowled. I turned back to this newly discovered memory and saw Gilly, puffing out his chest in pontification, a silly, lovelorn look on his face.

I saw myself at fourteen—laughing at him. Not just laughing at the speech—which I vaguely remembered as being funny—but laughing cruelly, laughing without even thinking about him, laughing loudly enough that I would distract Grant and Audrey, make them pay attention to me, make them involve me in their two-person world.

I didn't remember exactly what I said, but I remembered that I had made sure to make it cutting enough for them to laugh with me. At Gilly.

I didn't remember what Gilly did after I laughed, or how he looked. I was a mean girl.

"You should have heard how Grant was talking about you that

night," Gilly said, pulling me back to the present. My melting heart hardened again—in a slightly different shape, maybe, but as intractable as it had been a few minutes before. He was still wrong. I might have hurt him, but he tried to steal my identity. And mean girl, bad girl, good girl, whatever—it was *mine*, not his.

He walked over to the antique safe and opened it, taking out a Ziploc filled halfway with capsules. He handed it to me and knelt on the floor, pulling my clothes out from under his bed. They were clean and dry and folded into a tidy pile with Rockford's knife lying on top.

Gilly gathered up the pile and passed it to me. I took it, dumping it and the pills in my bag.

"I already had access to your profile," he said, quietly, still not meeting my eyes. "I had been checking it. I knew it was shitty to do, but I couldn't help it. I wanted to know more about you. And that night when I grabbed the stash—I never meant to do it, to make it look like you took it. Really, I didn't. But the way Grant was talking about you, the way he was describing you—"

"Don't tell me," I told him. "It doesn't matter."

Gilly finally looked into my eyes. "I got home that night and just—spiraled. All I could think about was you and Grant, and you and Audrey, and you and Ellie, and every time you made me feel . . ." He couldn't seem to find the word. He gulped and finished, "I could make you hurt, so I did."

I felt sick to my stomach. I didn't answer and headed for the door.

When my hand was on the doorknob, he spoke again. "I regretted it fast, Kendall. After we talked. I really did. And, then, after you got a plan, I tried to stay out of your life. Remember, I tried?"

I remembered. I remembered feeling bereft and abandoned that day after he'd given me his sweatshirt in the rain, the day he wouldn't even look at me at school. *That* was him trying? My throat was dry, but I managed to hiss, "Good to know." I turned the knob.

"Are you going to tell him who it was?" he asked.

"Any reason I shouldn't?" I snapped back. He didn't answer.

Gilly was facing away from me, slouched in defeat. I remembered him pulling his raincoat over my head. I closed my eyes and saw him put his head against mine, begging me to be careful. Sadness fell over me in a sour, heavy wave, until it felt like I was going to drown in it.

"I'll try not to," I said, and pushed out of his room.

CHAPTER TWENTY-FIVE

I DIDN'T TURN GILLY IN. I flushed the capsules. And I took to carrying the knife around in a locked pouch in my backpack. It didn't seem to matter if I got caught with a weapon and it seemed increasingly likely that I'd need one someday.

Saturday afternoon when I got to the basement office, I stopped short in the doorway. Mason was standing in front of a full-length mirror trying on ties. My eyes traveled up his thin profile, every inch in tight-fitting, eye-devouring black, a button-down hanging loose over his hips, a bone slightly visible there when he raised his arms to his neck.

He turned to face me, revealing a smirk, and, where his shirt opened, a triangle of red ribbed cotton undershirt. His eyes were flashing. He knew he looked good.

"What do you think?" he asked, holding up two ties. "Maroon or black-and-white pinstripes?"

"Depends on the occasion," I eventually answered. "Who are

you trying to impress?"

"Why, I'm trying to impress you, my dear," he said, inclining his head toward me. "But since I don't think that's going to happen, I thought I'd settle for your classmates. And mine."

"What are you talking about?"

"You and I are going to a party together tonight," he said, turning back to the mirror.

"Really? I don't believe dating you is in my employee contract," I spat as he frowned at his reflection and started to unbutton his shirt.

"Dating! God, you are in high school, aren't you?" he said, chuckling. "I forget sometimes."

"Yes, I'm very immature," I said, crossing my arms over my chest. "What is this party and why are we going?"

He shrugged out of the shirt, flexing a little. The pale hairs on his arms caught the light, making it impossible not to stare at the dark tattoos twisting around them. "Do you remember James Greenberger?" he asked.

The question surprised me. "James Greenberger? Yeah, he went to Howell. He was a senior when I was a freshman."

"And now he goes to Columbia. His twenty-first birthday party is tonight. It's going to be a blowout. Most of your class is invited. Well, the important people in your class."

"I'm not."

"You didn't have to be," he said smirking again. "I am, and the general assumption was that you would come with me. Get changed."

"Into what?"

He walked to the cupboard and pulled out a Nordstrom bag. He handed it to me.

I took it gingerly. "What is this?"

"It's a present. Happy ten-week anniversary."

I almost laughed. My life had unraveled so completely in just ten weeks? I unwrapped the tissue paper inside the bag and found a strapless dress made of raw silk, with an asymmetrical hem and a built-in push-up bra. It was bright red.

"How do you know it will fit?"

"I made a guess based on some concentrated observations," he said, folding his arms over his chest and leaning against the desk. "Try it on."

I looked at his face, at the hint of a smile. He was waiting to see if I would break. I wouldn't.

Looking him in the eye, I kicked off my shoes. He didn't blink and so I unzipped my sweatshirt and let it fall to the floor, quickly followed by my jeans. Still looking right at him until the moment the fabric blocked my eyes, I pulled my T-shirt over my head.

I shook out the dress. I hated not wearing a bra, but it wasn't as if I had a strapless just hanging out in my backpack. I again caught Mason's eye. He was looking at me admiringly and not just at my body—although there was a flash of that in there, too. Determined to brazen this out, I reached behind me and unhooked the bra, tossing it to the floor, before stepping into the dress. Mason stepped behind me and zipped up the back.

I went to the mirror. The dress fit perfectly.

"You never told me which tie," he said.

I turned and surveyed him. That red tank top matched my dress to a tee. "No tie," I told him. "Put the black shirt back on and wear it unbuttoned."

He came over to stand with me in front of the mirror and shrugged the shirt back on. He looked at the two of us standing next to each other in the mirror.

"Perfect," he said, appraising us almost clinically. "Shoes for you are in that bag, too."

I checked and there were indeed black stiletto boots. And a bottle of pills.

"Did I forget to tell you?" he said, smoothing his hair over his forehead. "You're working tonight."

"As what?" I muttered, staring at the boots.

His phone went off. He reached for it automatically, but when he saw the number, his shoulders shook a little and he threw the phone onto the couch, as if he were tossing off a beetle that had landed on his arm.

"Who was that?" I asked, genuinely curious. I had barely ever seen him rattled.

The phone was still ringing. As Mason watched it go off, a smile of sorts, simultaneously satisfied and grim, settled onto his face. He gave his phone the finger. "Let him wait for once," he said, to no one in particular.

He turned back to the mirror and looked at his reflection—and then at my reflection next to him. "That was my father," he said carefully.

He was still looking at my face in the mirror. He seemed to be waiting for a reaction, so I said, "Oh?" and busied myself with my hair.

"Do you get along with your parents?" He turned to look at me.

His face looked almost sincere, so I answered him honestly. "I used to."

He nodded. "That must have been nice," he said. "While it lasted."

We both turned back to the mirror. We looked good. We looked like a match.

James's parents had rented out the Rainbow Room, a former society haven of a restaurant turned high-ticket party venue. I could tell right away that the caterers were a private hire, because everywhere black-tie-wearing servers were carrying drinks to kids in my grade.

Mason and I were already a little late. Simone was leaning against a window frame chatting with the cutest waiter. We caught each other's eyes and she gave me a surprised smile and wave. But when Mason came up behind me, her face went dark and she turned away.

"So who am I delivering to?" I asked, turning toward my date, my stomach cramping with anxiety, suddenly aware that I couldn't keep this up forever. Simone would find out about the video or she would decide she hated me for not turning Mason in. I was going to lose her.

Mason grabbed my hand with his far hand and pulled it across his chest and me into his side. "Like I said. We're working to-night," he said with a smile.

I shuddered but muscle memory took over, and I shook the girl in the picture into my face. Involuntarily, I felt myself relax. I moved my hand upward from his chest, curling my fingers around his jawline. His smile got wider.

Mason led me over to a group of girls dressed uniformly in tight black. Addressing the girl with the longest hair and the short-est dress, Mason said cheerfully, "Madeline. How's tricks?"

The other girls melted away. Madeline cocked her head to the side, making her blond hair, paler than mine, bounce. "Mason," she drawled, swaying a little. She side-eyed me but kept her smile, and attention, aimed at Mason. "Who's your charming companion?"

Mason only snorted in response.

"I'm Kendall," I said, extricating my hand from Mason's and holding it out to Madeline. "It's nice to meet you."

She very lightly took my hand but didn't shake it. "Maddie," she said. "I've heard so many interesting things about you, Kendall."

"How *is* Jo?" Mason broke in before I had a chance to thank her.

Maddie let go of my hand and turned back to Mason, crossing her arms over her chest. "She's pissed, Mason," she said sweetly. "What do you expect?"

"Not much at this point," he said, chuckling.

She nodded. "That's good to hear. I'd rather you didn't expect any additional favors from my friend."

Mason's smile remained intact. "Madeline, darling, would you be so good as to show Kendall to the ladies' room? She's never been here before and I know you always know your way around."

"With pleasure," she cooed, her voice dripping with acid. Mason kissed me on the cheek and took off. I looked after him murderously and turned back to Maddie. She was staring after him with the exact same look.

Once in the bathroom, Maddie hopped up onto the counter. "Show me what you've got, kid," she said. I did what I was told and retrieved the pills from my clutch.

Maddie held it up to the light and quickly counted, judging by the way she pursed her lips six times in quick succession. "Thanks, darling," she said brightly, unzipping her designer combat boots—too cool for me to identify the label but obviously expensive—and sliding the bottle down to the heel.

She hopped off the counter and arched sideways, zipping the boot back up. She straightened up and handed me a wad of bills from her cleavage.

"Well, see ya," she said and headed to the door. When her hand was on the handle, she stopped and turned back, looking at me with a resigned expression on her face. "It was nice to meet you, Kendall," she said softly. "Good luck."

As soon as the door swung shut, I heard a flush from one of the closed stalls. I spun around. There hadn't been any feet visible under the doors when we walked in. A quick look told me there still wasn't. And then a single, black suede, lace-up platform lowered itself to the floor. Its twin followed a second later. I stashed the money in my boot and moved toward the door, but wasn't quick enough. The stall opened and Ellie Kurtz stepped out.

She looked great. That was something easy to forget about Ellie: She was very pretty. Her voice was barbed and discordant, and her eyes hard and suspicious, but if she was looking away and keeping her mouth shut, Ellie's face had a baby doll sweetness:

heart-shaped lips, button nose, rosy cheeks. And that night she had let her ash-brown hair out, keeping the natural curls, rather than employing the aggressive straightening that usually made her look so severe.

She went to the sink and started washing her hands. "How's business, Kendall?" she asked.

I joined her by the mirror and pretended to examine my hair. "I'm not sure what business you're referring to, El," I said, keeping my voice as even as possible.

"The business with the girl in the painted-on dress," Ellie said, turning to me.

"Oh, that business!" I slapped my forehead and turned to face her. "You mean *my* business. So sorry. You can understand why I wouldn't assume that."

Ellie glowered at me, pursing her lips with something that looked like disapproval. Disappointment. I couldn't take that from Ellie, of all people, so I added, "But I'll tell Maddie that you liked her dress."

Her eyelashes were so long that when her eyes narrowed, they cast little shadows across her cheekbones. "Do," she said crisply. She slipped past me, muttering as she went, "And tell Mason Frye that I like his dress, too."

I looked down at the red dress and tugged up the neckline. It was very low.

Mason scooped me up as soon as I left the bathroom and spent the next hour introducing me to a merry-go-round of kids styled to look like grown-ups. I stayed on autopilot throughout. My grin and slink was like body armor at this point: I could move freely under the skin of the girl in the photograph.

I felt itchy from my encounter with Ellie in the bathroom. I had never had to be the girl in the photograph with any of my classmates, to say nothing of people who used to sleep over at my house (Grant excepted). I didn't like the feeling that I had been ignoring how I might be looking at school. It scared me. And Ellie was the last person I wanted to be able to frighten me.

Ellie and I had always known just where to press each other. Actually, Ellie had always known exactly where to press anybody, a kind of mean girl superpower. Thinking about it now, I realized that the time we had fought in the hallway, she had purposefully pushed me into a rage with the crack about the liquor store—she knew about the bourbon bottle hidden in my bedroom. It was retaliation. I had surprised her when I zeroed in on her feelings for Audrey. She had thought that was hidden.

Mason led me back to the bar. I ordered and quickly downed a shot of whiskey. I still didn't like to think about Ellie's face when I said the thing about her and the girls' locker room. It made me feel small and sad.

I looked across the room and Ellie vanished from my mind. Because, in a corner by a window, Grant was hanging over Simone, grinning and chatting at her like a freight train—chatting at her, not with her, because from what I could tell Simone was answering in one-word sentences, if at all. She was looking away from him, her back straight as an iron rod, her face totally immobile.

"Give me a minute," I said to Mason, leaving his side to try and find an angle where I could see her better. She looked like she was walking away from Grant, but a cater-waiter blocked my view.

By the time he moved, Simone had her back pressed against the wall and was white as salt. Burke had joined Grant, and the two were flanking her, arms around each other's shoulders in jovial camaraderie, laughing and gesturing at Simone.

No. They did *not* get to talk to Simone.

I lost control.

I barreled over to the corner, steamrollering past everyone in my way and threw myself bodily at Grant and Burke, knocking them away from Simone. Burke stumbled out of my reach, but I managed to catch Grant by the shirt collar and slammed him up against the wall, in the same space Simone had just vacated.

"You don't get to speak to her," I hissed, cutting him off before he had time to speak. "And I will make you sorry someday. If it's the last thing I do, I'll make you sorry."

Grant pushed me off of him, scowling. "You crazy bitch," he grunted, but not quietly enough. We were starting to draw an audience.

I shoved him right back. "Yeah, I'm a crazy bitch. That's absolutely correct. I'm a crazy bitch who knows exactly what a cowardly, sniveling, pathetic little criminal you are."

He laughed bitterly. "Oh, I'm the criminal? Look in the mirror, Skipper. Look at who you're at this party with. Shit, who's the one who *sold* me those pills, what, like, a week ago?"

"Not *those* pills," I growled. "I didn't sell you the pills you gave to Burke and Pete two years ago to administer to whomever they wanted, whether they were aware of it or not, you complete asshole." As the color drained out of his face, I turned around and saw a semicircle of spectators surrounding us, with Audrey right out front.

I froze.

She was standing very straight and very still, watching carefully. She ignored Grant pulling himself together in the corner and just looked at me. It was the first time Audrey had looked at me like that in months, absent malice or carefully controlled rage. Or hurt, I suddenly realized. Our eyes locked and she inclined her head toward me as if she were asking a question.

Before I could answer, someone yelled out, "Police, this is a raid!" And all hell broke loose.

CHAPTER TWENTY-SIX

THE CROWD SCATTERED LIKE CONFETTI. I ran with the rest but not fast enough. Someone caught my wrists from behind and spun me against the bar.

The cop, a broad-shouldered, dumb-looking guy, called out, "Is this the one?"

A younger, slimmer uniform jogged up and stared at me. "Matches the description. Small, blond, red dress. Check her ID."

The first cop turned back to me. "Hand it over, kid."

My ID said that I was seventeen, but my blood alcohol level did not. I didn't move.

He rolled his eyes and pulled my bag off of my shoulder. He took out my wallet and flipped it open. "It's her," he said. "Kendall Evans."

The younger one smirked and pulled out cuffs. He stepped in front of the other cop and, grabbing my forearms, turned me around, pressing me down until my boobs were squashed against the bar.

"Kendall Evans, you have the right to remain silent," he intoned, jamming my wrists into the bracelets. "Anything you say can be used against you in a court of law . . ."

Outside, it was bedlam: a deluge of teens in designer clothes and not enough outerwear frantically hailing cabs, with cops detaining every eighth one, seemingly by random selection. I heard Grant yelling for Audrey to call a lawyer, to get out her wallet—basically to come get him out of trouble—until one of the uniforms got annoyed and threw him against the trunk of a squad car, cuffing him and tossing him in the backseat.

And then there was Ellie. She was leaning against a lamppost, watching me with her arms crossed. I got closer and realized she wasn't just watching me; she was waiting for me. I caught her eye as I went by her, my arms restrained behind my back, a cop's hand between my shoulder blades. Ellie uncrossed her arms and raised a hand in my direction. She paused, smiled, and then lowered the two middle fingers.

Mess with the bull, you get the horns. Our gym teacher used to do that in middle school. We thought it was hilarious, me and Ellie.

The cop shuffled me toward the squad car and I craned my head around to see if she was still there. She was.

I nodded at her through the window. Ellie and I had played the same game for a long time. We both knew the rules.

I had never really considered the effect of losing Ellie. I thought of the picture I knew used to be tacked up on her bedroom wall.

It was of me, Ellie, and Audrey, posing with our arms around each other. Audrey was of course in the middle, with Ellie on the right and me on the left. We were on the beach, not quite sixteen, dripping with saltwater and sunshine. Audrey was pursing her lips in a mock-model pose, her eyebrows raised to the sky. Ellie was sticking out her tongue. I looked annoyed.

I nodded at her again and she nodded back. I had broken détente. Mutually assured destruction meant that if I exposed her biggest vulnerability, she exposed mine.

It was almost fair.

She stayed there the whole time, our eyes locked, as the car drove me away.

Half an hour later, I was in an interview room, yet again. I was waiting there for a long time, alone, pacing, but eventually the beefy cop joined me.

"What exactly am I under arrest for?" I asked before he said a word.

"Settle down," he said, sitting opposite me. "I just want to ask you some questions."

I joined him at the table. "Excellent, we have something in common: questions. Why was I targeted by name?"

He smiled cockily. "Your friends aren't as loyal as you think they are. One of them sold you out."

"Ohhh," I said, folding my arms. "So, the reason you sought me out, specifically, in a room full of drunk teenagers, most of whom don't seem to have been apprehended, was that some other teenage girl told you to. Is that right?"

He grimaced at me.

"What did Ellie say I was doing?" I asked.

"Who said anything about an Ellie?"

I smiled. "I almost got suspended from school for starting a fight with her a few weeks ago. Seriously, call my school, ask anyone. If someone was going to spin some bullshit about me, it would be Ellie Kurtz. She's not exactly reliable."

The door opened and Rockford stepped inside the room.

"Are you Kramer?" Rockford asked, looking past him to where I sat.

"Yeah. Who are you?"

Rockford stepped forward into the light. He looked like shit. He was in a rumpled dress shirt and I wouldn't have been surprised if he hadn't shaved or slept since I left him in the *last* interrogation room I was in.

"I'm Detective Rockford from 1PP," he said in a clipped voice. "I'm taking over this investigation. Go talk to your captain if you have a problem, but he'll tell you the same."

The other cop left. Rockford shut the door behind him and turned back to me.

"You look nice," said Rockford, meanly, coming forward and standing on the other side of the desk. "What are you doing here, Kendall?"

I shrugged and looked away. "You tell me. I just went to a party."

"As Mason Frye's date."

"Having bad taste in boys isn't a crime."

He slammed his hands down on the desk and then hung his head. He closed his eyes and stood still and silent for a moment. When he looked up again, his eyes were blazing, but his breath was even. "You sold drugs at this party," he said, softly, if a little shakily. "And now, unless you do every little thing I say, you're going to get charged for it."

"Wait. There were *drugs* at that party? I had no idea."

"Listen, thug junior—"

"No, you listen," I hissed, leaning into his face, cutting him off. "You're not going to find a single person at that party who saw me giving anybody any drugs, let alone selling them. If Ellie says she saw me do it, she's lying. You're the one who's going to have explaining to do, not me."

There was a knock on the door. "What!" yelled Rockford.

The door opened and a curly haired woman in uniform poked her head in. "You have the underage drinker in here? Kendall Evans? She made bail."

I laughed out loud. I stood up and walked past Rockford, who looked ready to pull his hair out.

"Is she really mad?" I asked the female officer as we walked out, sobering up and realizing just how pissed my mother was going to be.

"Is who mad?"

"My mother. She posted my bail?"

The woman laughed. "I don't think so, honey. That takes babies having babies to a whole new level. But she is eighteen, so she could bail you out, no trouble."

I turned the corner and locked eyes with Audrey, standing alone and still in the middle of the crowded police station. The cop lifted up my hands and unfastened the cuffs.

"That's you done, hon," she said cheerfully. "Don't let me see you back here."

She dropped my wrists and I walked slowly toward Audrey. She held out my purse, confiscated when I had first gotten to the station. I looked down at it and then up at her.

Audrey was rarely visibly ruffled, and this was no exception. But her brow was furrowed and her mouth turned down at the edges. She looked like she hadn't been sleeping. She looked sad.

I took the bag from her as gently as I could. She seemed satisfied with that and nodded at me a little. I nodded back at her and we started to walk toward the door, side by side, her long legs slowing a little and my short ones skipping to keep up—almost as if we'd done it every day for a decade.

"Audrey!"

We both turned and saw Grant struggling against a cop in the doorway of a side room. "Thank god you're here," he called out. "Do you have my bail?"

Audrey broke away and strode over to him, facing away from me. He relaxed as she came near, breaking into a smile.

"Babe," he said, relieved.

There was a sound of sucking back saliva and then an impressive glob of it was rolling down Grant's gob-smacked face.

Audrey turned back toward me, neatly scraping spit off her lips with a fingernail.

"Let's go," she said. All I could do was nod.

Before I left, I glanced back at Grant, wiping the spit off his face with his wrist and sneering, not at Audrey, but at me. "So I'm the asshole, but your new boyfriend gets a pass? Fucking hypocrite."

Once outside, in the fresh chill of the air, Audrey turned to face me. Her hand twitched by her side. If we were guys, she might have stuck it out for a firm, fence-mending handshake. But we weren't guys, we were girls, and we had hurt each other. I grabbed her hand, holding it fast by her side.

I squeezed it, not looking at her. After a moment, she squeezed it back.

We dropped hands and crossed the street in different directions.

All I wanted to do then was go blank, but when I opened the front door to my house, I heard familiar voices in the kitchen: familiar voices mingling in an unfamiliar way.

My mother and Mason were sitting across from each other at the table, each with their hands clasped around steaming mugs of tea.

Mason noticed me first. "Kendall! I lost you at the party. I heard it got a little crazy—you make it out OK? No problems?"

My eyes darted over to my mother, but she wasn't looking at me. Her focus was fixed steadily on Mason.

"I'm fine," I answered, nodding so he would know that his business was fine, too. "What are you doing here?"

My mom answered. "When Mr. Frye got separated from you at the party and couldn't get you on your cell, he got worried. He said he was in the neighborhood and thought he would check in on you here."

"That was nice of him," I said mechanically.

"Wasn't it? I thought so." Her voice was pleasant and her mouth was smiling, but her eyes never left Mason's face and they were as hard as I'd ever seen them.

Mason stood up. "Well, since Kendall's OK, I won't keep you anymore, Mrs. Evans."

"Oh, you're not keeping me." She began to stand as well, but he held out a hand to stop her. To my surprise, she looked at me, a question in her face—she was looking for my lead. I nodded slightly and she sat back down.

"No, really," Mason said, smiling. "I do have to go. I have to meet my father."

"You do?" I asked, surprised.

"Sadly, I do. But it was really nice to meet you, Mrs. Evans." He stuck out his hand.

"And you, Mr. Frye," answered my mother, reaching over the table. "And thank you again for being so concerned about Kendall."

He smiled. "Nothing concerns me more."

"I'll walk you out," I said, breaking into their handshake. It had lasted a few seconds longer than seemed necessary.

When we got to the front door, I followed him out onto the porch, wrapping my bare arms around my chest in the cold.

"What the hell are you doing here?" I hissed, looking over my shoulder. "I live here. You can't be here."

"Trust me, I realize that nothing about tonight has been ideal," he said glumly. "I wouldn't have come, except I have to ask you a favor."

"And it couldn't have waited until tomorrow?"

"No." He pulled a bulging manila envelope out of his inside

breast pocket. "I really do have to meet my father. But he's in Texas. So I need you to take care of something while I'm out of town."

I took the envelope from his offering hand. "How long are you going to be gone?"

"Not sure. But this can't wait any longer. I have to see him now."

"Are we shutting down?" I asked hopefully.

"Far from it. I mean, yes, you won't be making deliveries while I'm gone, but what you will be doing is ensuring that you can make more when I get back. Open it."

Inside were four plain white envelopes. They were addressed to different people at different addresses in the New York metropolitan area.

"You want me to mail four letters? That's your favor?"

"Kiddo, I want you to hand deliver them. You are my courier, are you not? I don't trust them in the mail."

I clutched them a little tighter. "What's in them?"

He didn't answer. Checking his wristwatch, he said, "I've got to get to the airport. Where's a good place to catch a cab around here?"

I pointed to the left. "Go to seventh and ninth. If you don't have luck there, walk down to fifth, but you shouldn't have a problem on a Friday night." I was relieved at how calm my voice sounded. Clearly, I needed him to leave, so that I could open those envelopes.

"Thanks," he said. Then he took a step up until he was standing very close to me on the landing. There was maybe an inch between us. He leaned in, closing the gap at our chests and our skulls.

"This is important, Kendall," he said quietly. "I'm trusting you."

"I know," I said quickly. "It will be fine, I promise."

"Look at me."

I brought my eyes up to his, where they locked into place. The shameless—and I mean, literally, without shame—appeal in his face completely disarmed me, just for a moment.

"I know," I said again, quieter.

He was close enough that I should have been able to hear him breathe, but I couldn't. He was that sure. "I don't trust a lot of people. You don't either."

"Mason. I know." I finally looked away and he stepped back.

"Well, have a nice week, or whatever," he said, turning and casually skipping down the stairs.

"Yeah," I said faintly. "You have a good trip."

"Thanks," he called. "I won't—but thanks." He went around the corner and was gone.

I stepped back into the house and shut the door behind me, pushing the lock firmly into place. My mother was standing there waiting for me.

She was leaning slightly forward and her hands were balled up into fists at her sides.

"Hi," I said, as gently as I could. "Mom, it's OK. I promise, it's OK."

My mom let out a ragged breath. "There's something going on here I don't understand, isn't there?"

I drew in a shaky breath, feeling like I might cry. "Yes."

She closed her eyes. "I knew it," she muttered. "I knew there was something wrong, but I couldn't see what it was . . ." She opened her eyes and looked at me, her eyes a force of nature. "There's something not right with that boy. Not right with how he came here, not right with how he asked where you were. He was lying, Kendall. Why would he lie?"

It was nice to hear it put so simply. *How could she already know that*? I nodded.

She stepped closer and looked at me sharply. It was the patented Judith Evans truth-serum glare and I never stood a chance. I braced myself to spill, to tell her everything—the hacked Facebook page, the stolen pills, Gilly, Simone, my search for the supplier.

"Tell me," she said, her voice even again, almost hypnotic. "I should have pushed before and that's my fault. I didn't know how to—" her voice cracked here and she took a moment to collect herself. "Tell me the truth. What are you doing?"

I felt my knees buckle underneath me. I looked at her pale face and wide eyes and whispered, "I'm not sure anymore."

Her face seemed about to shatter like a broken wine glass. "OK," she said softly. "It's late, anyway. I think you need to sleep. But *this*, whatever you're doing with this boy; this can't go on. Will you *promise* to tell me when I can help you?"

I made a decision. I nodded.

She grabbed me then, in a hug unlike any hug she'd given me in years. I found my arms reaching around her too, holding on for dear life.

Mom let go. "Now go to bed," she ordered. She turned around, but I caught sight of her wiping her eyes. "I mean it, Kendall."

Back in my room, I tore the seal off of the first envelope and hungrily pulled out its contents.

It was a single piece of paper, with a long string of numbers and symbols. They meant nothing to me. I opened the next one. It, too, was a single sheet of paper with the same string of numbers and symbols. The third one, same deal.

"Fuck," I muttered, tossing them on my bed. I threw my hands into my hair in frustration. This whole thing was nothing but dead end after dead end.

I caught sight of myself in the mirror. I looked tired and pale. Diminished. I'd even lost weight. But then my eyes fell on the magazines sticking out from under my bed: my *Discover* and *Scien-*

tific American issues.

Biting my lip, I went back to my bed and took a closer look at the papers. Then I started to smile. This wasn't some kind of code. It was a formula. It was math.

I could do math.

I grabbed my chemistry textbook, my algebra textbook, and my computer and got to work.

The formula was written in a convoluted way. There were a lot of archaic symbols, mathematical blind alleys, and some really indecipherable handwriting. It was starting to get light outside when I finally translated it into a simple, chemical formula. Even after that, it took a few minutes for what I was looking at to soak in. I was tired and it seemed too simple. But there it was: a classic GHB formula, crossed with ecstasy and modified with sedatives. I opened my nightstand drawer and took out the note Mason had left on me after he'd drugged and dumped me on the steps of Howell. The handwriting matched.

I started laughing—a dry, choking sound after a night of no sleep. Mason didn't just sell this drug, he *was* the drug. And here was proof.

Nancy Drew would have slapped the shit out of me. And Simone was going to kill me.

Because, I suddenly knew that I had been wrong. Simone was strong enough to withstand a video. She had nothing to be ashamed of. I had said that I refused to participate in slut-shaming and then acted like she would or should be ashamed.

Simone would forgive me for letting the video get out. Mason had to go down.

CHAPTER TWENTY-SEVEN

By the time my mom came down the stairs the next morning, I was waiting for her with a cup of coffee and her briefcase.

She stopped in the doorway of the kitchen. "What's this?" she asked. We weren't the type of people who made coffee for each other—well, maybe my dad was, but my mom and I certainly were not.

I pushed the coffee toward her. "I need your help."

I started at the beginning.

Within a few hours, I was sitting once again in an interrogation room at 1PP, only this time, my mom was sitting next to me. Rockford was in street clothes, a gray hoodie and skinny jeans, scrutinizing the addresses on the envelopes. The formula sheets in Mason's handwriting were strewn across the desk. I clutched a notebook containing my careful translation.

When he had first walked in, he deliberately put his hand out toward me, his eyes serious. I had shaken it. Now, he looked up at me, his face neutral, professional, and his voice respectful. "How many of these addresses do you know?"

I looked at my mother. "You will follow my every direction," she had commanded as we left the house. "This is nonnegotiable. The moment you resist, I pass you off to another attorney. Is that understood?"

My mother nodded, so I turned back to Rockford. "This one is the Fish Hook," I said, pulling the first envelope toward me. "And this one is a Columbia University library."

"Those I know," he said, with a little grin. "Remember?"

He slammed me against a brick wall once. I remembered. But I needed him to be my ally, so I simply nodded. He nodded back. "What about these other two? These, I don't know."

I picked up the third one. It's in Chelsea. "I don't know this one," I said. "I've never delivered there and it's not one of Mason's spots that I'm aware of. But this one," I picked up the fourth envelope. "This one is interesting."

He took it from me and read out loud. "P.O. Box 346, Cold Spring, NY 10516. I can track the P.O. Box, but can you tell me who it belongs to?"

I shook my head. "But I do know that Mason held a meeting with someone named Leon Cohn at 1286 Brook Trail, in Cold Spring."

Rockford went still. "Leon Cohn?"

"Yeah. It was an important meeting, too. Mason was being *re-*

ally careful. He wouldn't text the address or even give it to Cohn in person himself. He sent *me* to deliver it to him, at the Four Seasons. Why, do you know who he was?"

Rockford leaned forward. "Does the name *Rodney* Cohn mean anything to you?"

"No. Should it?"

He hesitated. "Has Mason has ever mentioned his father?" he asked, a wary catch in his voice.

I sucked in my breath. "Is that his father? Rodney Cohn?"

"So he has mentioned him."

"Not much," I answered, adding up what I knew about Mason's father in my head. "I know that he owns a brownstone in Brooklyn Heights, among other properties. I've always sort of assumed he's at least on the condo board of Simone's building. I mean the one on the Upper West Side, where he has an office. I know that Mason doesn't get along with him. And that he's visiting him in Texas. Right now."

Rockford stood up. He gathered the envelopes and the formula sheets together. "Is it all right with your lawyer if you hang out here for a while?"

His voice sounded like a jump rope pulled tight. My mother eyed him carefully and finally said, "We will do everything we can to cooperate. For now."

Rockford nodded at her and left.

My mother and I were left alone. I looked at her, but she was scrolling through her phone. Her mouth was hard and set. I looked away.

"Who's Simone?"

"What?" I turned back to my mom. That was not a question I expected. "What do you mean?"

She was still looking at her phone, but I noticed that there was nothing on the screen. "You called the building where that awful kid runs his business 'Simone's building.' So who's Simone?" I realized I hadn't ever mentioned Simone by name. I had referred to the girl in the video just as my friend—maybe she'd even assumed it was Audrey. She didn't know anything about my life these days, not even the name of my only friend.

I kept looking at her, wondering when she was going to make eye contact. "She's the girl in the video Mason is using to blackmail me. She's my friend. Or she was."

"So her name is Simone. Your father mentioned the girl who came over cheerful and left considerably paler and slouching."

"He noticed that?"

My mother finally looked up. She turned to me. "He did," she said, uncharacteristically gently. "He does. We both do. We just . . . don't always know what to do about it."

I didn't have a response to that, so I told her, "She doesn't know about the video. She probably thinks I just chickened out of going to the cops and that I'm a scumbag roofie dealer now."

My mother nodded but didn't say anything. She started to put her hand on my shoulder, but Rockford opened the door and she pulled it back, snapping into Judith Evans, Esquire. In a strange moment of synchronicity, I snapped into the girl in the photograph.

Rockford sat down. "So, I sent your calculations with the formula to the Medical Examiner. If she agrees with you, as I suspect she will, we can proceed."

My mother cleared her throat. "Proceed with what, precisely?"

Rockford waited until he caught my eye. And then he grinned. "We can take Mason all the way down."

"And how do we do that?" I asked.

Rockford pulled out a file and opened it to a picture of a dark-haired middle-aged man with sparkling eyes. "This is Rodney Cohn. He and his wife, Louisa Cohn, had one son, Leon. Louisa died of ovarian cancer eight years ago. Twenty-one years ago, Rodney had an affair with a twenty-two-year-old ballerina named Therese Frye. And nine months after it ended, she had Mason."

I looked closer at the picture of Rodney Cohn. The coloring was completely different. Mason must have gotten the blue irises and the blond hair from Therese. But the squirrelly smile and the cheekbones—the blunt stare—that was all from his dad.

"Yeah, I know," said Rockford, reading my look. "It's a little creepy once you see it."

"So, Leon Cohn is Mason's brother?" I pulled the file toward me. "I would never have guessed that."

"I suspect Leon didn't either. As far as we know, Rodney never introduced his sons. They know of each other, but they were kept carefully apart. Therese signed a nondisclosure agreement and received a *very* generous child support package, which, from what we can tell, she used primarily to turn herself into a new money society babe. Don't get me wrong, Mason wasn't materially neglected either. He was sent to the best schools, lived in the best neighborhoods, really had the best of everything. But I doubt that there are a lot of people in Therese's social circle that even know Mason's her son. Rodney kept in touch with him but at a very clear distance. Mason never laid eyes on Louisa, or on his brother."

"So what does Mason want from Leon now?"

Rockford closed the folder and shrugged. "Can't say for sure. But Leon has a gambling problem and he's the CFO of one of his father's companies. My guess is that Mason wanted to involve his father's money in his business. And where his money is, Rodney Cohn is never far behind. My guess is he lured in Leon to implicate Rodney in his affairs."

My mother broke in. "This is fascinating, but what is it you want Kendall to do?"

"Exactly what Mason told her to do."

"What?"

"Deliver the envelopes."

"But . . ."

"No one's going to make any of those 'doses,' Kendall," said Rockford, making conspicuous, contemptuous quotation marks with his fingers. "Mason didn't even give *you* a readable formula. At least he didn't think he did. He keeps that close. I think those notes are a signal. That Columbia address—we found the remains of an old lab in a private study carrel six months ago. The Fish Hook we've known for some time has housed a mobile lab for Mason. Components need to be acquired, new equipment bought. Now that we know to whom these signals are going and when, we can sit on them, collect the evidence. We can actually forge a trail through Mason's whole operation."

I looked at Mom. "And all Kendall has to do is deliver the letters?" she asked.

Rockford hesitated. "Hopefully." My mother raised an eyebrow. "If Mason comes back to town, we need Kendall to stay . . . in character. He can't suspect that we're tracking him. Or he'll clear off. He's done it before."

"He was in Houston," I whispered. They looked at me. "I'm just remembering something Mason said. About hanging around Rice all summer."

Rockford grimaced. "I almost had him last year. But . . ." he looked away. "But, I missed him. I let him get away. I stayed undercover to catch Vin."

The pieces started to fall together. "And you almost got Jerry to roll on him last year, too."

He nodded. "He's been a criminal informant, a CI, for a while. But we couldn't use him as a witness without blowing the case and he was never involved in the actual *drugs* anyway—never even saw them, in fact. Mason was careful. Jerry gathered materials, set up meetings, rented locations, moved money. But he never touched the drugs. So I was directed to drop the Frye investigation."

"Why didn't you, then?"

"Well, I had," he said. He looked at me and smiled,, a genuine smile this time. "Until Jerry came to me and Vin with a story about a high school girl who had gotten involved in Mason's operation. A girl who, it seemed, might be on *my* side."

My mother broke the silence. "I'm going to need to get something on paper with the DA before I agree to let Kendall do anything."

"She's on her way," he said, standing up. "But, for what it's worth, you have my assurance that if Kendall helps us get these guys, she's going to walk away clean." I snorted. He looked at me. "What?"

If I had learned anything this year, it was that *clean* was a relative term. "Nothing," I said.

An hour and a half later, my mom and I walked out of the precinct with a deal. We got in the car and drove off in silence.

"Thank you," I said, once the precinct was out of sight.

She exhaled and looked over her shoulder at me. "You're going to have to be very careful. I want you taking zero risks, do you understand?"

I shrugged. "I know how to handle Mason by now. He likes me. He's not going to hurt me unless he can gain something from it."

Mom winced and shook her head. "That's not what I mean." She turned back to the road. "You're not completely out of the woods, legally. If all goes according to plan, the DA isn't going to charge you with any of what you've already done. But, Ken Doll, if you go off-book here? If you do something that can be construed as abetting Mason and they *don't* catch him? There's a real chance that they *will* charge you. And you turn eighteen in six weeks. I won't be able to get you tried as a juvenile."

It hit me like a volleyball in the nose. But all I could say was, "You called me Ken Doll." She hadn't called me that in weeks.

Mom turned onto the West Side Highway. I looked around. "Why aren't we just getting on the bridge?"

"Because I'm dropping you off at Simone's apartment."

"What? Why?"

She looked at me. "You need a friend, Ken Doll," she said softly. "And it seems like this girl was taking care of you. Better care of you than I was anyway."

"Mom . . ."

She took her sunglasses down from the mirror pocket and slipped them on. "Don't worry," she said. "The guilt's not debilitating. And if I can't take care of you in some ways, I can at least help you with this. I'm a good lawyer, Kendall. And I don't want you to go, but I'm getting you to YATS if it kills me." She turned to me. "You do know that I don't want you to leave, right?"

I hadn't known. I should have, but it hadn't even occurred to me.

I took the elevator up to Simone's apartment and, for the first time, rang the doorbell without the noxious presence of Mason rumbling upward from the floorboards.

A nebbishy man, slightly balding, with thick glasses, opened the door. He looked puzzled to see a teenage girl there but smiled nonetheless.

"Yes?" he asked. "May I help you?"

"Hi, Mr. Moody. My name's Kendall Evans. I'm Simone's friend. Is she home?"

His face softened. "Oh. Kendall. It's nice to meet you. Simone's here, but, is she expecting you?"

"She's not." I frowned. "Is she OK?"

He rumpled his curly hair. "She's OK. She just . . . had a little bit of a long night, I think. Let me just go see if she's up."

"It's OK, Dad," said Simone, strolling into the foyer. She hooked her arm into his briefly and, very slightly, laid her head down, swinging her long, silky hair over his arms. He gently pushed her hair back and she straightened, smiling up at him. Something in me started hurting a little.

"I'm feeling better than I was last night. And I want to see Kendall."

Mr. Moody stood aside and then shut the door behind me. Simone grabbed my hand and followed her father into the open plan dining and living room. He went into the kitchen and Simone sat me down at the table.

"So you got out OK, yesterday?" she asked.

I nodded. She looked calm but tired. When I looked carefully, I saw that her eyes were red around the edges.

Simone spoke first. "I think I should have made sure you were OK last night. I'm sorry, Ken."

I laughed. "No, you shouldn't have."

"No?"

That one word was full of all the arch incredulity at another's very existence that used to terrify me so much about Simone. But now I was overjoyed to hear it.

"I have to tell you something," I blurted out.

"Yeah, I think you do." The scorn was still in her voice, but there was also a bit of raw hurt tucked beneath it. She noticed the crack in her façade and busied herself taking a sip of coffee. I could tell she was itching for a cigarette.

I closed my eyes and whispered the truth:

"Pete and Burke took a video. Mason has it."

I opened my eyes. The coffee cup was still hovering at her lips, her other hand still clutching the tablecloth—Simone hadn't moved an inch.

Butter sizzled in a pan. Simone swallowed what had to be an enormous mouthful of hot coffee and set down the mug.

"Did you hear me? Simone?"

"I heard you," she said quietly. She got up and walked over to the kitchen counter, pouring herself a fresh cup of coffee, plus a second one for me.

"You don't have to do that—"

"Shut up," she cut me off, elegantly balancing both cups, plus a plate of bacon, on her arms and pivoting on her toes. She took the two or three steps back to the table quickly and set down the dishes without a single clink. She sat back down, her back perfectly straight, and reached for the creamer.

Her father came in after her and quietly set down a plate of pancakes, kissed her on the head, and left, reminding me so much of my own father I thought I might cry.

"Do you have any . . . questions?" I asked. "Anything to say?"

Simone finished mixing cream and Sugar In The Raw into her coffee before finally looking at me. "I don't have any questions," she said. I started to say something else, but she put up her hand, stopping me. "I honestly don't, Ken. I understand perfectly what happened. And I don't have anything to say. There's nothing to say."

I took a breath. "Mason's threatened to send it to the whole Howell listserv."

"And that's why you didn't turn him in." It wasn't a question, but I nodded anyway. Simone nodded back. She made a face that was almost a smile. "That was very sweet of you, Kendall. I don't know that I would have done that, though."

I felt myself begin to shake and clutched the cup in front of me. "It felt like the first time I had the chance to do something good for someone else. Like, the first chance since high school started."

"Is that what life's been like?"

I thought a moment. "I don't think I'm as nice a person as I thought I was. And now I'm screwing you over, too."

She waited patiently while I told her about this morning's meeting with Rockford.

"I don't know if it's going to work," I finished glumly. "I don't even know if I'll be able to stay out of jail. But I do know for certain that everyone we know will see that video. Mason will make sure of it."

Simone thought for a moment. She picked up a pancake with her fingers and took a bite of it. Eventually, she started talking.

"Of course I wish that night never happened. Or rather, I wish that they hadn't done what they did. Because of course, it didn't just *happen*. Burke and Pete made a choice to rape me. Grant made a choice to let them. Mason made a choice to exploit it. But the funny thing about that night is that it gave me a kind of emotional shortcut. When it first started to hit me that this was real—that it had really happened—the very first question I asked myself was 'What did I do?' What did I do to make Burke and Pete think that it was OK to drug me and then have sex with my body? I did drink. I had messed around with guys before, even though the rumors far outstripped the truth—I was a virgin at that point. Oh." She raised her eyebrows. "That surprises you. Of course it does. I'm sure it surprised them, too. But had my innate interest in experimenting with my boundaries, in kissing boys, in dressing in clothes that made me feel confident, been the reason they thought it was OK? In other words, was it my fault?"

She paused a moment and looked down at herself. Simone was still in pajamas, or what passed for pajamas with Simone: an ankle-length slip of gold silk, with a slit up to her thigh.

When she looked up from herself, she was smiling for real. She licked syrup off her palm. "I am who I am, Ken. And I like sex. I like to feel good in my skin. And once it really sank in that that night was their fault, *their* problem, and not mine, I got a gift. I got to never, ever feel bad about being myself again. If anyone thinks I deserve to be shunned or denigrated for being the way I am, as long as I don't hurt anybody, I now know, *in my core*, that they can go fuck themselves. So let Mason send out that video. Let him. Let people watch it. If anyone watches that video and thinks anything bad about *me*, they can go fuck themselves. That video is not an indictment of my sluttiness, it's evidence of a rape. I'm not embarrassed by what happens in that video. I'm angry. And anyone who isn't angry after seeing that video should be the ones who are embarrassed."

I didn't know what to say, so, after staring at her blazing eyes, stunned, for what might have been five full minutes, I just said what I was thinking, which was: "I wish I could be like you."

She laughed, a real, genuine laugh, growly and barking. "I know." Her cell phone, laying a few feet away on the other end of the table, went off. She reached for it and then recoiled. "Christ, it's Mikey." She looked closer. "Texting to ask if I've talked to you. Again." She looked at me, exasperated. "What did you do to him?"

"Um, I did fucking nothing to him, except maybe keep him out of jail!"

Simone's brow furrowed. "Wait, what? What did Mikey do?"

"It's really disorienting to hear you call him Mikey. And, not much: He only stole Mason's stash and hacked into my Facebook profile to frame me for it."

Simone dropped her pancake. It fell on the ground, and a little dachshund I don't remember having seen in my previous visit to this apartment scurried out from nowhere and started to eat it.

"No way," said Simone. "He couldn't have."

"He did. Didn't even try to deny it."

Her jaw fell open. "Why would he . . .? I mean . . . how did you even figure it out?"

"Ellie, of all people." Ellie. Sensible, secretive Ellie, protecting me even as she was hating me. "She saw us, um, smiling at each other—we had kind of hooked up, a little bit—"

"You *what*? Gross. Never mind. We'll deal with that later. Continue."

I told her the story, along with Gilly's subsequent, pathetic justification. She sat back in her chair with a wrinkled nose.

"I take it back," she said, the arch contempt fully restored to her voice. "That sounds exactly like something Gilly would do. He feels emotion and, like a Neanderthal, he lashes out. He's been doing it since he was a baby."

"What happened between the two of you, anyway? Can you tell me now?"

"It's stupid. I imagine Gilly hasn't told you because it makes him look bad. But I haven't told you, because it's just dumb." She sighed. "He read my diary."

I laughed. "You're kidding." Her face remained serious and strained. "That's it? He read your diary. And so you two didn't speak for five years. Really?"

She scowled. "He said I was acting snobby, like I thought I was a hot shit high schooler, and so he read my diary out of 'concern.' And then he told Joey Long that I had a crush on him!'"

"Joey Long? That eighth grader who moved back to England before high school?"

"Yes! I had very limited time to get him to like me and Gilly showed him my diary entries about him! Because Joey was 'too old' for me and he was 'worried.' Punk. Like I needed his protection from *myself*. Grow up."

I didn't know whether to laugh or cry. We just wouldn't let him be the knight in shining armor he so desperately wanted to be, would we?

Simone was right. Punk needed to grow up.

CHAPTER TWENTY-EIGHT

OVER THE WEEKEND, I DELIVERED MASON'S LETTERS AS PLANNED, EVEN TAKING METRO-NORTH UP TO COLD SPRING ON MONDAY; MY MOM ALIBIED ME WITH HOWELL, CLAIMING I HAD THE FLU. I wore a wire each time and a little camera that Rockford showed me how to fit into a buttonhole. Rockford was too well known in Mason's milieu, but another cop, dressed in street clothes, named Mendoza, always tailed me there, so they could set up a monitoring plan.

I debriefed with Rockford after each delivery, handing over the wire and the camera, but, honestly, there was never very much to say.

"So, how's it going?" I asked, as I unscrewed the button cam after my third delivery, to the mysterious Chelsea address, which turned out to be an HVAC repair shop. The guy I had delivered the letter to had been a very pleasant, older gentleman who had offered me tea. He clearly didn't know what he was hosting.

"What do you mean?" asked Rockford. He was distracted, plugging the recording device into his laptop.

"There's nothing on that tape, Rockford." He looked up at me.

"That's why I'm asking how it's going—'it' being the investigation. Because, from where I'm sitting, we're not getting anywhere."

He sat down across from me. "We're not there yet. But we are getting somewhere. We subpoenaed the bank records of every person you've followed and isolated payments from an account on Saint Lucia in the Caribbean. If anyone in the United States transfers funds there, we can track it. Even if it's through a dummy account, there will be a paper trail we can follow. We're working with campus security at Columbia and we've cataloged everything that kid you delivered the note to has set up in his study carrel. And we're very close to flipping Trev. He just operates the bar for his cousin, who it seems is the one that originally made contact with Mason."

I absorbed that information and then realized that he was leaving something out. "What about the PO Box in Cold Spring? Do we know who picked up the letter?"

He coughed. "Leon Cohn picked that up. He seems like he's staying in the area, but he's stopped using plastic, so we're not sure where."

"What about the address I gave you?"

"It's a bait and tackle shop. The manager there had never heard of Mason Frye."

"So . . ." I thought through everything. "You have everyone *except* Mason."

"Mason and his father. Who is more connected with a few suspicious import/exporters than we'd like, so we'd like to bring him down with his kid if we can. Which we think was the point of Mason bringing in Leon and his dad's money by proxy. If shit hits the fan, Rodney has an incentive to protect Mason, because it's also protecting himself."

It made sense to me. Mason liked insurance policies. "But you have nothing directly connecting Mason to any of this," I clarified. "Except my word."

He nodded. "We need his name on an account or his voice on tape, or we need you to actually see him fabricate, sell, or otherwise traffic the drugs. Otherwise, his father has enough expensive lawyers to make it possible that he walks."

"And I've pretty much only seen him play video games, flirt, and menace high school girls," I said glumly. *And my reputation makes it so that I'm not a credible enough witness on my own*, I silently added.

"Right. He's good at this. But this is how you build a case and we're going to get another shot at him."

"How do you know that? I haven't heard from him."

"Because I have a friend in the TSA who tipped me off that Mason got on a plane to Newark this morning. He should be back in Manhattan by now."

Just then, my backpack started vibrating on the table. My real phone was in my pocket.

The backpack vibrated again. I reached across and pulled out the Barbie phone. Rockford raised his eyebrows at the pink case and I put my finger to my lips.

I pressed accept.

"Mason," I said, throwing my head to the side and flipping out my hair without even thinking about it.

"Kendall, dearest," came back his honeyed tenor tone. "Miss me?"

"No," I answered. "Enjoyed the break. Did some homework. Spoke to people who weren't sleaze-balls. You know."

"Well don't worry, they were sleaze-balls inside. Everyone is. What are you doing tonight? Are you busy?"

My heart sped up. "I didn't think we were back in operation." Rockford leaned forward eagerly.

"You don't know a dinner invitation when you hear one? You really are such a *kid*."

A plan snuck into my head and shook off its clothes.

"Kendall, you there? Are you sifting through your dance card?"

"No, no, I was just distracted by something on the TV," I said quickly. "I can go to dinner."

"Good," he said. "I wanted to thank you for taking care of those little errands for me this week. They *are* all done, right?"

"Yes, master," I snapped. "I told you that they would get done and they did."

"Fine, fine. Untwist your panties. Can you get to Laundromat in an hour? I'm starving and if we get there any later, it'll be hours before we eat."

Laundromat was a trendy restaurant a couple of blocks from Howell. It was only twenty minutes away from the police station by subway. "Sure. See you in an hour." Mason hung up.

"What's going on?" asked Rockford as soon as I put the phone back in my bag.

"I'm meeting Mason for dinner."

"Is that . . . ? Were you guys going out to dinner a lot?"

His voice was pert and judging. I was about to give him the finger, but then I remembered how I had twined my arm around Mason's neck at James Greenberger's party and decided to pre-emptively shut up.

"If I can get him to the Fish Hook lab, or on tape talking about making the doses, can you be ready to nab him?"

Rockford's eyes narrowed. "What is it you're planning to do?"

"I'm going to tell him that I figured out the formula."

He drew in his breath. "No. You're not going to do that."

"Why not?"

"Because it's dangerous and your mother will kill me."

I lifted my head, sure that I was right. "You don't understand my relationship with Mason. That I'm suspicious of people and a sneak is what he likes about me. If I play into that, I think I can draw him out."

Rockford took off his glasses and rubbed his eyes. "How does a girl like you get to be a girl like you?"

I was really tired of everyone telling me what kind of girl I was. "Just lucky, I guess."

He put his glasses back on and set his jaw. "No. I will wire you up and we will be waiting outside of the restaurant in case he says anything that gives us probable cause. You will, however, not go with him anywhere. It's my ass if anything happens to you."

We had been friendly lately, but the image of him flipping a pocketknife in front of my face flashed before my eyes. I made a snap decision and lied. "Fine," I said. He didn't care about my ass, so why should I care about his?

I let him wire me up and then left the station on my own steam. The uniforms would be waiting for me there. It wouldn't do to let Mason see me in a police car.

The air on the street was sharp and I could see my breath, blue and misty, as I sprinted down the pavement to the station. When I turned the corner, the police station out of sight, I ducked under scaffolding overhanging an anonymous corporate building.

I did not intend to obey Rockford, not if it meant I could end this. They had everyone ready to go down, except for the one person that I wanted to go down. I had come too far to risk Mason getting away.

Quickly turning my back to the street, I unzipped my backpack and plugged the code into the combination lock on the pouch, half-forgotten, buried at the bottom of my bag. I took a breath and pulled out Rockford's knife. Then it was back into the cold, the hilt of Rockford's knife beating against my chest from where it lay sheathed front and center in my bra.

By the time I got to Laundromat, Mason already had a table. I slumped into the chair, sweaty and heaving. I had run all the way from the train.

"You're early," Mason said with a smile. "I haven't even had a chance to hit on the waitress yet."

I drank about four-fifths of my water in one gulp. "Don't let me stop you," I gasped, before drinking the rest of it.

He shrugged. "Nah. It's no fun now that you're here."

Finally catching my breath, I shook off my coat. "Sorry. You'll just have to hit on me instead."

"It's been a very long game."

I gave him as cold a look as I could summon through the sheen of sweat on my face and he laughed right in it.

We ordered and I scanned the room, looking for Mendoza. I found him in a dark corner of the bar.

"So how was your trip?" I asked.

Mason's face went a little slack and then blank. It was as if he had shaken an Etch A Sketch, so that nothing showed up in his features. "It was fine. Like I said, I was seeing my father."

"This is the father you don't get along with."

"You remembered. That's sweet."

We had nearly finished the appetizer—which I had bolted down, suddenly realizing that I was starving—by the time he spoke again.

"I never had the chance to ask you: How was jail?"

"Oh, it was super fun," I said, mildly. Again, I lied, telling him something I knew he'd be amused to hear. "I loved sweet-talking Grant into bailing me out. It's always fun to prostrate myself in front of him."

Mason smiled wickedly. Fondly. My stomach turned. A soft, comforting, secret bundle in the pit of my stomach that I hadn't wanted to acknowledge, a satisfaction at being seen, even by *him*, was dissolving. I was betraying him. He didn't know me.

No one does. Not even me. What am I doing here?

A familiar laugh and gasp made me twist my head around. My jaw fell open.

Behind me, at the maître d' stand was an incongruous knot of Howell kids, including Audrey, Ellie, and, of all people, Gilly. What could they possibly all be doing together?

"I thought this was a date, Kendall," said Mason, his voice dry. "What are all of your friends doing crashing our happy reunion?"

"Not a clue," I answered, honestly. I looked closer at the group and it clicked. Naya and Luca were in the group and so were Drew and Dave Lemon. It was November already.

"It's the dress rehearsal of the play," I said out loud. "They all go out to a fancy dinner before, even the stage crew guys. I went when Naya was in *The Crucible* last year. They won't sit together." And sure enough, Audrey, Ellie, Naya, and the other "acceptable" theater kids (basically the ones who did track or baseball in the spring and skipped the musical) sat at one table, and Gilly and his gangly, mopey cohort sat at another.

"That's fascinating, Kendall. There's nothing I find more enthralling than the social intricacies of high school extracurricular activities."

Gilly had seen me right away and was looking at me with tortured, liquid eyes. I tore my gaze away, back to Mason. "I'm sorry, Mason. What would you prefer to talk about? The state of the New York art scene? Favorite books? Mid-season replacement TV shows we're excited about?"

"Aw come on, kiddo, you can do better than that. Come on, dazzle me with those mean girl wits. Give me something good."

This was my opening. "I can tell you about how I broke your code."

His smile stayed in place but drained out of his eyes. I saw Mendoza touch his earpiece. Rockford had heard me. I might not have much time.

I spoke faster. "Is that why you wanted to use a kid like me, instead of other college students? Did you think I'd be too entrenched in the social intricacies of high school extracurricular activities to be curious? Or did you just think you were smarter than me?"

Mason leaned forward, his eyes a diamond-tipped drill. "Maybe I wanted you to figure it out."

I met his eyes. "And why would you want me to know that you're the one that makes the pills?" *Come on, come on. Say you make them. Lean forward just like that, so I can get it on tape.*

That would have been too easy. Mason just smiled and said lightly, "I like seeing you live up to your potential, Kendall." I caught eyes with Mendoza who sympathetically shook his head. That wasn't an admission of guilt.

I was suddenly furious. "You like seeing me live up to my potential? You couldn't just leave me alone? I had worked very hard to be a certain girl and I was very good at being that girl, until I wasn't. And I fucked up. But that was going to be *fine*, because I chose someone else I wanted to be, someone who could use her brain to escape Grant, and Audrey, and Howell, and just go study space and *you're* the one who fucked *that* up. *You* made me be the girl in the picture!" My voice was getting louder, the rest of the dining room quieter. I saw Audrey lift her hand to quiet her table. She was listening intently. It didn't matter.

I looked back at Mason. "All this because I wasn't living up to your estimation of my potential." I shook my head, disgusted. "When will people stop telling me what kind of girl I am?"

Mason looked confused. He opened his mouth to say something but was interrupted.

Gilly was standing at my elbow.

Mason looked up at him curiously. "Can I help you?" He looked a little closer. "We've met, right?"

Gilly didn't even look at Mason. His eyes were set directly on me. Suddenly he went down on his knees, put his hand over his heart, and started speaking.

"Daylight and Champaign discovers not more," he said, in a rich, unctuous, *hilarious* voice. "This is open. I will be proud, I will read politic authors, I will baffle Sir Toby, I will wash off gross acquaintance, I will be point-devise the very man. I do not now fool myself, to let imagination jade me; for every reason excites to this, that my lady loves me." I remembered this. This was the monologue I had laughed at.

Gilly gestured at himself, pride in every line. "She did commend my yellow stockings of late, she did praise my leg being cross-gartered," he continued. "And in this she manifests herself to my love, and with a kind of injunction drives me to these habits of her liking."

I felt my jaw hanging open like a fish, but I couldn't make it shut. I didn't want it to. This was the weirdest thing I had ever seen. This was the best thing I had ever seen.

Laundromat was silent. Gilly worked the room, sighing and gazing across the tables until his eyes fell on me. He lowered them to my lap, and took my hand, saying, quietly, softly, "I thank my stars I am happy. I will be strange, stout, in yellow stockings, and cross-gartered, even with the swiftness of putting on. Jove and my stars be praised!"

There was a silence until the tech table exploded into raucous applause and whistles. Gilly tried to bite down on a smile but couldn't quite conceal it. He looked up at me, appeal and warmth and something else I couldn't identify radiating from his eyes. Something . . . *loving*?

Ick? Or . . . maybe . . . aw? I knew I should be able to tell the difference, but I couldn't.

Gilly got to his feet, still holding my hand. "That was very good," I told him. "Very funny." He smiled again, a full-bloom grin this time.

Mason cleared his throat. "I love dinner theater as much as the next guy—meaning I'll tolerate it if someone else is paying—but, as it happens, I intend to be the one paying for this meal, so can you go away, please?"

Gilly flinched and dropped my hand. I tried to warn him with my eyes to go away. He wouldn't break eye contact, so I ventured to shake my head, using movements as miniscule as I could manage.

Gilly seemed to understand a little, because his face got scared. His gaze flickered to Mason and he practically snarled. Then he walked back to his table, and the clamor of the restaurant resumed.

Mason observed all of this closely, sipping his drink the whole time. He did that so he seemed casual, but I knew his eyes well enough to know that he hadn't missed anything about that interaction.

"So who was that?" he asked. "*What* was that?"

I focused on my water glass. "That was . . . my friend. Sort of. He's weird."

"Clearly. He's a new friend?"

"Kind of. Why do you ask?"

"Because your old friends are staring at you."

Audrey and Ellie were indeed staring at me. Audrey had her eyebrows arched and her lips pursed, in a tolerant condescension that I recognized. Ellie just looked like she was trying not to laugh.

I forced my focus back on Mason. "What were we talking about?" I asked.

"You were yelling at me for objectifying you."

He started to speak, but then sat back and stared at something behind my shoulder. I turned just in time to see a black Crown Victoria pull up outside the restaurant. I could make out Rockford in the passenger side.

Mason looked around the bar and caught sight of Mendoza just as he put his hand down from his ear. He turned back to me, his eyes full of ice.

"What did you do?" he hissed.

"Nothing," I whispered back. "You're paranoid."

Mason grabbed my hand and jerked me out of my chair. The menace that had always been under the surface of his crooked smile and pretty eyes was written in every muscle of his face and radiating through his fingers to my rapidly bruising wrist.

With his other hand, he pulled out cash, lots of cash, more cash than the bill would have been, and threw it on the table. "We're going to walk toward the bathrooms now," he said in a low tone. "You're going to walk with me like we're about to hook up. Now."

I looked behind me. The Crown Vic was still there. They had told me to play the part, so I got up, my wrist still held in Mason's hand like a vise, and led the way to the bathrooms downstairs. Once there, Mason changed directions and bolted toward the service entrance on the other side of the hall. It was the kind restaurants used for deliveries and led up a rickety, narrow set of stairs directly to the back alley. He pushed me in front of him, his arm across my waist, almost like an embrace, and in a few steps, we were outside.

I had left my coat inside and started shivering. He had, too, but didn't seem to mind the cold. He pushed me forward until we reached a Prius—the same Prius from the photo on my Facebook album.

I had never given that picture to Rockford, even though it had plates in it. It had seemed irrelevant. It hadn't occurred to me.

This suddenly seemed deeply stupid.

He unlocked the door and I opened my mouth to scream for Rockford, but Mason did the last thing I had ever really expected him to do.

I thought he might drug me. I thought he might punch me. I even thought he might cut me—if I had a knife, anyone could have one.

What I hadn't expected him to do was pull out a dull black and terrifying handgun.

CHAPTER TWENTY-FIVE

OUR RIDE OUT OF THE CITY WAS SILENT. Which was too bad, because the receiver in Mendoza's ear and Rockford's car had a limited range, and I would have liked the wire strapped to my chest to transmit some useful information for once. But once Mason pulled out a gun, there was very little left to say. He kept one hand on the wheel and one hand on the grip, a finger hovering centimeters behind the trigger. The barrel rested on the cup holder, aimed up toward me. I didn't have my cell phone. Once Mason got me in the car, he made me throw it out the window.

We'd been on the road for almost an hour before Mason finally spoke, just as he exited the highway onto the more poorly lit and less populated roads of upper Westchester County, New York.

"Don't you want to know where we're going?" he asked.

"Do you want to tell me?" I was pleased my voice came out steady.

"We're going to just outside Cold Spring," he said, turning onto a wooded, dirt road. "My father has a compound. He uses it for fishing mostly."

"And that's why you have a P.O. Box in Cold Spring."

"It's why I set one up in Cold Spring, but I think you'll find that my name's never been connected to it. And there's no address on the compound, because it was built on a private parcel of land. My dad's name isn't on the deed. They'll trace the ownership eventually, but you and I will be gone before they do."

I felt myself start to breathe fast. I counted the ruts in the road as the Prius bounced over them. *One, two, three. One, two, three.*

My heart slowed enough for me to grasp at self-preservation. "They?" I asked as airily as I could. "Who's they?"

"Don't play dumb, Kendall. I might be the only person in your life who doesn't like it."

I looked at him. He was driving slowly, his hand gripping the gun so tightly his knuckles were white.

"You want me to stop playing dumb, Mason? Fine, I will. But stop playing gangster. Put the gun down and focus on the road. It's pitch black out and freezing. I don't have a coat. I don't have a phone. I don't have any knowledge of the area. I'm not going to jump out of the car and try to make a break for it. Relax."

He looked over at me, his eyes wary, crunching the numbers. Ultimately, he shook his head. "It's a nice try. But I keep my hand on this gun until I can put it in a place where you can't get at it," he told me. "Appreciate that I don't underestimate you, Kendall. It's why I wanted to keep you."

Mason turned up a steep incline and reached into his pocket, bringing out what looked like an old-fashioned pager. He hit a button on the top and a huge, iron gate I hadn't even noticed opened in front of us.

He tossed the button on the dash and drove us through. The gate shut behind us.

So this was Mason's dad's complex.

I pressed my face to the window, trying to memorize the lay of the land.

"You said we'd be gone before the cops found us," I said. "Why even bother stopping here?"

I felt the dirt road underneath the car turn into smooth pavement and turned to face the front. We had pulled up to a low but sprawling midcentury house of blond wood and glass.

Mason shut the car off and threw the keys on the dash. "Because this house has a helicopter pad."

The lights were on throughout the house. Mason pulled me out of the car and through the unlocked front door.

Clutching my arm with one hand and hitting the safety on the gun with the other, Mason called out, casually, "We've got company, bro."

Leon walked out of the kitchen, looking disconcertingly homey and reassuring in bare feet and sweatpants. He had a tentatively pleasant smile on his face, which drained to alarm when he saw me. He stopped short.

"What is this?" he asked, standing still. "What is Kendall doing here? Why are you here so early?"

Now that I knew they were brothers, I could see the resemblance. Leon must have gotten *his* coloring from Louisa Cohn, which might have been why I had missed it. He had neither the twisted Disney prince affect of Mason nor the Bond villain styling of his father. He was a soothing beige type: lightly tanned skin, softly curling, light brown hair, and those calming gray eyes. But the angles in his face matched Mason's exactly, and the confident way he moved.

The initial hit of charisma was the same. But where Mason was an ice pick, Leon was a back massager.

I looked up at Mason. He was looking at his brother with a mixture of disgust and affection. *I'd be jealous, too*, I thought. Leon had simply lucked out.

"Exigent circumstances," answered Mason, shortly, handing me over to Leon, who gingerly took my arm, much more gently than his brother had. Mason walked the gun over to a wall safe and started turning the knob. "Your good friend Kendall has been working with the police."

Leon turned white. He turned to me. "How much do they know?" he asked.

Mason, assuming the question was directed to him, shrugged.

"I imagine they don't have enough to arrest me or they already would have. I don't know what they know about you, Leon. But Kendall and her potential testimony are coming with us to Saint Lucia, anyway, so we're safe."

"What?" Leon and I asked in unison. We looked briefly at each other.

"I'm not going to Saint Lucia," I said, my voice trembling against my will.

"That wasn't always the plan, was it?" asked Leon, confused. "Why would she?"

Mason didn't answer us. He put the gun in the safe, shut the door, and walked toward us. He looked at where Leon was still holding my arm. Leon saw him looking and dropped it like it was electrified. "Call Dad," said Mason, not unkindly. "Tell him we need the chopper here, now, as soon as possible, and the house ready and waiting for us, or he's risking his own skin."

Leon bit his lip and took a step closer to me, as if he wanted to protect me. "What are you going to do with her?" he asked, and I realized that he was scared of his little brother.

Mason knew it, too. He narrowed his eyes at his brother. "Feed her," he told him, in a tone of voice that said this should be obvious. "Find her a sweater and some caffeine. It might be a long night." He sighed and rubbed his temple. "Make the call, Leon. He'll like to hear from you more than he would from me."

Leon looked his brother in the eyes for a moment, as if searching for something. Eventually, he sighed and rubbed his head in almost the exact same gesture Mason had used and headed to a side room, pulling a cell phone out of his pocket and sneaking a last backward glance at the two of us before shutting the door.

We watched him go. When we were alone, Mason turned back to me. "Do you actually want some coffee?" he asked.

"Not really."

"Well, I'm making us some anyway. I want to be ready to leave."

He walked into the kitchen and, having nowhere else to go, I followed him. It was straight out of a cooking show, all gleaming surfaces and wood accents. I surveyed the room and my eyes landed on a wall phone.

Mason walked into a pantry and I made a beeline for it, but had only gotten through to an operator saying, "911, what's your emergency?" when a finger reached over my head and hit the hang up button.

I looked up at Mason, who shook his head and said, "No dice, kiddo."

He walked to the fridge and stuck his head in it, staring blankly at its contents. "So, we're running away together, huh?" I asked.

Mason laughed, but he didn't sound like he thought it was funny. "Guess so," he said. "My little partner-in-crime."

He looked me in the eye and I got a faint hint of the magnetism

I had felt that first afternoon in the basement of Simone's building, and at his party. I could still feel it, buried under everything else I felt about him. It made me angrier than ever.

"There's something very . . . unnerving about you, Kendall," he continued, reaching into the fridge. "You are a very scary little girl."

"Yes, you seem terrified."

Mason chuckled. "I'm bigger than you. That helps. Also, you like me. That helps, too."

"I don't like you," I muttered, clenching my fists. "I never liked you."

"Oh, no?" He pulled out a baking dish of macaroni and cheese and set it on the kitchen island. He took off the top and started eating it cold with his fingers. He offered it to me, but I didn't respond. "Maybe you *don't* like me. Turning down mac and cheese. What kind of teenage girl are you?"

"None of your business."

He reached for me, but I stepped out of range. "You know why I want you with me even though you're a scary little girl who claims not to like me?" he asked, his voice controlled and casual.

"*No*," I said emphatically. "Mason, I don't know. Why can't you just leave me alone?"

He stood upright, pressing his palms against the counter. He looked down. "Because you're *me*. Because I see you. I see the part of you that you like to pretend doesn't exist."

"You see that, huh?" I scoffed. "And what part is that?"

He smiled a bittersweet smile. "You're a destroyer of worlds. You just started with your own." I drew in a sharp breath. "You realize, of course, that you could have crawled back to Audrey Khalil. You knew what you had to do. You had the skill set. You could have groveled and you would have gotten most of your life back. But you didn't do that. And that's not even mentioning how you deliberately blew it all up in the first place." My head shot up and again he smiled. "Come on, Kendall. Grant Powers? *Grant Powers?* If you really wanted to protect your world, Grant Powers would never have been incentive enough to risk it all. You know that. You always knew that. In more ways than one, he was a tool. You used him as an improvised explosive device."

I absorbed every word. They sank into my skin like fat, slow raindrops. Every one of them was true.

I looked at Mason and saw him for what he was. He was a skinny kid, only a few years older than me, and he was all alone.

Of course, that wasn't all he was. He was also a criminal—a blackmailer and an accessory to rape. He was cruel and callous. He was lacking in empathy. He had done immense damage and felt no remorse about any of it. He was ruthless.

Give me another couple of years. I bet I could become that ruthless. I could become cold.

Mason must have sensed a weakness, a softening of the tension, because he moved closer to me. "I blew up my world, too," he said. "And I don't regret it any more than you do. It doesn't mean I don't want any company."

The air between us, too narrow to be an effective perimeter, crackled. I angled my head backward and remembered something I had forgotten the moment Mason pulled out that gun.

I had a knife in my bra. And, of course, a wire—of dubious functionality so far from the city—a few inches below that. If I used the former to escape, hopefully I could use the latter to finish my job.

Leon walked into the kitchen, stopping in the doorway at the sight of the two of us, locked in whatever it was we were locked in: embrace, challenge, war? I wasn't sure.

He cleared his throat. "The helicopter will be here within the hour. Do you have enough cash on you?"

The spell broke. Mason straightened up and turned back to the mac and cheese. "I need to gather some basics together, but I've got things set up in Saint Lucia. It will be good enough for me anyway." He pulled out his phone and made a few quick maneuvers with his spindly fingers. "I'll go get them now. Stay with her, will you? Make sure she doesn't use the phone."

Leon nodded but seemed unwilling to look at me. Mason brushed past his brother into the hall and then doubled back, turning to me. "Kendall?" he asked.

"What?"

"Just so you know, what I just did on this burner? That was me sending out the video of Simone. I've had it set up as a draft email for weeks, for just this occasion."

Even though I knew Simone would be fine, my fingers itched for the knife. I forced them down, curving them around a kitchen stool. "Why did you have to do that? I can't hurt you anymore."

"Because we had a deal." He tapped his very utilitarian phone. "I don't break my word, even for you." He turned around.

Still gripping the stool, I craned my neck, watching as he returned to the wall safe. He unlocked it and retrieved the gun before bounding up the stairs.

Leon coughed. "I'm sorry about my brother. I'm sorry you're here."

I looked away. "Not sorry enough," I told him through clenched teeth. "Or else I wouldn't be here."

Now that Mason was out of the room, Leon seemed to find it easier to make eye contact with me. He stepped closer and stretched out a sympathetic hand. "Believe me, if there was anything I could do—"

"Save it. You're a coward and I'm not interested in you. Just lock me in a room without a telephone and leave me alone."

He sighed. "I'm not going to do that."

"Why not? You're going to put me on a helicopter against my will, without any ID or money, without telling my parents. Do you know how old I am, Leon?"

He cracked a sad smile. "Younger than you look, you said. But smarter than you seem."

Frustratingly, I felt myself softening at his smile. "How did you let yourself get mixed up in this?" I asked him. "Did you get so in the red with gambling debts that this was your *only* choice? *Really*?"

He eyes widened with surprise, but, to his minor credit, he didn't bother to deny it. "Yes," he said simply. "I used the corporate account to pay off a debt—one of a few. I embezzled, but I made the withdrawal in my father's name. Somehow Mason found out who else I owed and bought out my debt. I don't know how he found it, how he *did* it, but the kid seems to be good at this."

"He is." I told him. "Although I don't know that he would appreciate being called 'the kid' by his big brother." Leon looked at me sharply. "When did you find out?" I asked.

"In our first meeting," he said. "He told me after I had already agreed to put my—*our*—dad's money into his business. But if I'm being honest, I knew the second I saw him. He looks so much like dad. He *is* dad."

"So then why did Mason want so badly to fuck him over?" I asked, not even meaning to say it out loud. Because of course I knew the answer.

I looked at Leon. "Your father's kind of a shit, isn't he?"

Leon stiffened. "You don't know anything about him. He was a good dad to me."

I laughed. "I'm sure he was," I told him. "To *you*."

Leon took a step away and looked at me closely, as if I was a picture that was coming into focus for the first time. And he didn't like what he saw.

"You're taking *his* side?" he asked, revulsion lining the pleasant timbre of his voice.

"You mean your *brother's* side?" I answered sharply. "No. But I'm not taking *Rodney's* side either. Now put me in a place without a telephone and leave me alone."

He sighed again. "There's no need for you to be alone. You're just a kid—"

"No, I'm *serious*," I said, cutting him off. "That's what I *want*." I looked at him and forced my face to go soft. "Please? I'm so nervous. It would be kind." I let my lower lip quiver a little. "Please, understand."

Leon's whole body seemed to yield like Silly Putty. He still looked at me suspiciously, but he also nodded and said, "Follow me."

I took his hand and let him lead me into a leathery study. "Thank you," I whispered.

Leon seemed to have cheered up a little, clearly relieved to have the opportunity to be nice to me. "Of course. I'll give you a minute."

I swayed a little and smiled a thin, watery smile. "I appreciate it," I said meekly.

He smiled and shut the door slowly, looking at me sympathetically the whole time.

As soon as I heard the lock turn in the door, I dropped my smile. I went into a corner in the back of the room, far from view of anyone who might be lurking outside the windows, and swiftly unbuttoned my shirt.

I got the knife out first. I checked the mechanism, flipping the blade out and in and out again, before setting it on a nearby shelf. Then I untangled the wire and looked at it.

I knew that once we had left the city, we were out of range of Rockford's receiver, but the red light was still on, so it seemed possible that it was still recording, even now. But what to do with it? It was sheer luck that Mason hadn't searched me yet. I couldn't leave it in my shirt. Mason wouldn't scruple to pat down my stomach or chest and he would feel the wire.

Was there anywhere he wouldn't search? I considered putting it in my underwear, but my pants were too tight. It would show through my jeans.

I couldn't let Mason destroy anything that might be evidence.

I scanned the room, looking for something to transport it in, but there was nothing I could credibly take with me. No bags or even hats to hide it under.

The lock started to turn.

I thrust my arms behind me and backed away toward the open window. The door opened and Mason poked his head in, a duffel bag slung across his shoulder.

"What are you up to?" he asked. "What are you doing all the way back there?"

I opened my fist behind my back and dropped the wire into the rosebush under the ledge.

"Nothing," I said.

CHAPTER TWENTY-SIX

MASON DID SEARCH ME AFTER THAT. IT WAS JUST A PAT DOWN, BUT THERE'S NOT A PLACE ON MY BODY I COULD HAVE HIDDEN THAT WIRE WHERE HE WOULDN'T HAVE FOUND IT.

As Mason bent over my calves, my eye wandered to the bookshelf where I had set the knife.

"You almost done?" I asked, still eyeing the knife. He stopped and I looked down at him. *If I could just distract him . . .*

"Why don't you just make me take my clothes off again?" I sneered. "Wouldn't that be easier?"

He stood up. "I never made you take your clothes off."

I raised my eyebrow. "No? When you bought me that dress before James Greenberger's party? I didn't realize it was so forgettable. And here I thought you liked me."

He laughed, this time for real. "I didn't *make* you take your clothes off. I handed you the dress and told you to try it on. You could have gone into the supply closet. Or just said no. You did that all by yourself."

"I did that because you were being an asshole," I said hotly. *I wasn't going to back down in front of you.*

"You did that because you weren't about to back down," he said, echoing the voice in my head. "And you liked it."

I didn't answer. Mason looked disappointed. He checked his watch. "It's time for us to head out, little girl. Our grand adventure begins."

He picked up his bag and reached out for my hand. I pulled back. This was happening too fast. It couldn't be happening this fast.

"Wait," I said, planting my feet, scrambling for any delay. "I don't have any clothes. I don't have my *passport*."

Mason just tightened his grasp on my hand. "You won't need one. My father will have taken care of all of that. We just need to be on that helicopter. Now."

I wrenched my hand away and backed up to the window.

Mason looked at me thoughtfully and dropped his bag. He stepped closer and closer to me, but I had nowhere to retreat to, so eventually he reached me.

He lifted a hand and smoothed back my hair. "Come on, Barbie," he said softly. "Be a good girl."

My trembling stopped. It was like someone had replaced a cracked screen on a laptop. I could see clearly. Mason continued to brush back my hair. I stared straight ahead and saw things. I saw the duffel bag that was Mason's only luggage. I saw the globe on a polished wooden floor stand. I saw the file cabinet with its shiny brass knobs. I saw the desk to my right: blotter pad, laptop, wooden box full of paper clips. And I looked to the left and I saw

Rockford's knife waiting for me on the bookshelf.

I looked at Mason. His bright blue eyes had never been closer. He had never been closer. "Why did you call me that?" I asked him.

"Barbie?"

"Yes. Only one other person has ever called me that."

"I called you Barbie for the same reason he called you Barbie. Because you're pretty, blond, and adaptable. But I also called you that because *I* know you're a survivor. You'll live through anything, you'll see. You're like a cockroach."

I smiled for real then. Mason noticed it and pulled his head back a centimeter. "What? What did I say?"

I put my hand on his cheek. I had never touched him for no-nutilitarian purposes before. His bones impressed themselves onto my skin and I felt a moment of gratitude and recognition, mingled with the customary disgust.

I looked at him hard. Whatever happened, this would be the last time I felt anything about him at all. I should try to remember it.

"What?" he asked again. His fingers tightened around my hair. "Are you ready to admit that I'm right? That this is the best way?"

I stroked his skin, smooth and supple, down to his collarbone. I held my palm there. "I've been called a lot of things over the past few months," I told him. "I've been called a good girl, a bad girl, a little girl, Ken Doll, Skipper, Ken, and Barbie. I've never been called a cockroach. And it's my absolute favorite."

I reached out my free hand to the desk, flipped the laptop up and smashed it into Mason's head.

Wailing, he careened into the bookshelf, shaking it and knocking the knife to the ground. I dodged as he fell to the floor and dipped to pick up the knife.

Mason was down. Still brandishing the laptop, I stepped around him and grabbed the duffel bag. Whatever evidence there was to salvage against Mason would be in it.

Mason was still down. He looked unconscious. I put down the laptop and peered out the window. He started to groan.

I jumped.

We were on the first floor, but the window was still several feet off the ground. I got tangled up in the rosebush, scratching my arms, and fell heavily on the damp grass.

The wire was in front of me. I grabbed it and clambered to my feet.

I instantly fell again. I had twisted my ankle.

Mason's groans got louder, so I ran anyway, wincing with every step.

It was cold and dark. The frost hit me like a punch, raising all the little hairs on my arms, and I couldn't see my feet as they grappled with the dying foliage littering the lawn.

I followed the line of the house until I got to the driveway, and then I sprinted to the car, wincing through the pain in my ankle, trying to ignore the crashes and yells coming from the house. I made it onto gravel and was feet away from the car when I heard a shattering of glass and a bang behind me.

I stretched my arm out for the driver's side door and wrenched it open, falling over my injured ankle. I scrambled to maneuver my body into the car, but there was a pulse of footsteps behind me, like a racing heartbeat, and Mason suddenly had his arms around me, almost like an embrace.

The momentum knocked me into the car, face down on the upholstery, and I lost hold of the knife. Mason's wrists were under my torso, pinned down by my hipbones. I pressed into them, trying to use them as leverage to twist my body around and free my legs. He growled.

"I was there that night, you know," he whispered in my ear. "With your friend."

I writhed and thrashed but couldn't escape. He only tightened his grasp and dug his fingernails into my shoulder.

"While Simone was lying in your boyfriend's bed, naked, I was standing over her, watching her," he continued, hissing like a snake.

"How?" It came out sounding like a sob.

"Powers fucked up," he sneered. "He let those little pricks snag the dose. It wasn't ready to be out yet and, of course, he panicked and called me. I had to scare him into line and get those other two out of there." He lifted a hand and ran his fingertip across my collarbone. "I didn't mean for that to happen, but it brought me to you, so I'm grateful."

I flinched at the freedom from his grip. I slowly flexed and leaned back into him, laying the line of my arm down his abdomen, fist clenched. His cell phone was in his pocket.

Mason pulled my hair back, wrenching up my face, twisting it so I was forced to look at him. "You don't have anything to say?"

I did what he wanted and looked him in the eyes. "We're not the same, Mason," I said, my breathing labored, as I struggled to maneuver. My arm was splayed out in front of me, Mason's entire weight pressing on my shoulder blades: I couldn't move them.

He put his mouth right up against the crease where my jaw met my throat. "You enjoy power. You scheme for it. You feel the urge to destroy, to wreck, to dominate. And you're mean and selfish. It's close enough for me. As close as I've gotten."

"I'm not a rapist," I hissed. I shifted, trying to reach the knife. "I'm not like you."

He laughed, manic. A drop of blood splattered onto my collarbone, and I saw that he was bleeding from the head. "I'm not a rapist either. I'm a scientist. I'm like you. I like to make things. Look at what I accomplished with you."

It was my turn to growl. "You didn't make me into anything."

He pulled my hair again. "No, I didn't. I gave you a way to be more yourself. And I made that drug because it's there to make. They're just chemicals. They're not choices or actions. It's just a set of chemicals that I put together a certain way. Whatever happens after that has nothing to do with me."

I moved my one free hand, experimenting with its range of motion. "And you like people to be afraid of you."

"Irrelevant. That's just human nature. We seek power. This was the power available to me."

I smiled. "And that's how we're different, Mason."

"How's that?"

I moved the hand down to rest over my heart. "Because I am more than one thing, more than the thing I am in the eyes of whomever I'm with," I told him. "I am a bad girl. I'm mean and I'm a liar and a schemer. I can be insensitive to the feelings of others, mostly because I count the number of people I actually like on one hand. But that's not all I am. That's not all I can do. They're just tools in the toolbox."

He drew in a breath and his grip relaxed. I darted my hand into his pocket for his phone, wrenching it out. He began to swear but before he had time to move I tightened my fist and slammed it backward into his groin.

Mason fell back. Controlling my body's spin as much as I could with his face still looming over mine and blood pumping through my ears, I grabbed the knife, spiraled onto my back, and jammed the point into his thigh.

He finally let go of me. I yanked the knife back out and scrambled on my back to the passenger side door, unlocked it with my thumb, and tumbled onto the gravel.

I hooked the duffel bag's strap with my good ankle and pulled it out, picking it and my body off the ground. Then I ran to the gate.

It was locked and too high to climb.

I looked to my right and saw a boat shed with a padlock on the door. I looked to the left and saw a rocky precipice overhanging the river.

"You fucking bitch!" Mason was limping out of the car, his fists balled up like clubs, his eyes blazing.

I whirled to face him and tightened my grip on the knife.

"Don't come any closer," I said. Mason stepped toward me, blood spreading down his jeans. I backed up toward the cliff's edge.

"I'm serious," I said, still walking toward the cliff, one hand holding out the knife, one desperately trying to unlock his phone.

Mason still didn't say a word. He just advanced on me, slowly and deliberately.

I tried every significant combination of numbers I could think of. I tried Simone's apartment building. I tried the P.O. Box in

Cold Spring. I tried the combination lock that was in his office. I tried the address where he had held the house party. None of them worked.

I stumbled over a rock with my bad ankle, nearly toppling to the ground. Mason took a closer step, but I held out the knife and he waited. He needed me on that plane with him.

Or dead.

Wildly, I plugged in the day we first met. And the phone opened.

Fingers trembling, I dialed 911. The call went through, but I forgot to turn it on silent, and in the dead silence of our stand-off, Mason heard it ring.

"911, what's your emergency?"

Mason rushed me.

He ran at me, with his arm out and barrel-rolled me to the ground. My fingers lost their grip and the phone rolled over the edge of the cliff.

"I didn't want this," he gasped, holding my arms down, angling me closer and closer to the edge. My hair fell over the rock face, lifting in the icy wind from the fast-moving river.

He pressed me harder, sliding me back and back until I was suspended over the chasm, only held upright by the hand he pinned to the ground and the other hand he thrust in the air, fighting for dominion over the duffel bag we both held in our grip.

"I should have gotten rid of you!" he shouted. "That would

have been the smart thing: to hurt you so badly that you were in no position to hurt me back. But I wanted you with me! I wanted you to *enjoy* this! Ungrateful bitch."

Mason pushed down harder. "I didn't want to go alone," he wailed.

My whole torso was hanging over the edge now. I dug my fingernails into the dirt, searching for purchase. My hand found something, hard and cold and slender.

I craned my neck up to look at Mason.

"Don't worry, Mason. You're not going anywhere alone."

I flicked my hand upward, stabbing him in the palm with the knife. He howled, let go, and, just before I careened all the way off the cliff, I grabbed him by the shirtfront and we fell together.

I didn't feel the falling, but I felt the landing. I slammed into the rock tailbone first and somersaulted the rest of the way down.

Then there was nothing.

The next thing I saw was the river rushing by. I lifted my head, but I couldn't see very well. It was as if I was trying to see through barbed wire—everything was blinding and gray, and it hurt to try. I shut my eyes.

When I opened them again, all I saw was dirt. My face was on the ground, and I couldn't seem to move it. I squinted and saw

Mason sprawled out several feet away. His eyes were closed.

I shut my eyes again and opened them in a different direction, looking upward. The phone had landed a little bit away from my head. It seemed intact.

I couldn't move my legs. I pushed against the dirt with my nose, inching toward the phone. I unlocked it the same way and, blessedly, it worked.

What's the number? I thought. *I don't remember the number I'm supposed to call. It's three numbers. Why can't I remember them?*

I learned it too long ago. That's the problem. I plugged in the last number I remembered learning. It rang.

"Who is this?" answered a nervous, rasping voice. A male voice. It was a voice I recognized, but couldn't quite place.

"I'm Kendall," I said. "I'm Kendall Evans."

And then I blacked out.

CHAPTER TWENTY-SEVEN

"So, Kendall." The reporter smiled at me, a warm, bright smile designed to make me feel at ease but also to completely dispel any suspicion that she was a threat. "We're going to start recording now. Are you comfortable where you are?"

As it happened, I wasn't comfortable. I had two cracked ribs, a dislocated shoulder, a swollen tailbone, a broken ankle, a sprained wrist, and various cuts and bruises. And I wasn't about to be on painkillers. I was going to keep my head clear for this particular conversation, thank you.

I smiled back at her, a demure, sparkling smile. "I'm fine, Katie. Thank you so much for coming here to do the interview. The doctors don't want to move me yet. They think I might have caught a minor strain of pneumonia when I was lying out there. It started to rain before Detective Rockford found me."

She motioned toward the cameraman. A red light went on.

"Let's start there," she said, leaning in. "What's the first thing you remember after going over that cliff with Mason Frye?"

"My parents standing over me in the hospital." Katie made an *awww* face.

Actually, it was my Dad. Mom was already in with the DA, trying to assure that I wouldn't be charged with aggravated assault, or even attempted murder.

When I woke up, Dad was there, calm and professorial, reading a copy of the *New Yorker*. He didn't even notice I had woken up until I started croaking, "I'm sorry, Dad, I'm *so* sorry—"

"Shhh," he said, putting his hand on my head, the closest unbandaged part of me he could find. "It's OK. You don't have to explain anything."

"But don't you want to know how—? You should ask me why—"

He shook his head again and patted my scalp. "Mom told me the facts. I don't need you to justify yourself. I'm sure you did your best. I believe in you."

I was struggling. "But . . . I should explain to you why I . . ."

He shook his head. "I don't need you to explain it to me. To be honest, I'd rather be a safe haven from this for you. Associate me with everything else. Talk to me about everything else. You'll need to talk about this year enough. You don't have to with me."

There was no need to lie about my parents in the interview and for that I was grateful. I looked back at Katie. "My parents have been with me the whole way," I told her. "I'm very lucky."

She pursed her lips. "I understand that your mother is representing you. Was there ever a discussion about you retaining out-side counsel?"

"Why do you ask, Katie?"

"Well, to put it delicately, there are some *sensational* aspects of this case, that I imagine might make it difficult for a mother to represent a teenage daughter."

I looked through the window of my hospital room and saw Mom, standing straight and still with her arms crossed. She was staring at the reporter with narrowed eyes.

Mom had been against me giving any interviews. But that was before someone in the State Trooper's office had leaked the report to the *New York Post*. An Ivy League drug dealer, a kidnapped prep school girl, a fight in the mountains—it proved irresistible. After someone in the hospital had leaked the photos of Mason and I as we were brought in—each of us prettier and blonder than the oth-er, bruises not withstanding—even out-of-state newspapers start-ed hounding the hospital, Columbia, Howell, everyone.

My mother had eventually conceded that we needed to spin the story ourselves. But she would probably have clocked the reporter if she'd heard that last question.

I pivoted. "I'm not sure I know what you mean by a 'case,' Ka-tie. I haven't been charged with anything."

"But Mason Frye has."

"He has. Detective Rockford tells me that he has been charged with possession, conspiracy to manufacture, and conspiracy to distribute, as well as kidnapping and contributing to the delinquency of a minor."

"And you *haven't* been charged with anything?"

I smiled. "I feel like you want to ask me something. Go ahead and ask."

Katie's eyes narrowed, but her otherwise pleasantly bland expression remained intact. "Well, let's circle back to that. Let's start by going over that night. How did Detective Rockford find you? I understand you managed to call someone who alerted the police?"

"That's correct. I was almost passed out, but he understood that I was in trouble and called Detective Rockford."

"Remarkable. Can you tell us about this hero?"

Again, my gaze drifted out the window. Behind my mother, Gilly and Simone were sitting in the waiting room. Simone refused to let me go on TV without her first doing my hair and makeup. And from what I gathered, Gilly was wherever Simone was these days.

"He won't leave me alone, Ken." Simone was the first nonfamily member and noncop to bully her way into my hospital room. After scolding me for not calling her before my dinner with Mason, and then for calling Gilly instead of her, she began her new favorite game: complaining about Mikey.

"He's insufferable," she insisted. "All he wants to talk about is

Kendall this, Kendall that, what does Kendall think. It's pathetic. He's so anxious, we actually had a *sleepover*, Ken. A *sleepover*. My mother made s'mores dip. We watched *Mean Girls*."

"What do you want me to do about it?" I raised the arm in the sling. "I'm not exactly mobile."

"Just say you'll go out with him or say you won't," she said bluntly. "Put him out of his misery."

I pointed at Gilly through the window. "That's the hero, right there, Katie," I said. "He's a friend of mine from school."

The second cameraman turned just in time to see Gilly knock an unlit cigarette from Simone's fingers. She glared at him as he ripped it to shreds.

Katie looked at him appraisingly through the glass and turned to me with a conspiratorial, all-girls-together grin. "Just a friend?"

I laughed. "Come on, Katie."

"You have to admit, it's pretty romantic that he was who you called."

I looked away from Gilly, back at her. Smiling again, forcing it more this time, I told her, "I totally see why you would think that, but, honestly, we're just friends."

"If you say so . . ." she singsonged.

I had. I had said so.

It had sucked. Gilly had bounded into the room, so relieved to see me, his face like one of those lamps you use to alleviate Seasonal Affective Disorder.

I had launched right in. "We're not going to date, Gilly. I'm grateful to you and we'll always be friends. But at the end of the day, you framed me. You hacked my profile. You spied on me. You lied to me. I know," I said, holding up my hand as he opened his mouth to protest. "I know you're sorry. I believe you. But I can't. I *won't*. I won't be the girl who just forgives that. And if that makes me a bitch . . . then I'm a bitch."

Gilly's skin had gone almost green and he had walked out of the room like he was the one with a concussion. But he had come back every day. He wasn't going away. I couldn't make him.

I smiled at Katie. "I know. I wish I had a better story for you."

Her face got serious. "Let's talk about boys, Kendall, if you don't mind."

I nodded. "Of course. I understand people have questions about my relationship with Mason Frye."

"I have a picture of you two here," she said, handing over an iPad. "You look pretty cozy in it."

It was a picture from James Greenberger's party. We were at the bar. I was standing with my back to him, and he was arching his torso around me like a snake. He was smiling down at me and I was looking up at him intently. I looked like the girl in the picture. I wondered if he looked like anyone he had made up, or if that was really him.

"I went to the police the very day after this picture was taken," I said quietly.

"And what made you decide to turn Mason in?"

I ran out of livable options. "It took me a long time to realize the damage that Mason was doing," I told her, casting my eyes down. "I'm not proud of how long it took for me to wake up. I can only say that I was young—I am young."

"What do you think should happen to Mason?"

Leon had cut a deal. It seemed like Rodney was going to cut a deal as well. But Rodney hadn't even sent a lawyer for Mason. Mason had done all of this to force his father into his life, but the gamble hadn't paid off. His father wasn't coming to protect him.

I almost felt bad for him. Almost.

"That's up to the courts to decide," I said. "I'm just glad that he's no longer free to make and sell those drugs that damaged so many lives."

"And what's next for you, Kendall? Are you going to be able to go back to your senior year soon?"

"Actually, I was accepted into the Young Astronomers Talent Search program. It starts in January. I'll spend what's left of the semester recuperating and doing my schoolwork from Howell Preparatory School remotely. If I pass all my tests, medical and otherwise, I hope to be in Texas, studying astrophysics this spring."

That was one of the reasons I was doing the interview. We

hadn't heard anything from YATS. As far as I knew, I was still accepted. But Dr. Forrester had come to visit me and warned me that the program was aware of my situation and not . . . pleased. I needed a boring interview, to answer the questions, make the press go away.

Because I still really wanted to go to YATS. It was a relief to be sure of that.

Katie asked me a few more questions about the kidnapping and my daring escape. All of that was in the public record, so I stuck to the facts. Luckily, they were violent and lurid. It was good enough TV on its own—hopefully they'd stick to that and focus less on how a girl like me got there in the first place.

"Well, you are a very brave young woman," finished Katie. "We wish you the best of luck with your recovery."

"Thank you, Katie. I can't tell you how much I appreciate that."

She looked sly. "I have just one more question."

"Sure."

"I understand that you were very popular at your high school, the well-regarded prep school Howell: star athlete, student government, liked by everyone."

I felt the girl in the picture, of her own volition, shimmy over me like a silk nightdress. "That's a very flattering portrait."

"But this isn't your first brush with scandal." She pulled out the iPad again. "Could you tell me about this picture?" I took it from her.

And there I was, clutching my shirt to my chest in the gym, bra straps sliding down to my wrist, skirt still on the floor.

Grant was standing next to me, but you couldn't see his face, just his shoulders and hips. The focus of the picture was me.

I put down the iPad and turned to my bedside. There was a glass of water next to a vase full of the most beautiful, full red roses. The bouquet was almost too perfect.

But then Audrey was like that. The note was fastidious and succinct.

Dear Kendall,

Please accept my best wishes for a quick and full recovery. You are in my thoughts. I think you should know that reporters have been patrolling Howell for quotes about you. I can't speak for everyone of course, but please know that I refused to comment. Ellie told them to go eff themselves. She sends her best as well and good-bye. She'll be in Paris next semester, studying art.

All my best,

Audrey Naeema Khalil

Ellie had also plotted an escape route. Good for her. Hopefully, I'd get to take mine, too.

I took a sip of water and picked up the iPad again.

I was blushing in the photograph and looked like I might be shaking. The image was the platonic ideal of a shamed girl getting caught in the act; the picture you would conjure up when you think "bad girl."

But I looked at it closer. I had always remembered that moment with me wide-eyed and panicked, struggling and fidgeting. But that's not actually how I looked.

My eyes were actually narrowed and my lips pouted. I didn't look panicked. And I suddenly remembered that, in that moment, I hadn't launched into my panic mechanism, counting the seconds—*one, two, three.*

I didn't look panicked in that photo. I looked annoyed. I looked angry.

That seems right, I thought.

I handed the tablet back to the reporter. "What's your question, Katie?"

She seemed taken aback, almost mad. "What would you say about the girl in that photo? What kind of girl is that?"

I shrugged. "Me."